JAMIE & GRACIE : THE HIGHLAND CLAN , BOOK 7
Published by Keira Montclair
Copyright © 2017 byKeira Montclair

Printed in the USA.

Cover Design and Interior Format

© KILLION
GROUP, INC.

Jamie & Gracie

THE HIGHLAND CLAN — SEVEN

KEIRA MONTCLAIR

BESTSELLING AUTHOR

DEDICATION

To my daughter, Christy:
Thank you for your patience. You have always been a blessing.

To my readers:
Thank you for continuing to push me for more, more, more…
This one is for you—two for one.
And remember—it can't be easy to be the lass who must follow in Ashlyn and Molly's footsteps.
I hope you enjoy!

THE GRANTS AND RAMSAYS IN 1280S

GRANTS

LAIRD ALEXANDER GRANT, and wife, MADDIE
John (Jake) and wife, Aline
James (Jamie)
Kyla
Connor
Elizabeth
Maeve

BRENNA GRANT and husband, QUADE RAMSAY
Torrian (Quade's son from his first marriage) and wife, Heather-Nellie
and son
Lily (Quade's daughter from his first marriage) and husband, Kyle-twin
daughters
Bethia
Gregor
Jennet

ROBBIE GRANT and wife, CARALYN
Ashlyn (Caralyn's daughter from a previous relationship) and Magnus
Gracie (Caralyn's daughter from a previous relationship)
Rodric (Roddy)
Padraig

BRODIE GRANT and wife, CELESTINA
Loki (adopted) and wife, Arabella-sons, Kenzie and Lucas
Braden
Catriona
Alison

JENNIE GRANT and husband, AEDAN CAMERON
Riley
Tara
Brin

RAMSAYS

QUADE RAMSAY and wife, BRENNA GRANT (see above)

LOGAN RAMSAY and wife, GWYNETH
Molly (adopted)
Maggie (adopted)
Sorcha
Gavin
Brigid

MICHEIL RAMSAY and wife, DIANA
David
Daniel

AVELINA RAMSAY and DREW MENZIE
Elyse
Tad
Tomag
Maitland

CHAPTER ONE

The Highlands of Scotland, 1200s

JAMIE GRANT KNEED HIS HORSE to action, hurtling out of the woods as if there were an army on his tail, moving toward his brother at full speed.

Jake Grant, Jamie's twin and elder brother by two minutes, immediately went on alert. Raising his sword arm, he prepared to defend himself—then swore when he realized it was just another of Jamie's games.

Kenzie, a lad of eight summers, guffawed from the front of his adoptive sire's horse. "I saw him sneaking away, Uncle Jake, but you missed it. Uncle Jamie, you startled your brother. 'Twas funny."

Laughing, Jamie turned his horse to ride next to his brother. "Just trying to have a wee bit of fun, Kenzie. Jake is too serious at times."

Jake glowered at him for a moment before shaking his head and smirking. "And you're never serious. Someday 'twill cost you."

Their father, Laird Alexander Grant, had sent the two of them, along with Finlay and Fergus and a few other guards, out for their regular jaunt around Grant land to check for anyone who did not belong. They had been experiencing a rash of reivers of late, men attempting to steal their cattle. Loki, Jamie's cousin, was visiting from his own keep, and he and his son Kenzie had joined the group.

They continued their ride through the woods and valleys, and were still laughing about Jamie's feint when the reivers *did* attack. It happened while they were traversing a ravine—the perfect place for an ambush.

Jake was leading. Though they were not prepared, his Grant war whoop immediately put them to attention. Sword arms swinging from their horses, Jake and Loki fought through the first two reivers, allowing their group to get out of the ravine, a most dangerous spot for a siege. Even so, a never-ending line of men continued to come at them from an unknown place.

Jamie had wounded two, mayhap three in the initial onslaught. "How many do you see, Jake?"

"Too many," his brother bellowed back.

Loki yelled, "Ten and five to our ten, but they keep replenishing from God knows where." He had just dropped Kenzie, who had been riding in front of him, to the ground. "To the trees with your slinger, lad."

Jamie watched the lad race over to a nearby oak and climb it in no time at all, his slinger out, his supply of stones at the ready. The lad had a dead eye.

Finlay yelled, "Jamie, behind you."

Jamie turned to see two men descending on him. He swung his sword overhead and caught one guard from the side, not a death blow but hard enough to unseat him from his horse. He was just about to take out the next fighter when Jake swooped in for the kill, leveling the fool from behind. Jake grinned, nodded, and turned away to fight two more.

One of them took a stone to his temple and tumbled off his horse.

"Keep going, Kenzie," Loki shouted.

Jamie came up behind Loki and called out, "Five more coming at you."

Loki's eyes widened. "Rat bastards. We'll get them."

The two fought side by side on their mounts, each taking on two of the reivers while Kenzie knocked the fifth off his horse.

The only two reivers left standing in the copse were fighting Jake and Finlay. Jamie pointed in one direction for Loki to check, and he and two other warriors rode off in other directions, scanning the area for more of the thieves.

That was when tragedy almost struck. Jamie heard a thud and a yelp. He spun around and his heart shot straight to his throat. Kenzie had fallen out of the tree and landed unmoving on his back. Appearing out of nowhere, a reiver headed straight for the lad, his sword arm raised. The Grant warriors were all too far away to get there in time. There was only one hope...

Jamie dropped his sword, pulled out his bow, and stopped his horse to draw his arrow. Narrowing his focus, he waited until the exact moment the attacker's sword arm rose to its highest point to discharge his arrow.

Kenzie, who had finally recovered from his fall, caught sight of the reiver just before the arrow plunged into the man's belly. The lad screamed and rolled aside as the man fell off his horse. The reiver landed next to Kenzie, his sword still gripped in his hand.

Jamie had spurred his horse the moment the arrow left his bow. Allowing instinct to drive him, he jumped off his mount and threw himself across the reiver, forcing him away from Kenzie. He put his fist in the lout's face, but the man still had his sword raised, and he seemed intent on burying it in Jamie's chest. As much as Jamie pushed back, he could not overpower him. Jamie's eyes narrowed on the arrow protruding from the fool's belly, and he leaned against it, causing the man to roar in pain, but it did naught to relieve the attack. The reiver twisted his sword toward Jamie's neck.

For about ten seconds, Jamie thought he was a dead man as the sword edge came closer and closer to his skin. Then a shadow crossed over the man's body from above and a blade sliced across the man's neck in a quick movement, shooting blood everywhere. The man fell backward, as did Jamie, clutching his neck to assure himself it was still there.

He looked up into Loki's eyes, panting and gasping for air, and was about to thank him when Loki whispered, "We're even. Kenzie would have been dead."

Kenzie let out a squeal and a sob, his emotions finally getting the best of him. He threw himself into his adoptive sire's arms. "I was almost dead. He was going to kill me. If Uncle Jamie hadn't stopped him, I'd be dead."

Jake appeared at Jamie's side and helped him up.

"Are they finished?" Jamie gasped as his brother clapped him on the back.

"Aye, all are dead. Don't know where in hell that last fool came from."

"Out of nowhere," Loki said. "I never saw him until it was almost too late. You've got a good eye, Jamie."

Finlay joined the group. "We got them, and we're still here. That's what matters."

But wee Kenzie's eyes were filling with tears, and that look on his face squeezed something in Jamie's chest. Grabbing the laddie around the waist, Jamie tossed him into the air with a whoop. "We got 'em, did we not?"

"Yeah," the lad said, wiping his cheeks, "we got the rat b…"

"Kenzie!"

Kenzie scowled at his sire. "We got the rat pig-nuts. Uncle Jamie, a winner's circle, please? Please?"

Jamie set the lad down and ruffled his hair. He loved playing with his cousin's son, and if there was aught he could do to keep this memory from haunting the lad, he'd do it.

"Aye," he said, "you've earned it." He moved behind Kenzie, shouting instructions as the lad giggled, trying his best to stay in one spot. "Arms up."

Kenzie pointed his hands to the sky.

"Hold still," Jamie said, though he knew that was about the same as asking a squirrel to stay put in the trees. The lad had more energy than ten men.

Kenzie did his best to control his wiggling, then Jamie grabbed his wrists and lifted him into the air, spinning in a circle as fast as he could, the lad shouting loud enough to be heard back at Castle Curanta.

"Kenzie," Loki said, "if you must heave when you're done, be sure to do it on Jamie." But as soon as Jamie set Kenzie down, Loki hurried forward and grabbed the laddie's feet. Together, he and Jamie tossed him into the air and caught him. Once, twice, three times.

When they finally set him down, his eyes shone as bright as two suns in the summer.

Kenzie grinned as he clambered onto his sire's horse. "I'm better now. We did get them, Papa. I helped."

"Aye, you did a fine job." Loki mounted behind the lad and patted his shoulder.

Jamie found himself glancing at his brother as he brought his hand up to rub his throat again. He'd almost lost his life in the middle of Grant land. Two more seconds and he could have been a dead man.

The others chatted while they headed back toward the keep, but he could not stop thinking about how close the point of that sword had been to his neck. He'd almost lost his life without doing any of the things he'd promised his mentor, Mac, he would do.

As soon as the old stable master popped into his mind, something else came to him: this month was the ten-year anniversary of Mac's death.

Nothing had affected him more than seeing his mentor die in front of him. Now he'd almost lost his own life, and it made him question what he was doing with it. He'd almost died, but he had no legacy to leave behind.

Ten years ago, he'd wanted to explore the lands south of the Highlands, travel to Edinburgh, find a lass to fall in love with, and make his sire proud by participating in a big battle. His sire and uncles had become heroes for their actions in The Battle of Largs, and Jamie and Jake had spent many years fighting imaginary Norseman, pretending to protect the women of their clan from them. In their games, Jake had always protected Kyla and Jamie had protected Gracie.

But those had been the dreams of two young lads. Since Mac died, he'd considered becoming a spy like Uncle Logan and Aunt Gwyneth. Now his cousin Molly and her husband Tormod had joined his aunt and uncle.

Mayhap it was his turn. He needed to make his mark on the world.

True, he had gone to Edinburgh in pursuit of one of the Scot's most notorious villains, but there'd been no lass, no major battle, and he certainly hadn't proven himself a hero.

After MacNiven was killed, though by Molly and Tormod, not by Jamie and his men, Jamie had felt a pull to go back to Uncle Logan's and talk to him about becoming a spy. But he'd had a group of men to lead, so he'd returned as duty dictated. Nearly every day since then, he'd thought about leaving, finding his destiny, doing something to make his sire and clan proud, but he'd stayed.

Was his near-death experience meant to tell him something?

About an hour later, Loki and Kenzie headed home to Castle Curanta with their guards. Finlay and Fergus, Nicol's sons, had joined Loki's keep, but they headed back to the Grant keep with the rest of the men. They'd been living at home since their mother, Inga, had fallen ill.

As they neared the keep, Jamie noticed Jake had fallen back from the others.

His brother waited until a decent distance separated them from the others before swinging around to face him. "I can tell that you're aggrieved about something," he said, waiting for Jamie to speak. "What is it?"

"I almost died back there, and I've done naught with my life."

"What do you mean? You just returned from the Ramsays. You were at Edinburgh. You've been a much larger part of chasing Ranulf MacNiven than I have. Ever since I married Aline, I've stayed close to home, but you've traveled quite a bit."

"Being the eldest, you'll be laird someday, and I'll be naught."

"Do not be ridiculous. You'll be right by my side, as Da has said many times. You may not have the title, but your work will be just as important."

True, their sire had said exactly that on many occasions. "I know, but…"

Jake arched his brow at his brother. "But?"

Jamie stared ahead, unable to explain his feelings.

Jake began to nod his head, increasing the emphasis of each nod as they moved ahead. "Now I understand." He glanced up at the clouds over their heads. "Aye. 'Tis Mac, is it not?"

Jamie could not answer him around the huge lump in his throat.

"Ten years ago this month, was it not?"

Jamie turned his head to his brother. "Aye. Ten years."

"You did not die, so you've plenty of time to do what you promised Mac." Jamie had told Jake long ago about all his promises.

Jake pointed off in the distance. They'd been too wrapped up in their conversation to notice the horse bearing down on them, a dark horse much like their sire's old horse, Midnight, its rider galloping at full speed, her dark hair flying in the wind behind her. He recognized their sister Kyla, the image of their sire except with their mother's blue eyes.

"I'll let you talk to her." Jake flicked the reins of his horse and took off toward the gates.

Jamie heard his brother shout at their sister. "He's thinking of leaving again. Talk him out of it, would you, please?"

His tone had changed, the way it always did when Kyla was around. Both brothers adored her fun-loving, carefree attitude. They knew Kyla was their da's favorite, not either of them, though their sister Eliza had done her best to change that, and now wee Maeve, the lassie their parents had adopted. Their youngest brother Connor was riding directly behind Kyla.

Kyla laughed. "Jamie, you are not leaving. We'll all be too upset if you did. You belong with us."

"What brought this on?" Connor asked.

"Mac," Kyla said in a soft voice. "He died ten years ago this month."

Jamie glanced at his sister, wondering how she could remember such details, but she always did. He nodded in agreement. He flicked the reins of his horse, and the others followed him back to the keep.

"Aye, and I almost joined him less than an hour ago," Jamie said. "Loki saved me."

Connor arched a brow at his brother but said nothing.

"Aye," Jamie said.

"At least you are allowed on your reiver jaunts. I am not. I'm tired of staying home like a bairn while you two are off fighting. Papa sees you and Jake as equals, not me."

"You almost lost a couple of us out there. You can be glad you were not with us."

Kyla said, "And it reminded you of Mac's death, did it not?"

"Aye." Jamie said. "I think 'tis time for me to leave. I care not what Jake says. 'Tis my time to do what I promised Mac. I wish to do something that matters."

"And helping the next laird in our clan does not matter? Hellfire, I'll take your place."

"Connor, 'twill be a long while before Jake takes the lairdship, and I have other things I'd like to accomplish. When he does, you'll be there just as Uncle Robbie and Uncle Brodie are with Da all the time. But I want something else, something that's missing. I'm not sure what, but I'm ready to talk to Uncle Logan. If Molly and Tormod can do it, I should be able to, as well."

Kyla said, "Then mayhap 'tis your time to explore."

Jamie nodded, pleased they'd accepted what he said.

Now, if he could only convince himself that becoming a spy was what was missing in his life. His gut told him it wasn't.

But he had no idea what it was.

CHAPTER TWO

G RACIE GRANT LED HER THREE charges to the small trestle table off to the side of the dais for the midday meal. Sometimes the lassies ate in their large chamber upstairs, and other days she brought them here to visit with Maddie Grant, the laird's wife. They were a bit early, so there were not many in the hall yet.

"Come sit by me, Morna," she said, "and Maeve, you may sit on the other side of me."

Maisie hopped onto the bench opposite them. "I'm a big lass. I can sit here by myself, Lady Gracie."

Gracie smiled. She did not feel she should be addressed as a lady, but her aunt Maddie, whose mother had been English, insisted. "I'll have my daughters and anyone else I can influence raised with manners, lass." So the wee ones addressed Gracie as "my lady" or Lady Gracie.

Maeve and Morna were both around three summers, and Maisie nearly five. While Maeve was the adopted daughter of Uncle Alex and Aunt Maddie, Maisie and Morna were the wee sisters of Jake's new wife, Aline. Gracie took care of the three lassies every day, and she adored them.

"Aye, Maisie, sit wherever you'd like. Now, you three stay here while I go fetch your food."

Gracie swung her plait over her shoulder as she hurried to the kitchens. The serving lasses were probably busy with last-minute meal preparations, and she did not wish to bother them. She was perfectly capable of fetching their food. Once inside the door, she waved to the serving lasses and then set about her work, doing her best to stay out of their way. Pleased to find fresh goat's milk and an apple to cut up, she also grabbed a chunk of bread and some cheese for the lassies. She bustled out with her hands full, pushing the door open with her back.

"Oh!" The door had been lifted off her back without warning, and she just managed to catch herself without spilling the goat's milk. "Goodness, what in the heavens?" She spun around and straightened, only to find herself staring into a pair of brown eyes and a huge grin.

"Good day to you, my lady," Fergus said.

"Oh, good day, Fergus. You startled me." Before she could say anything else, a scream from the hall rent the air. The tray of food still in hand, Gracie raced out to see what had happened to the girls. The cry had come from Maisie, for certain.

No one would hurt her wee lassies.

Fergus's voice carried from behind. "I'll help you, Lady Grace."

As soon as she rounded the corner, she knew who'd caused the trouble—Airril. While not a bad laddie, he liked to tease others. Airril, who was only four summers himself, had taken ahold of Maisie's braid, and was tugging it from behind while Maisie screamed. He had almost pulled her off the bench when Gracie came up beside him, set the tray on the table, and reached for his hands. Airril's aunt, Peigi, was laughing at a nearby table.

"Airril, stop that. You'll not be hurting others!" Hair-pulling…how she hated it. She grabbed his hand to wrench it away from poor Maisie, but Airril's aunt swatted her hand.

"Unhand him, Gracie." Peigi stood over the bairns, ready for battle— Gracie could see it in her face and her countenance.

Gracie scowled. Not one to ever raise her voice to others, she was hesitant to confront another member of the clan, especially in front of witnesses, but she would not allow her charges to be mishandled. "Your nephew needs to unhand Maisie." She made sure to say it in her sternest voice, glaring at Peigi.

"He's just having a wee bit of fun with the lassies. Leave them be." Peigi's hands parked on her hips.

"Nay, I'll not leave them be." She turned to the laddie and lifted him into the air. "Drop your hands, Airril."

Fortunately, Airril's face crumpled up and he dropped Maisie's hair, but not before he broke into a howl that could be heard across the nearby mountaintop.

Chaos erupted in a matter of moments. Airril continued to holler,

Maisie still sobbed, and Fergus, who had followed Gracie from the kitchens, started lecturing Peigi. The lass paid him no attention at all. She'd grabbed her nephew and was spouting cuss words as fast as a warrior who'd sliced his own finger by accident.

With all that noise, no one noticed Jamie come in the door until he was upon them all, shouting for everyone to be quiet, waving his arms overhead.

Everyone stilled, but Gracie picked up Maisie in an attempt to soothe her crying.

"What goes on?" Jamie glanced from Gracie to Peigi to Fergus and then back again.

Gracie pursed her lips, refusing to speak. She backed up to the trestle table, making a sheepish look.

Fergus said, "I came out to help Lady Grace. Peigi's nephew was hurting Maisie and…"

Jamie's gaze narrowed at Fergus. "Were you not sent here by my sire?"

"Aye, I came for linen strips. He needs them right away."

Jamie tipped his head and crossed his arms, still staring at Fergus.

"Och, aye. I'll get them now." He scuttled back to the kitchen, casting a furtive glance at Gracie before he left.

Jamie gave his attention to Peigi and Gracie. Gracie lifted her chin a notch, but said naught. She would do as her mother had taught her and only speak nice words.

Peigi felt differently. "Some people, people who just arrived here in the keep, think they can direct others. My nephew was playing with Maisie, and Miss Lady here thinks she can order him about. I was letting them play."

Gracie lifted her chin another notch and sat on the bench next to the wee lassies, setting Maisie down beside her.

"Gracie?" Jamie leaned toward her.

"Forgive me, but I did not think it was playful. I was just protecting Maisie." She refused to look away from the bairns. "The lass was crying."

She heard Jamie say, "You've a fine-looking nephew, Peigi, but I'd like to speak to Lady Grace alone, if you do not mind."

Peigi picked up her nephew and strode to the door, mumbling, "Lady Grace, indeed."

Maeve glanced up at Jamie, wrinkled her nose, and whispered, "Greetings, 'amie."

Gracie broke the bread and cheese into portions and cut the apple into small pieces, giving each bairn an equal amount.

"Pay her no mind, Gracie," Jamie leaned over to whisper to her. "You were correct. She's just a wee bit spiteful that you have gained the position she wished for—my mother's helper."

Gracie was still so furious, she could think of nothing to say. The door to the hall opened and Jamie's mother strode into the room.

Maeve bounded up from her seat, her arms outstretched. "Mama!"

Maddie gave the wee one a quick kiss and said, "Come eat this good food Lady Grace has prepared for you."

Once the children were settled, Maddie asked, "Did I not hear some yelling before? Maisie, why are your cheeks wet?"

Gracie glanced at Jamie before replying, "Naught to concern yourself with, my lady. I took care of everything."

Maddie winked at her. "I saw Fergus leaving just now. I fear you've melted another lad's heart. Fergus manages to find his way here at least once a day, does he not?"

Gracie sighed and looked down. "Aye, he does."

"Och, well, 'tis the way of lads, and he has a good heart."

Jamie grinned and nodded. "Gracie has set many hearts afire, lately."

"I can see why. Gracie is a lovely lass. Do you not agree, Jamie?" Maddie looked at her son expectantly, and Gracie wished nothing more than to run into the kitchens to hide. Instead, she blushed and cut up more food.

Jamie paused before he spoke. Gracie did not dare lift her gaze to his because then she would blush an even darker shade of red. Why was he hesitating so? Did he not think she was lovely?

"Aye," Jamie whispered in a tone she hadn't heard before. "Gracie is most lovely."

She lifted her gaze to Jamie's blue eyes and her heart skipped a beat, she was sure of it. He was staring at her, something she'd never noticed him do before.

"The girls are doing well with their reading," Maddie said, drawing her attention away from Jamie. "I'm so happy you agreed to help me with them. I do not know what I would do without you."

Gracie nodded. "I do love them so."

"How is your sister doing?"

"She is still sick in the morn, but I keep reminding her about the bairn in her belly. I hope it does not last much longer."

"You will be such a help to Ashlyn when the bairn arrives." Maddie broke off another piece of bread for Maeve. "Excuse me, I must return to the kitchens for something."

After Maddie left, Gracie noticed the hall was filling with more people as the time for the meal drew closer.

Every time the laird's wife told her how much she appreciated her help, Gracie's sense of hope deflated more. Her dream was to have a family of her own, but Maddie was so good to her. How could she ask for permission to marry when it meant she might have to stop caring for her charges? Ashlyn had suggested that she speak with their sire, but she was afraid to do that since he was her adoptive sire. It was something she'd need to discuss with her mother first.

Gracie's gaze found Jamie. He was tall and broad-shouldered, just as his brothers were, but it was his blue eyes and kind smile that always reached in to touch Gracie's soul. He was by far the most handsome of all the warriors, though she'd never tell him so. They hadn't seen much of each other before she'd moved to the keep to take care of the lassies, but now they saw each other daily.

"Gracie, how was your morn before Peigi?" Jamie leaned his elbow on the table, smiling at all the wee ones. His fair hair swung around his face in wild disarray.

"Verra nice. I thank you for your help."

"I have to admit I've never seen you quite like that, Gracie. You did a fine job defending your charges. I do not think you needed me at all."

She opened her mouth to say something derogatory about Peigi, but then changed her mind and snapped it shut. Her mother's voice echoed in her head: *Only speak nice words.*

Thankfully, Jamie had turned his attention to his wee sister Maeve, who had stood up on the bench and held her arms out to him. "Kiss, 'amie?"

Jamie laughed and gave Maeve a kiss, flipping her upside-down and smooching her until she giggled. "Where's 'akie?"

Tossing her up in the air, he said, "Jakie is taking on anyone he can in the lists."

"Again, 'amie!"

Jamie obliged her and tossed her in the air two more times.

How Gracie loved to watch him with the lassies. They all adored him. He had a fun-loving side to him that she'd rarely seen before she moved to the keep. How had she not noticed it?

Maisie stood up from her bench and then Morna joined her, both with a chorus of "Jamie, kiss?"

As soon as Jamie obliged the three wee ones with kisses and tosses, Gracie said, "Sit, lassies, and finish your bread and cheese." She patted the table and they all took their seats again.

Jamie's blue gaze met hers, and she found she could barely breathe. "Gracie, how do you like living up here in the keep instead of in the cottage with your parents? Do you not miss the loch?"

"I love it here." She dipped her head and blushed. "I loved living with my parents, too, but I've met many new friends."

He gave her an odd look and said, "So I've heard. The lads are all happy to have you here."

She sat up, pondering what he'd said, remembering the comment he'd made earlier. "They do? Who do you mean?"

"No one in particular," he said abruptly. He stood up from the table. "I suppose I should get the supplies I need and return to the lists. My sire is still training us as though MacNiven is loose and on the attack." The clan's longtime enemy had finally been defeated in the middle of winter.

Maeve said, "I wuv you, 'amie." She waved at him.

"Love you, too, wee one." He hugged Maeve and hurried toward the door.

Gracie's gaze followed him, just as the wee ones' did. How she wished things could be different. For there was another problem that had been troubling her, one she hadn't dared confide in anyone. Now that she was at the keep every day, she'd decided exactly who she wished to marry. The lad she loved with all her heart was *Jamie*. True, he was not a blood cousin—Jamie's uncle was her stepsire—but they'd known each other ever since she and Ashlyn had arrived at Clan Grant.

Still, her heart knew what it wanted. She wished to marry Jamie Grant.

CHAPTER THREE

G RACIE TUCKED HER HANDS INSIDE her mantle against the cold
spring breeze. She lifted her face up to the sky, wishing the clouds
would part to reveal the radiant blue that she so loved, but it wasn't to be
today.

This was her day with her family. She'd hugged Maeve, Morna, and
Maisie before leaving the keep, a bit wistful to be leaving them behind,
but she looked forward to spending time with her sister and her mother.

She had a very important topic to discuss with them—marriage.

She was ready to ask her mother if her stepsire would consider finding a husband for her…and she also planned to tell Ashlyn how she felt
about Jamie. Though it unnerved her to think about bringing it up, she
trusted her sister to be both honest and kind. She had to know if the clan
would accept a marriage between cousins, especially since they were
not blood cousins.

"Grace? Hold still. I must speak with you." Though she was almost to
the stables, she pivoted to face the voice that had called out to her.

Peigi hurried toward her, her face to the ground as if she wished to go
unrecognized.

Though she would sooner speak with anyone else in the clan, Gracie
waited for the other lass to come closer, and when Peigi motioned for
her to move away from the stalls so they could converse in private, she
heeded her.

"Good morn to you, Grace," Peigi finally said.

Gracie nodded to her, unsure of how to reply.

"I've noticed you are enjoying your new role in the keep with the wee ones."

"Aye, I am. The bairns are lovely and sweet." She smiled at Peigi, hoping to overcome the sourness of their last meeting, but the gesture was not reciprocated.

"I hope you stay in that measly role," the other lass sneered at her. "It suits you. Most children are quite dirty."

Gracie's smile left her face as quickly as it had come. "Nay, they are not."

Peigi crossed her arms, glaring at Gracie. "I notice you have become interested in Jamie Grant. I tell you now, he will be mine when he is ready, and you are to stay away from him."

Nothing Peigi could have said would have shocked her more. She had been so careful to hide the way she felt. "You know not what you saw."

"Lie to me and even to yourself if you like, but I know what I saw. You are interested in him, and I'm telling you to stay away. Jamie is confused right now, but when he's ready to settle down, he'll be coming in my direction. Do not think to distract him from that."

"Peigi, I have no interest in Jamie other than as part of my stepsire's family."

"Just make sure you heed my warning. If not, I'll see that you regret it." Peigi gave her a sly grin that was entirely lacking in goodwill and then whirled around, heading back toward her own cottage.

Gracie was stunned, both by Peigi's suggestion that she was interested in Jamie and by the girl's assertion that Jamie was hers. And what exactly had she meant when she'd said Gracie would regret it if she pursued Jamie? The lass was surely daft.

Her head spinning with questions, Gracie trudged across the dirt over to the stables, pleased to see one of the lads had already saddled a horse for her. She rode straight for her sister's cottage, determined not to allow Peigi's words to frighten her. No matter what, she'd always known Clan Grant to be a safe place. It had become a haven for both her and Ashlyn, and she would not allow a jealous lass to take that from her.

Ashlyn's husband, Magnus, waved to her as soon as she arrived, and his two Scottish deerhounds, Mada and Sim, ran out to greet her. Once Magnus had helped her down from the horse, she lavished some attention on the two animals. She tipped her head up to her sister's husband. "She is still heaving, Magnus?"

He sighed, then tossed a stick off into the distance for the two dogs to chase. "Aye, I wish I could help her, but she sends me out, telling me she wishes to heave in private. Sometimes I relent to her tender sensibilities..."

Gracie laughed. "My sister does not have tender sensibilities."

He broke into his usual grin as he reached for the stick Mada had brought back to him. "Och, she does, but only occasionally. I think this bairn has changed my wee fighter. Come in for some porridge. I just finished making a pot. 'Tis why she's heaving, you know. She looked at my cooking."

"Oh, Magnus, do not tease me so. Ashlyn loves your cooking because she hates to cook. I just wish she would feel better. Seems 'tis way past time for her to stop heaving. She is well beyond three moons in her time."

Magnus pushed the door open and held it for Gracie, who added, "I'd love to try your porridge, if you do not mind."

No sooner had she sat down and grabbed a bowl of food than her mother came knocking at the front door. Caralyn bustled inside, and after kissing Gracie on the cheek, she headed toward the bed chamber to speak to Ashlyn.

"Gracie, are you not here a bit early?" she asked over her shoulder.

"Aye, but I wished to speak to you and Ashlyn before we had our midday meal."

The sound of Ashlyn heaving in the bed chamber made Magnus turn a shade of green. He flashed them a grin as he headed back out the door. "I'll leave you alone so you can talk in private. Tell Ashlyn that I take Mada and Sim with me up to your sire's home. We'll go see what the lads are doing."

When Caralyn opened the bed chamber door, Ashlyn was already standing behind it. "I do not blame him for running," she said, wiping her face with a linen square. "He must tire of listening to me heave."

Caralyn ran her hand through Ashlyn's hair. "Mayhap Gracie and I will wash and plait your hair today. 'Tis a mass of knots."

"I know, Mama. 'Tis just too hard for me to plait it."

Her mother ushered her over to a chair in front of the hearth. "Your husband has the cottage all warm for you. He takes such good care of you." She found a plaid and covered her with it.

"Aye. I only wish this bairn would hurry along."

Gracie had to admit she'd never seen her sister so pale. She stopped eating her porridge, her stomach twisting with what she was about to say, and moved to a chair by the fire. "If you do not mind, I've come with some questions for you and Mama. Mayhap 'twill take your mind from your sickness."

Ashlyn snuggled under the plaid. "That sounds wonderful. I do not wish to talk about me at all. Go ahead. I hope you are not unhappy with your new role at the keep. Aunt Maddie loves having you there to help her."

"Nay, I still love the bairns. They are so sweet, but…"

Gracie's mother quirked her brow at her. "But…?"

"But." Gracie stared at the flames dancing in the hearth and took a deep sigh before she continued. "But now that I have seen your happiness, Ashlyn, I'd like the same for myself."

Ashlyn stared at her sister and drawled, "You call this happy?" She stared down at the night rail she still wore.

"Ashlyn, you adore Magnus and he adores you. You are so wonderful together."

Ashlyn switched her position so she could lean her head against the back of the chair, her knees tucked under her. "I know. He is wonderful. I just wish I could show him how I much I love him instead of feeling so sick. Aye. I *am* happy, and would wish the same for you. What do you think, Mama?"

Her mother smiled. "Naught would please me more than to see you both well married. But who do you have in mind, Gracie?"

Gracie thought for a moment, trying to decide how honest she should be, but Peigi's words echoed in her mind. "No one in particular. I just wondered if Papa had a suggestion. Seems everyone here usually finds their own partner, much like Ashlyn found Magnus. There's no courting as there is in the burghs."

"Mayhap you shall be the first," her mother said. "Your sire can talk to Uncle Alex about finding you a husband."

"But would he allow me a choice? I would prefer not to have someone forced on me." She couldn't help but wonder if Jamie would pursue her if he knew she was interested in marrying. Things had changed between them lately—he was friendlier, and when his mother had asked him about Gracie's looks, she'd heard something in his tone. Was it possible that he was interested in her, or was her mind playing tricks on her?

"Uncle Alex was told by his mother that he was to allow Aunt Jennie and Aunt Brenna to choose their own husbands. I'm sure he would allow you the same." She grinned at her. "If not, Aunt Jennie would certainly remind him of his promise."

"Do you think so? I do not wish to force someone to marry me, especially if I do not know him."

"I'll talk to your sire," her mother said, reaching over to touch her cheek. "But you know what the problem will be, do you not, Gracie?"

Gracie glanced at her mother, then her sister, shaking her head in denial. "Nay." Alarm shot through her. Did they know how she felt about Jamie?

Ashlyn tipped her head toward her sister. "Aye, you do. I know you wish to deny it, but you cannot. Surely you've seen how the lads act around you in the keep. They've been so different now that you are living there."

"They're just being nice. You interpret things differently. I still do not believe that what you say is true." Even so, Gracie had felt herself blush. It wasn't the first time she'd been told as much. Aunt Maddie had commented on it more than once, and even Jamie had said something about the lads' interest in her...

"Believe it, daughter," her mother said. "Offering you for a possible betrothal will cause a stir here in the Highlands."

"And probably in the rest of England, Mama," Ashlyn added.

"Why must you exaggerate so?"

"Daughter, 'tis not an exaggeration. You'll see for yourself if we announce that we are looking for a husband for you."

Gracie closed her eyes as she tossed her plait over her shoulders. Why did they insist on embarrassing her?

"You have the same reputation Aunt Celestina had years ago," her mother said.

Ashlyn smiled at her. "You are by far the most beautiful lass in all of the Highlands, just as the minstrels say. All the lads believe it. Their mistake is to believe 'tis true because of your white blonde hair and your blue eyes, but 'tis not why."

"What do you mean?" Gracie asked, her cheeks burning.

"You've earned that title because of your beautiful heart, not because of the color of your hair or your eyes."

Caralyn nodded, and both of them beamed at her. Gracie could only scowl. How could a lass ever live up to such a title?

Later that eve, Gracie's stepsire escorted her back to the keep. She stopped her horse for a moment because something had struck her. "Papa? Wait for a moment, please?"

Robbie pulled his horse to a stop next to hers, following her lead.

She'd tipped her head back to stare at the stars above them. "They are most beautiful tonight, do you not agree?"

"Aye." He glanced at the stars, then back at her. "Daughter, everyone says your hair is gold or yellow or white, but to me, 'tis like the stars. A brilliant silver."

Her heart filled with gratitude at this wondrous gift she had been given years ago, her stepsire, Robbie Grant. How she loved him.

Her bond with her stepsire was so strong that she considered him her true sire, yet questions about her birth still niggled in the back of her mind. Her mother would only tell her that her true sire had been a friend of Malcolm's, the cruel man who'd controlled Caralyn for a time after the death of Ashlyn's sire. Gracie's sire had only visited once after she was born and never come back.

Why? Had her father believed there was something wrong with her? Or was her mother hiding something worse from her? Could Malcolm be her true sire?

Robbie asked, "Which grouping of stars do you like the best?"

Gracie tipped her head back, taking the time to examine the stars carefully. She could understand why Aunt Jennie and Uncle Aedan were so entranced with the night sky. It looked like a scattering of gems above her.

She knew which one she loved best. Her finger pointed off to the farthest corner of the sky, a star off by itself, away from the others, yet still shining. "That one."

"Why that one?" Robbie tipped his head to stare at the distant object, his gaze narrowing.

"I'm not sure, but it calls to me." She did not understand why.

Gracie flicked the reins of her horse, indicating she was ready to head back.

Her sire called out to her, "Do not worry, Gracie, you'll find someone."

She didn't know how to tell him that she already had.

CHAPTER FOUR

JAMIE WIPED THE SWEAT OFF his brow as he collapsed on the ground in the lists. The sun was almost gone, and he knew better than to use his sword in the dark and risk hitting someone. Besides, he'd lost all his motivation. Battling with his brother was still a challenge, of course, and neither one could beat their sire yet, which seemed to be the driving motivation for them both. Still, now that MacNiven was dead, the skirmishes had ended.

After his near-death experience, Jamie had decided it was time to take action. He'd sent a message to Uncle Logan, requesting to speak to him about working for the Crown. That had been a couple of days ago. Now he was anxious to hear his uncle's response, though it was way too soon.

Finlay fell down next to him, "You're losing your arm, lad. I almost took you down twice."

"Nay, not losing it, just…" He reached up to rub his neck. He couldn't stop thinking about the sword that had been a hairsbreadth from killing him, how its cold metal had felt pressed against his skin.

"Just what? I've seen a look in your eyes. What is it?"

Jamie took a deep breath and let it out slowly. "Bored, I guess. Now that we've no villain to chase, what shall we focus on?" He wasn't quite ready to tell all to his friend yet.

"There are plenty of men trying to steal your cattle. Do you not recall what happened the other day? You need more than twenty men with swords aimed at you? How many? Fifty? Four score? Ten score?"

Jamie grinned, his eyes lighting up. "Ten score. 'Tis what my sire and my uncles went up against. My uncles Robbie and Brodie never stop talking about the Battle of Largs. Can you imagine being part of that? I wish I could have seen my da in his golden helm on his chain-mailed horse."

"He let you try on his helm. It must have been heavy. I'd rather fight without it."

"I cannot argue with that. 'Tis too heavy for my taste. But I'd like the chance to prove myself for all to see, just like Da and Uncle Brodie and Uncle Robbie did."

"Why not like Molly and Tormod?" Finlay said, referring to the pair who had finally managed to best Ranulf MacNiven. Molly was a Ramsay, and Tormod was one of their own, though he'd stayed with the Ramsays to marry Molly. "Consider their reputation. You need not have everyone witness your skills."

"Tormod's own brother does not believe what we told him."

"Lyall's a fool, as you well know. All the Scots know what Molly and Tormod did. Come. Get off your lazy arse and I'll get you an ale at the hall."

Jamie pushed himself off the ground with a grunt.

Finlay chuckled. "That difficult, aye? We're almost the last ones to leave."

Jamie laughed. "Nay, I just need something…" They strolled back toward the keep.

Finlay narrowed his gaze and pointed his finger at his friend. "Wait a moment. I've seen that look before. You're planning something. What have you done?" When he did not answer, Finlay answered for him. "You're leaving, I can tell. But for where?"

What could it hurt to tell his closest friend? "I sent a message to Uncle Logan. I want to work for the Crown."

"You did?" Finlay stopped walking for a moment before he began again. "Och, I cannot believe it. But I'm happy for you. Would you care for company? I hated staying back when you went to Edinburgh."

Jamie could see exactly how his friend felt about this idea, the excitement ready to bust out of him. "You wish to work for the Crown?"

Finlay shrugged his shoulders. "I've not given it much thought, but I might like to talk to your uncle. I'd be interested to hear what he has to say. As long as…"

"I know. As long as your mother is doing well."

"As long as she's not near death's door. I'd still come back once a moon to check on her. But I'd get to travel with you this time."

Jamie nodded. "If my uncle invites me for a visit, I'd be honored to have you by my side. We'll see what he says. Until then, I know not what I want except for the messenger to hurry."

"A lass?"

Jamie barked, "Nay, not a lass."

Finlay clasped his shoulder as he lumbered next to his friend. "Aye, a lass. 'Tis exactly what you need. You're jealous of Jake and Magnus and Tormod." He glanced at the fast-moving clouds overhead. "And Loki and Kyle. They all have someone to go home to at night. You're tired of your hall and your family."

"Saints above, I love my family and my clan."

"Aye, but you'd have more fun with a lass." Finlay winked at him as they neared the hall.

"You need the same."

"True. Mayhap 'tis time we searched for a couple of lasses for ourselves."

Jamie snorted as he opened the door in the hall, surprised to see almost everyone had finished their meal and left, though there was a group of his family huddled around the hearth. He glanced at Finlay, who shrugged his shoulders.

"I'll get the ale if you find us something to eat," his friend said.

Jamie nodded, and a few moments later he and Finlay were sitting at a trestle table with their dinner, listening to the group around the hearth.

"My judgment is to keep it inside the clan for now," Jamie's sire said. "You agree, Robbie?"

"Aye, I think someone within the clan would suit her best."

Jamie frowned, then glanced at Finlay. "Suit whom?"

Finlay had his back to the hearth, so he glanced over his shoulder at the members of the group.

Jamie's gaze was drawn to them as well. He saw his mother and father, Uncle Robbie and Aunt Caralyn, Uncle Brodie and Aunt Celestina, Ashlyn and Magnus, and one more. Gracie.

Finlay whispered, "Gracie? Are they discussing Gracie's future?"

Without thinking, Jamie bolted out of his chair and sidled over to the group. Leaning on Uncle Brodie's chair, he said, "I know I'm prying, but is this a discussion I should be involved in?" After all, he was a member of the family, though it did not appear that Jake, Kyla, Connor, or Eliza were present. Maeve was too young.

"Nay," Jamie's sire shot back.

Jamie's mother reached for his sire's hand, something he'd seen her do many times. It was her signal that he should reconsider his answer. Though she was skilled at turning the laird's opinions, she never spoke against him in front of others. His mother said, "Jamie, Gracie is interested in getting married. We are considering whether or not we should announce this to anyone outside the clan, or just keep it inside."

Jamie stood up straight, his gaze boring into Gracie. "Gracie? You wish to marry? But you only just started helping my mother."

Maddie cut in quickly. "Jamie, she may continue to help me once she's married. She needn't change her entire life, especially if she marries someone within the clan."

But Jamie only gave her part of his attention, still unable to tear his gaze from Gracie. She'd blushed the deepest shade of pink he'd ever seen, and she turned away from him as if embarrassed about her request. She had every right to marry, but he'd never considered the possibility.

For some odd reason, he didn't like it.

His father squeezed his mother's hand, another silent cue. "This is not Jamie's concern, sweeting."

"Nay, but mayhap he is aware of someone who is interested in Gracie. You know how lads are. Have any of you heard of someone in the lists who might be interested in courting Gracie? There must be someone. Fergus? Gracie, how do you feel about Fergus?"

All the heads turned in tandem to stare at Gracie, who looked as if she was about to burst into tears. He had to put a stop to this.

"Nay, Fergus is totally wrong for her." Jamie crossed his arms and leaned against a table.

"What about Ned or Struan? They are both nice lads." Maddie gave Gracie her nicest smile.

Jamie couldn't even wait for Gracie to answer. Why would they torture her about some of these lads? "Struan? Nay, he would not suit. He's as homely as a hedgehog. Look at Gracie. She's beautiful. You cannot marry her to a hedgehog."

The grin on Uncle Robbie's face was wider than he'd ever seen it. His uncle leaned back in his chair and said to Jamie, "Aye, but I think Ned would be a good match."

Uncle Brodie smirked and said, "I agree. Ned is perfect for Gracie."

"Nay," Jamie could feel his heartbeat speeding up as he listened to their foolishness. "Ned is terrible in the lists. How could he ever protect her?"

He glanced at Gracie, who was now staring at her hands as a tear rolled down her cheek. Suddenly, he was angry.

He looked from his sire's stone face to his mother's wide-eyed stare, then at his two uncles, who still had smirks on their faces. "What is wrong with all of you? Why are you doing this to her?" He waved his hand toward Gracie, reminding them she was seated nearby. "Can you not see how you are upsetting her? Why are you forcing her to marry if she does not want to? Da, did you not say that Grandmama wanted everyone in the family to agree to the person chosen for them? The same should be for Gracie. She should be able to choose. Stop forcing this on her. Look at her face. Why are you doing this?"

Gracie stood, her hands folded in front of her. She lifted her chin so she could gaze directly into Jamie's eyes. "Because I requested this meeting. I would like to marry, and I do not need your approval."

Jamie threw his arms up in the air, spun on his heel, and walked out the door.

Gracie watched in a fury as Jamie left the hall. What in blazes was that about? Clearly, he was not interested in marrying her, but why would he try to stop her from finding someone else? Did she not deserve happiness? She waited to see if anyone else would speak after he slammed the door behind him. Finlay, whose mouth had dropped open during Jamie's rant, gave them a wave as he chased his friend out the door.

No one spoke, so Gracie said, "Forgive me, but I'd like to return to my chamber."

Uncle Alex stood, "Gracie, please stay for a moment. I fear your uncle and sire were goading your cousin on. Lads can be foolish when they are young. Jamie only wishes the best for you."

Maddie said, "Aye, please do not take offense."

"What should I do? What have you decided?" She wrung her hands, glancing at her sire. He and Uncle Brodie were still grinning at each other. Apparently, they were still sharing a joke about something. "Papa?"

Her mother said, "Robbie, enough. Look what you are doing to the poor lass."

Uncle Brodie said, "Gracie, forgive us. We were playing with the lad. 'Tis hard not to poke at him a little. Jamie is a born protector. 'Tis a wee joke between your sire and your uncles. We goaded him into losing his temper."

Her sire nodded. "Aye, 'tis true. Jamie is so even tempered until he's called to protect the weak or…"

"Papa, I'm not weak." Why did they see her as a child still? Was *that* how Jamie thought of her?

Robbie gave her his full attention. "Gracie. We all know you are not weak. Forgive us. We were teasing your cousin. I think we've agreed that the best way to handle this is to spread the word amongst our clan-mates first." Robbie turned to his wife.

Gracie's mother jumped in. "Aye. Why do we not see if there is some-one at Clan Grant who would be interested, someone who will suit you. We will not force a marriage on you. We promise to respect your opinion." She cast a glance to Uncle Alex, who nodded.

Uncle Alex said, "Aye, we will respect your wishes. If you cannot find a lad here who suits you, we shall move to our neighboring allies—to Loki's Castle Curanta first, then others. Take your time, lass."

"How does one make this type of announcement?" she asked the group.

"Magnus can help," Ashlyn said. "He'll know who to speak with about this."

Maddie added, "And we shall hold a gathering soon for all to attend. The word will be out by then." She moved over to Gracie and wrapped her arms around her. "You shall see. It will be a lovely eve for you."

She prayed that at least one man would attend.

CHAPTER FIVE

JAMIE GRITTED HIS TEETH ALL the way down the staircase to the great hall. Gracie's night was finally upon them.

Gracie's night. What the devil did that mean?

The night Gracie could become betrothed. Nay, he couldn't, *wouldn't* believe it was possible. He moved his jaw back and forth, a sad attempt to relieve the tension there. If he could only stop grinding and gritting his teeth, he'd feel better, but it seemed to be happening more and more of late.

He could not deny that he knew why. He did not wish to see Gracie betrothed, nor did he wish to see the line of lads who would undoubtedly be here to court her. A sennight had passed since that night he'd overheard the discussion in the great hall, and in that time, more than one person had asked him why the possibility of Gracie becoming involved with a man so unsettled him. His parents and uncles had asked him, and Finlay would not stop pestering him about it.

So many people had asked him that he'd finally put that same question to himself. Unfortunately, he found he could not answer. The surprising part was that no one had asked him if *he* was interested in marrying Gracie, though he expected the question would come soon enough.

How would he answer?

Nay.

That was a true statement. The thought of marrying Gracie or anyone did not settle well with him. While his sire had joked about him being the next to marry, he knew in his heart that he was not ready to marry. He had to prove himself first. Mayhap once he was working for the

Crown, he'd never wish to come back to live on Grant land. Besides, there was the small fact that Gracie was a part of the Grant family, though not by blood.

As soon as his feet hit the floor in the great hall, his mother flew to his side. "Jamie, you look so handsome in your leine and your strong plaid. The red becomes you with your fair hair and your blue eyes." She gave him an appreciative glance from his toes to his nose. "Funny how you look so different from your twin, yet when I look into your eyes, I see the same fire burning there."

"What?" That was something he'd never heard before. Everyone had always said he and Jake were as different as the sun and the moon, the mud and the snow. What he always wondered was which one was he?

He guessed he was the mud.

"There is something about you and Jake that is so much alike, but I guess only a mother can see it. Why, even in the cradle, you and Jake would do things exactly alike. You rolled over at the same time, you sat up at the same time. It was not until you were older that your differences became more noticeable to us." She kissed his cheek and said, "You enjoy yourself tonight. 'Tis Gracie's night."

"Aye," he said, a little sourly. "Finlay is here, so I'll join him." But his sire clasped his shoulder before he could take another step.

"I hope you lose that frown tonight." Alex chuckled as he leaned over to give Maddie a kiss.

Jamie shook his head and stepped away. What frown? He was not frowning.

Finlay approached him and said, "Not having a good day?"

"Aye, I'm having as good a day as any. Why would you ask such a thing?" Damn, but people were already annoying him.

"By the frown on your face."

"I'm not frowning." When he felt the scowl in his eyebrows, he made a point to relax his face and smile. "There. Is this not better?"

Finlay drawled, "Truly, much better." Finlay had the art of sarcasm down well.

They made their way over to the trestle table heaped with drink to grab an ale, then sat at the nearby table with a few other lads: Ronan, Fergus, Ned, Struan, and Sean. Jamie decided he could keep his eye on the fools if he sat nearby.

"So," Finlay said as he looked at everyone seated around the table. "Is anyone interested in courting Lady Grace?"

Fergus cleared his throat and looked at his brother. "I am. But you probably knew that."

Jamie asked, "Anyone else, or is Fergus going to be Gracie's betrothed?" The more choices Gracie had, the better it would be for her, though he did not think anyone at the table would be a good fit for her.

A chorus of "I am" and "me" greeted him from various lads.

Jamie asked, "Is there anyone *not* interested in Gracie?" Silence greeted him. "All of you?" He glanced at Finlay to gauge his reaction, but his friend did not appear surprised by the revelation.

"Why would we not be? Lady Grace is the most beautiful lass in all the Highlands," Ronan said.

"In all of England," Sean added.

"And the sweetest," Ned declared with a nod.

"And the nicest," Struan said. "Look around the hall, Jamie. We're *all* here for Lady Grace."

Jamie had his back to the crowd, so he hadn't noticed who'd come in. When he scanned the great hall, he had to admit he was shocked by the sheer size of the crowd.

"All of them?" Jamie roared, though no one noticed because the clamor in the hall drowned him out.

"Are you not interested?" Finlay asked, doing his best to hide his smirk.

"Nay, she's my cousin."

"She's not a blood cousin." Finlay shrugged his shoulders. "Seems you're clutching any excuse you can, aye?"

"Why are *you* not interested, Finlay? Something wrong with my cousin?" Jamie shot back.

"Nay, she's just not for me. Lady Grace is wonderful. You're sure you are not interested?" Finlay wore that smug look again, and though they'd been friends for as long as he could remember, Jamie found himself wishing he could reach over and punch Finlay just to get rid of the damn thing.

What the devil was wrong with him? If he kept this up, he wouldn't even like himself. He rubbed his chin and then shook his head at the same time as Ronan tossed out his opinion.

"I do not think you would suit for marriage," he added. "Lady Grace deserves someone verra special."

Jamie was about to jump out of his seat and grab Ronan, but an eerie quiet settled over the hall. Everyone stopped talking and started elbowing each other, and Jamie stood up and moved to the other side of the table to see what had caught the others' attention.

Gracie.

Gracie floated down the staircase as if adorned with faerie wings, each step as smooth and elegant as that of any royal queen. Her gown was a pale green with a lavender surcoat, just tight enough to show off her curves. Tiny pink and green flowers were woven into the blonde hair cascading over her shoulders. The sweet smile on her face made her even more stunning, if that were possible.

Her sire moved to her side, then escorted her around the room, introducing her to each of the guests, something Uncle Robbie had suggested they do to ensure they did not miss anyone who attended.

When Robbie and Gracie reached their table, Gracie's gaze settled on him for just a moment before she whispered, "Jamie."

"Gracie, you look lovely tonight." A truer statement he'd never made.

"Aye, lovely."

"Stunning."

"Just beautiful."

Jamie couldn't tear his gaze from Gracie, so he had no idea who had made each statement or who had stammered the most. He'd become lost in a pair of pale blue eyes and a smile that beckoned him to come closer, close enough to kiss her delicate pink lips…

An elbow struck him in his side and he swung around to see who had dared to interrupt his thoughts.

Finlay said, "Mayhap you should consider…"

Uncle Robbie said, "Pleased to see you here, lads. Enjoy your night. We'll move on to meet the others."

Jamie followed them as they moved around the rest of the hall, but he spared enough attention to chastise the friend who'd accompanied him. "Stop suggesting what I think you are suggesting, Finlay. Nay. She's my cousin."

"Not a blood cousin."

There was that damn smug expression on Finlay's face again. True, Jamie was aware it was a flimsy excuse, at best. But that smile of Finlay's? Och, it was testing his patience. "Nay, I said."

Fortunately, Uncle Robbie and Gracie finished their journey around the room, and Uncle Robbie led her to a spot at the dais while Jamie's mother motioned for the serving maids to bring out the food. His sire motioned for two of the minstrels to start their performance. One sang, and the other played the harp.

Jamie moved to an emptier table to eat, and was joined by Finlay, Kyla, and Connor.

Kyla started on him as soon as they finished eating. "Jamie, are you not going to dance with Gracie once?"

"Nay, she's our cousin," he said, repeating his chosen refrain.

Connor snorted. "As you well know, there's no blood relation. She is a gorgeous lady. Look at her. The men are following her like a swarm of bees after their queen."

Finlay pursed his lips into that same smug expression. "Aye, he *does* know, he'll just not admit it."

"Leave off, fools. All of you." He glowered at the three of them.

Kyla said, "If you insist in being so foolish, then I'll go talk with Gracie. Sit and fume."

Connor went along with her. "I'll check on the other lassies, who are feeling quite neglected by now." He winked at Finlay before he left.

"He's right," Finlay said. "If you look around, there are plenty of lassies on the outskirts of the room, just waiting to be noticed by any lad. 'Tis hard to compare against Gracie this eve."

Jamie growled, finding no words that would be appropriate.

A few moments later, Finlay managed to throw another sarcastic barb his way. "Nay, you're not interested in Gracie at all, are you? Not at all." He gave Jamie a wide grin and nudged him. "And if you clench your fists any harder, you'll not have any skin on the palms of your hands by morn."

"Mind your tongue, foolish arse." Jamie refused to look at his friend, especially since he knew Finlay spoke true. He could not tolerate watching Gracie talk with so many different men. The dancing had started, and her laughter echoed through the hall as she moved from dancer to dancer, twirling and whirling in delight. "Do not forget that I plan to meet with Uncle Logan soon. All this will be behind me."

"Aye, my thanks for the reminder. That will end it. And when you return, you will meet Gracie's new husband." Finlay stood and said, "I'm off to mingle. Do you want aught?"

"Aye, another ale, if you please." He'd drink the night away. Anything to make it go faster, though he did not know which was worse, watching Gracie carry on with different men or feeling this confusion well in his gut.

Why was it that Finlay knew just the right thing to set his blood to boiling? Come back to meet her husband. He bolted out of his seat, but then changed his mind and sat down again. He hoped Finlay got his drink quickly.

His mother sat down beside him. "Good eve to you. How is your night going? Is Gracie not the loveliest ever?"

"Aye, she is, Mama. Why are you not dancing with Da?"

"His bones are aching too much. Besides, we are both of the age to enjoy watching the young ones in our clan. I remember you all when you were wee ones." She sighed and rested her chin on her hand, staring out over the dancers in the middle of the hall. "Jamie, do you not recall how you were with Gracie when she first came to Clan Grant? She rarely spoke."

"Nay, I do not. Why?"

"I'm not surprised you do not remember it. You were only three or four summers and Gracie was around two summers, I think. It may have been a year or so after Uncle Robbie first married Caralyn, but you gave yourself the title of Gracie's protector."

"I did? What about Jake?" Jamie folded his hands on the table in front of him, unclenching them for the first time.

"Jake was busy with the laddies. You were smitten with Gracie. One time Gracie wandered off, and everyone was searching for her."

"Where was she?"

"Not far from you. Robbie's horse had taken a liking to Gracie and Ashlyn, and she'd gone to the stables to pet him. Mac was watching her."

"I miss Mac." It still hurt to hear his name.

"We all do, and I especially miss his wife, Alice. He was the best stablemaster. I was so pleased when Alex invited them to stay after we married. Mac felt at home at the stables."

Jamie stared out over the crowd, not really seeing. Even all these years later, he still missed his old friend.

His mother continued her story. "You followed her into the stables and led her to the right horse, using your wooden sword to warn the other horses away from her. She was so little compared to the horses."

"Did I?" Jamie grinned, wishing he could recall it. Half-formed memories from his favorite spot danced through his mind. He had always loved the smell of the horses, of the hay, listening to the animals nicker. And, oh, how he'd loved Mac and all his stories, though he'd realized that Mac liked to tell tall tales to him and Jake. The old man would tease them with stories of lassies and love and such. Jake would throw his hands up and walk away, but Jamie used to stay, absorbing every word of Mac's wisdom as he carried pails of water and buckets of oats for the horses.

"Mac said he went with you just to be sure you were both safe, but you turned your sword on him several times to warn him back from Gracie. You did the same to all the stable lads. When your father walked in, you had several of them at the end of your sword. Gracie was standing up on a bale of hay, feeding a carrot to Robbie's horse. Mac was not far from her."

"She must have been the size of Maeve. I cannot imagine Maeve or Morna near the horses, especially Midnight. Mac allowed it?"

"Only around a couple of horses. As I said, Robbie's horse took a liking to Gracie and Ashlyn. Your father said you even tried to tell *him* to stay away from Gracie."

Jamie laughed at the thought of standing up to his father at such an age. "And his response?"

"He said his heart was in his throat at the sight of Gracie near Midnight, but your father has always been so soft-hearted around wee lassies. He stood with Midnight so Gracie could feed him, too."

"I wish I remembered, Mama, but I do not. Why do you tell me this?"

She leaned over to kiss his forehead before she stood up. "I've noticed you're a bit surly tonight."

"Surly?" When had his mother ever spoken to him in such a way?

"Aye. I've seen it happen on rare occasions, but this time it concerns me."

"When have you noticed it before?"

Her voice softened. "Whenever you are forced to reach deep into your heart. You do not realize it, I'm sure, but it discomfits you."

Jamie had no idea what she was trying to tell him, but he continued to press her. "So what worries you tonight?"

"Because something about Gracie is bothering you. In your heart, I think you'll always be her protector."

Jamie mulled over her words for a bit, wondering if there could be any truth to what his mother said.

CHAPTER SIX

GRACIE MADE HER WAY TO the side table near the front door. She was eager to escape for a moment to compose herself, but she did not think it was possible. If she stepped out the door, she'd probably be followed by at least ten lads, and she did not want that to happen. Her face hurt from smiling so much, and her poor feet had been stepped on multiple times.

The next man who approached her was as friendly as the rest, but his intentions were quite different. "Lass, you look cornered."

She laughed. "Not quite cornered, Father MacKenny, but confused."

"Too many lads for you?" Father split his time between Loki's castle and Clan Grant. She did adore him, though she was surprised he was here for these festivities.

"May I give you a wee piece of advice?"

"Of course, Father."

"Follow your heart, lass. Your heart will tell you which way to go."

How she wished that could be true. "Many thanks, I'll try to keep it in mind." The only problem was her heart told her something that could never be. Jamie had made it all too clear that he did not wish to court her.

A mug of ale appeared in front of her. "My lady, an ale for you."

And a goblet appeared from the other side. "My lady, I found a fine wine for you."

Two others lads appeared in front of her, so she took the second wine, thanked Ned for it, and attempted to turn away from them all. They followed, though, and Father MacKenny disappeared into the crowd.

Kyla appeared in front of her, taking over. "Go away for a few minutes, gentleman. The lady needs a brief respite. I'll take her to the hearth, and you are to stay away for a few moments."

Multiple groans and grumblings met Gracie's ears, but she could not have been more pleased to see Kyla. "Many thanks, Kyla. 'Tis too warm in here, and there are too many people." She waved her hand in front of her face.

"Would you like to step outside?" Kyla asked. "I can tell our family to leave us be. Uncle Brodie and your sire are not far. I'll tell them you need some fresh air."

Once outside, Kyla led her over to the stone bench in the garden. "Tell me what you think? Has anyone caught your eye? Surely, one of the lads must make your heart beat faster than the others."

Gracie sighed and sat down with a flounce of her skirts. She was not about to tell Kyla the truth. The only one who caught her eye was Jamie. Jamie in his leine and the bright plaid that made his hair look like spun gold. His eyes, a darker blue than hers, were hard to read, but there was the promise of strong emotion in them, too—emotion that Jamie would not allow to escape.

Why did he keep everyone at such a distance?

"Gracie?" Kyla leaned into her visual field, trying to get her attention. "Gracie, I know that look. Who is it?"

Gracie spun around to give Kyla her complete attention. "Of what do you speak?"

"That expression on your face. You're in love with someone. Who is it? Tell me and I'll do whatever I can to arrange a quiet rendezvous with him."

"Hush, Kyla. There is no one for certain. I've seen a few of interest, but many I'm not interested in at all. If I could just summon the courage to turn some away." She bit her lower lip, wondering how she could be so cruel and dash someone's hopes so quickly.

"I say turn some away. Why not choose three and let those three pursue you further? There is no reason to lead the rest on if you are not interested. 'Tis better to tell some now so they do not get their hopes up. Choose three."

Gracie thought for a moment, then said, "I cannot. I've no idea who to select." Except for the one name she refused to utter.

"All right. We shall work from the back way. Tell me one you are not interested in. One at a time."

Hope surged within Gracie. This she could do. "Struan. I've no interest in Struan."

"Good start. I'll agree with you. The lad is homely. I wish someone would…never mind. Choose another." She patted Gracie's hand.

"Ronan."

"Ronan? Why him? He's not bad-looking."

"Kyla, you're not helping. I feel awful saying so, but Ronan's breath is horrible."

"I'll accept that. I've not been close to him before."

"How about Sean? I'll put him in my list of three."

"Good. That's a start. Sean it is. How about Fergus? He has such a good heart. They say he is wonderful with his ailing mother."

"All right," Gracie said, "I'll keep Fergus." The poor lad had been dealt enough bad news in his life. Maddie had said his mother, poor Inga, would not live for another year.

"Great! That's two. Sean and Fergus."

"I cannot choose another. You choose for me." Gracie held her breath, waiting to see what Kyla would say. Would she choose her brother? Had she guessed as Peigi had?

"All right. Allow me a moment to think…Ned. How about Ned?"

Doing her best to hide her disappointment, Gracie whispered, "Ned will be fine. Sean, Fergus, and Ned."

"Are you ready to return now that you've made a decision? I'll find a nice way to suggest the three men without hurting too many feelings. You just go on and find one of them." They both stood, and Kyla led her by the hand toward the door.

Gracie breathed a sigh of relief. This was too difficult, too hurtful, too everything. She was shyer than she had wished to admit to herself. Each encounter tonight had felt strained and unnatural, and it was ever so tedious to come up with topics to discuss with suitors who wished only to compliment her eyes, her hair, her form. If she had her choice, she'd be done and in her bed within the hour. But she could not overlook everything Aunt Maddie had done to prepare for this eve. It had all been done for *her*, so she must bear the pain of being on display. Still, she was more than willing to allow Kyla to take over for her and make all the decisions.

Already exhausted, she trudged toward the door, trailing behind her bolder friend. Before they reached it, someone stepped out of a dark corner in front of them.

"Sean, you startled us." Kyla took a step back, but kept ahold of Gracie's hand.

"I...I..." he stammered. "Would I...could I...would you stroll with me for a few moments, Lady Grace?"

Kyla gave her back to Sean so she could smile at Gracie. "Aye, go with him."

Gracie nodded, though her heart was not in it. She mustered enough energy to give Sean a smile, but there was a sinking feeling in her stomach as she watched Kyla leave.

"Lady Grace, you are stunning this eve. Your hair...someday I hope to be able to run my fingers through the silky strands." His gaze followed her hair from the crown of her head all the way to where it ended, just above the swell of her bottom. She quirked her brow at him.

"Och, forgive me. I did not mean to be rude. Come, walk with me. I'd like to know you better."

"All right." He held his arm out to her, so she tucked her hand inside his forearm, hoping he would keep her hand warm. He covered her hand with his and tucked it in close. Sean's wavy brown hair was nicely complemented by his brown eyes and wide smile. Not overly handsome, but pleasing to the eye. He was just...average.

Stop, Gracie, stop. His only fault is that he's not Jamie. Now talk to the man.

"I was so surprised, but pleased, to hear of your wish to marry. You have no idea how much I wish to be your betrothed."

"Why is that, Sean?" She couldn't help but ask the question. Since she'd spent most of her life in her parents' cottage near the loch, she hadn't met Sean before this eve. He seemed pleasant enough and polite. He wasn't as broad-shouldered as Jamie, but...

She chastised herself again. It would not be fair if she continued to compare them all to Jamie.

"I'd be honored to have such a lovely lass at my side. A lass to take care of my needs, to love and cherish me. I hope you'll consider me."

She nodded as they moved down the path toward the herb garden, an area certain to be empty at night. It wasn't surprising to hear him say it, but it was still disappointing. He wished to marry her because she was lovely.

Was that her only value? Did she have any skills besides cooking and taking care of bairns?

But there was no time to think on it. A second later, Sean's lips descended on hers, a rough onslaught of tongue and saliva that seemed to cover most of her face. While she had never been kissed before, if all kisses were like this, she wanted no part of it. She shoved at his shoulders, but he resisted, putting more pressure on her lips, almost hurting her. Before her distaste could elevate to alarm, an unknown force lifted the lad and tossed him into the bushes.

Jamie.

Jamie stood over him, his hands on his hips. "The lady pushed you away. Get your arse away before I kick it all the way to the gates."

Gracie wiped the saliva from her face with her linen square, staring at the man in the bushes. There was no sign of guilt on his face. Still shocked by Sean's behavior, she did not know what to say.

Sean stood up, brushing the dirt off his sleeves and casting a glance over Jamie's shoulders at Gracie. "Mayhap the lady does not wish for me to leave."

"I'm giving you an order to leave. If Lady Grace wished for you to stay, she would have offered her thoughts by now."

Silence. No one moved. Gracie's gaze dropped to the ground as the start of a blush began to creep up her neck to her cheeks. Jamie took one menacing step toward Sean, and the man ran off. As soon as the lad was out of sight, Jamie spun around to face her. "Is that what you want? Because if it is, I can demonstrate how it should be done right."

Jamie grabbed her around the waist and tugged her close. Angling his mouth over hers, he teased her with his tongue until she parted her lips enough for him to slip his tongue between her teeth.

Jamie growled and wrapped his arms around her, his body now flush with hers. This was different, so different that it muddled her thoughts. She loved the taste of him, a touch of ale, a touch of mint, and something else. Something wonderful. Darting her tongue out to meet his, she gave him what he wanted, their lips dancing together. This was *right*, being here in his arms, and it felt like nothing mattered except for them. There was a hardness beneath his waist, and she wanted to run her fingers across his chest and down his abdomen to an area completely unknown to her.

But the best part of this? Jamie desired her. There was no denying how much he wanted her. She could feel it in his touch, in the sound of his voice—she could feel it everywhere. His hands moved up to cup her face. He ended the kiss, his panting matching her own as he leaned his forehead against hers. "That's a proper kiss, my lady. Do not allow Sean to touch you again. He was wrong. You must be careful, Gracie.

Men will take advantage of your innocence." His voice, though only a whisper, held a veiled threat against the man who had brought her out here unsuspecting.

She wished more than anything to ask Jamie why he'd kissed her. This night had caused her so much confusion. She gazed into his eyes, wishing he'd hold her forever. Her heart urged her to tell him that she had no interest in Sean at all, that the only lad she was interested in was *him*, but how could she say such a thing? The fear that he would walk away or, worse, pity her, stopped her lips. While Jamie seemed to desire her, her innocence had given her little experience in such matters. Now he was chastising her for doing with Sean exactly what she'd done with him. What was she to make of it?

Nothing. She had no inkling what the kiss from Jamie had meant, but the more she thought about it, the more she doubted herself. Jamie still saw her as the same little girl he used to protect.

She knew whom she wanted to marry, but she was further than ever from having the family she wanted.

He kissed her nose, then took her hand and led her back to the keep, only stepping away when they reached an area where they could be seen.

Uncle Brodie stood by the door, his arms crossed in front of his chest. "Everything all right, Jamie? Sean came running through here as if he'd been attacked by a boar."

"Everything is fine. I was just escorting Gracie back to her party."

Gracie, her mind functioning once more, folded her hands in front of her and said, "Aye, 'tis a most wondrous night. Do you not agree, Uncle?"

It was a night she'd never forget.

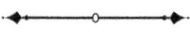

Much later, when Jamie lay on his new pallet of heather, he stared at the ceiling and relived his encounter with Gracie. Saints above, but Gracie had stirred something in him he'd never felt before. He'd been foolish enough to think that if he kissed her the proper way, just to show her and mayhap help her, his urge to kiss her would go away.

How wrong he had been. Now he wanted Gracie more than ever, and this want was not the kind of desire to leave a man—not for a long, long time.

Mayhap never. He'd heard the elders speak of the Grant men and how they each loved one and only one woman forever. Was Gracie his match?

Why had all this happened when he was preparing to leave? As soon as he heard from Uncle Logan, he and Finlay would leave the next morn. He needed to remain focused. If he wished to work for the Crown, traveling the land as his aunt and uncle did, he could not take a wife. His aunt Gwyneth was a rare woman. Gracie would not be interested in dressing in a tunic and leggings and traveling in the cold.

What was he thinking? Nay, he was not the man for Gracie.

He couldn't sleep, so he moved into the passageway and down the staircase, hoping to find something to eat in the kitchens. Many nights he slept with the warriors outside, but had sought out the privacy of his own chamber because his thoughts were too jumbled.

Before he could run across the hall to the kitchens, he noticed a small figure by the hearth, rubbing her hands in front of the embers still burning inside. He could not tell who it was, but he heard the sniffling from the distance. It was definitely a lass, so he changed directions to see who stood crying by the hearth in the middle of the night.

He was almost upon the lone figure when she straightened and pivoted to stare directly into his eyes.

"Gracie?"

She swiped at each cheek before she spoke. "Jamie, forgive me if my presence causes a problem. I shall return to my room."

"Problem? This is where you live now. Why are you alone down here?"

"I did not wish to bother the wee lassies in my chamber."

"Why are you crying?" Her gaze dropped to the floor. Another tear found its way down one of her cheeks, so he reached over to wipe it away. "Did you not enjoy your party?"

"I'm so confused. I know not what I want. I know I've been protected, but I did not expect all that transpired…"

"Gracie, forgive me." Damn it, but he'd been too rough with her, frightened her for sure. She was an innocent. "I should not have…I was too forward. Och, I should not have been so rough with you."

"Nay." Her head shook in short bursts. "I did not mean…"

"I was just so angry when I saw Sean press himself on you. 'Twas wrong…and I should not have kissed you the way I did." He'd forever be embarrassed by how quickly he'd lost control with Gracie in his arms. He ran his hands through his hair before settling them back on his hips. "That was wrong, too."

"Nay, Jamie. You were not wrong. I liked it, I…" She paused to gather her thoughts. "'Twas the only thing about the night that I did like."

Jamie did his best to hide his shock. He needed to hear more to understand what she meant, so he waited for her to continue.

"I had no idea so many would come to court me, and I do not know how to turn them away. Mayhap I've made a huge mistake. Mayhap I should never marry. And I never thanked you for watching over me, for pulling Sean…"

He could see the pink rise in her cheeks as she dropped her gaze to the floor. Now he understood. He lifted her chin with his hand, bringing her gaze up to meet his. Those eyes of hers seemed to hit him straight in his gut of late. "Sean took advantage of you. You need not feel bad about how he was treated. And I took advantage of you at a vulnerable time. My apologies. I hope you will forgive me."

Suddenly, something else occurred to him. "Gracie, come sit next to me for a moment."

She followed him over to two chairs in front of the hearth. "Has anyone spoken to you about how foolish lads can be?"

She shook her head, dropping her gaze to her lap. "Sean surprised me. I did not know how to handle him after he ignored my attempts to push him away. At first I thought a stroll would be nice. Kyla encouraged us to go, but I became uncomfortable quickly."

"Lads are fools. Many lads will do anything to toss a lass's skirts up, get under them. Lads all talk about the best way to do that. I'm embarrassed to tell you this, but you must know. You need to be able to protect yourself. Being Robbie's daughter should keep you safe, but there's bound to be some fool or another who will try to get his hands underneath your gown, anywhere to feel your bare skin…"

Gracie stared at him as if she had no idea of what he spoke.

"Hellfire, I'm making a mess of this. Look, I'm probably not the one who should be telling you about lads. Ask your sister or my sister, but I can tell you this. When any man does something you do not like, there is an easy way to end it. 'Tis not a nice way, but every lass needs to know how to protect herself."

"What is that?"

Jamie scowled, feeling as if he was giving away the secrets of his brotherhood. But Gracie had to know. Someone else would try to take advantage of her. "You kick them."

"Kick them? In the shins?"

"Nay, you kick them in their bollocks."

Gracie sat up straight. "In their…"

"Aye. This is a difficult conversation to have, so let me end it with this. If a man is hit in his bollocks just so, 'twill end whatever he is doing. 'Tis so painful, he will be frozen for a moment, and you'll have time to run. Do what you must to keep yourself safe." Jamie stared at her, the innocent expression on her face making him wish to wrap his arms around her and carry her upstairs to her chamber. "Gracie…"

Her pale blue eyes locked on his, and all he could see were her pink lips, those delectable pink lips that he suddenly felt belonged near his own, somewhere he could always gaze upon them, feast on them. In fact, he wished to taste them just one more time.

He leaned down and touched his lips to hers, tenderly, a kiss for an innocent lass, unlike the one from the night before. She relaxed against him, leaning into him, so he increased the pressure of his lips, hoping she would open for him. When she did, he groaned and wrapped his arms around her, invading her mouth with his tongue, tasting her again.

The flimsy material of the gown she wore did nothing to hide her curves, instead giving him exactly what he would have begged for, the feel of her soft breasts against him, so close that he could almost feel the quivering in her skin at his touch.

He ended the kiss because something fierce had gripped him—a terrifying feeling that had made him wish to push away from her and run for the nearest loch. And yet the feeling would not release him, even after he pulled away.

He had to fight the weakness that he felt around Gracie. Mayhap he should start by telling her the truth. "I need to tell you something else."

"What is it?"

Damn, but he could stare at her beauty all day if she were his. "I've decided to seek out Uncle Logan," he said, running a hand through his hair. "I'd like to travel with him for a time, see if I'm interested in working for the Crown. I…'tis impossible to explain, Gracie, but I'm looking for something. I'm not sure what 'tis, but I won't feel whole until I find it."

"Oh?"

Hell, but he couldn't even think straight when she stood in front of him in that flimsy gown, her enticing lavender scent wafting all around him, tugging him closer. "If Uncle Logan agrees, I will leave Grant land immediately."

Her face changed, but then returned to normal. Was that disappointment he'd seen?

"Well, I hope you will find what you seek with Uncle Logan. Please be careful."

He brushed his thumb across her cheek and kissed her sweet lips one more time, one to take with him. He gazed into her eyes again, lost in the trust he saw there, ashamed that he'd taken advantage of her yet again. "Forgive me, lass. I should not have done that. I'm sorry. Allow me to escort you back to your chamber."

Gracie did not argue. She rushed toward the stairs, tucking her night rail around her as she hurried up the staircase.

When they reached her door, she turned around. He opened his mouth to speak, but she put two fingers to his lips and shook her head.

"Please do not apologize again. 'Tis too painful." She disappeared into her chamber so fast that he stood and stared at the door for a few moments in shock.

He did not know what to make of that.

CHAPTER SEVEN

G RACIE HAD REQUESTED NOT TO go to the great hall the following day. It would be unthinkable to face all the suitors who'd
followed her around at the party. She moved her charges to their special
chamber for their letter learning—furnished with a table and four chairs,
a stack of Maddie's picture books that the wee lassies adored, and a few
toys.

Maddie stuck her head in early, so Gracie took the opportunity to put
her question to her. Kyla came behind her mother.

"If you please, my lady, would it be too much trouble for us to take
our meals here today?"

"Of course that would be acceptable." Maddie embraced Gracie
before doing the same to each of the girls in turn. "Poor dear, you must
be exhausted after all the fuss that was made over you last night. Were
you not pleased to see all the lads interested in you?"

"Everything was lovely. Many thanks to you for the festivities. I was
quite surprised by the number of lads in attendance, but I'm fine." She
would not say anything bad about the evening since it had been spe-
cially arranged for her.

"And did you find anyone who caught your interest?"

"Did you kiss a lad, my lady?" Maisie whispered sweetly.

Maddie leaned over to speak to Maisie. "We will not ask her that
question. That would embarrass her, so we shall simply ask her if she
had a nice time and if she thought anyone was special."

Maisie, properly chastised, stared at the ground. "Forgive me for my
rudeness, my lady." Gracie could see the wee lassie fought her tears,

but Aunt Maddie stepped forward before she could react. She scooped Maisie into her arms, bussed her cheek with a kiss, and said, "You know I love you."

Maisie lifted her gaze to Maddie's. "But I was naughty." Her face scrunched up and turned a deep shade of pink.

"Nay, do not say such a thing. You just needed a wee bit of guidance, lass. You are as sweet and kind as ever."

Maisie's expression switched back to a huge smile, so Maddie hugged her once more and set her down.

"Now why do you not tell a story to Morna and Maeve with my picture book while I talk with Gracie and Kyla."

"May I? Please?" Maisie clapped her hands, her exuberance showing in her every movement.

"Aye, you may choose your favorite. Just talk quietly so we can speak here."

Maisie ran off to the table, followed by the two bairns, while Maddie ushered Gracie over to the side of the chamber.

Maddie took Gracie's hands in hers. "So tell me, did you find anyone you are interested in?"

She knew which man she wished to marry, but it wasn't anyone they expected her to name. Gracie opened her mouth, prepared to tell a lie, but found she could not. She stared at her feet for a moment before lifting her gaze to her beloved aunt's smiling face. "Aye, but I'd rather not say yet. I am not sure…"

"My sweet, do not concern yourself. I need not know all the details yet. I'm just so pleased that you have found someone that interests you. How wonderful. Do you not agree, Kyla?"

Kyla nodded. "Last eve, she thought there were three who might interest, but you talked to one of them enough to be more certain? Truly, Gracie?"

Gracie could only nod, afraid if she spoke, tears would fall down her cheeks at the hopelessness of the situation. How could she tell Maddie she was in love with her son, especially since he clearly believed their short relationship had been a grave mistake?

Not only had he regretted kissing her, but now he planned to leave Clan Grant off for another land. How long would he be gone? Was he running from her? Could he tell how she felt?

Three times he'd kissed her, and he'd apologized and said it should not have happened. Her hand moved to her lips reflexively.

Kyla, who missed nothing, caught the subtle movement, and her eyes widened and her mouth turned into a perfect circle.

"Mayhap," Gracie finally answered. "I am not sure yet. Last eve was truly confusing. I'll need more time. Would that be possible?"

"Of course, of course," Maddie said. "We shall have another festive night for you, though I'll call it a night for all the Grants. We'll schedule it in three days to give you some time to collect your thoughts. How does that sound?"

Gracie wished to scream. The last thing she wished to do was spend another night running away from strangers declaring their love for her. She did not wish to be the one to dash a lad's hopes. What a terrible burden to be placed on anyone's shoulders. Not revealing her true feelings, she nodded and said, "That would be wonderful, Aunt Maddie."

"I do not want it to focus on you this time, but it will still give you the opportunity to mingle with the men you met. Would that suit you?"

"Oh, 'twould be lovely." Gracie replied with a smile. "I would love another night to help me decide." No, her gut dropped to her toes at the mere thought of it. She should never have brought up the idea of marriage since her goal had failed. She'd hoped Jamie would choose to pursue her, but now she knew that wouldn't happen. If only she could cancel the entire event.

"Then it's settled." She patted Gracie's arm and then pivoted toward the door. "I must go speak with Cook, so be on your best behavior for Lady Grace, lassies. Kyla, when you're finished here, please come see me in the kitchens. Gracie, before I see Cook, is there anything special you would like at the next party? Fruit tarts? Meat pies?

Apple pies. How she loved anything with apples in them. But she did not feel she could ask for anything else from Maddie, who had done so much for her. "Nay, whatever you choose would be wonderful."

Maddie hurried out the door with a wave.

The very moment the door closed, Kyla grabbed Gracie's hands. "Someone kissed you and you liked it! I can tell."

Gracie could feel the blush creeping up her face again.

"You're blushing, so it must be true." Kyla grinned.

"Why do you never blush? I hate that I blush at all the worst times."

"Because you are much fairer than I am. Your yellow-white hair means you blush easily, just as my brother does."

"Which one?"

"Jamie."

Gracie ignored the flutter of her heart at the mere mention of his name. "Are you not interested in someone, Kyla? You are of an age to marry. There must be someone pleasing to your eye."

"I've had my eyes on a few, but I wish to wait and see how you do with all the lads. You get first choice."

"What if I cannot find anyone? What if I find someone and he changes his mind? Suppose I'm interested in someone who is not interested in me?"

Kyla leaned over to whisper in her ear, squeezing her forearm. "We'll make him change his mind." She stood up straight and declared. "Besides, Gracie, that is just a preposterous statement. Everyone loves you."

Everyone but the lad she wanted—Kyla's brother.

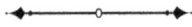

Jamie couldn't recall the last time he'd been so out of sorts. He had no fever, no wound, no belly ache, but he was more miserable than he'd ever been before. Unfortunately, he had a sinking feeling that he knew the cause of his surliness.

As usual, his mother had been right.

Gracie. He had feelings for Gracie. But he still wished to pursue his plan, and he expected a response from Uncle Logan any day now.

Regardless of these new feelings, he did not feel ready for marriage. His gut told him to seek his adventure now, and he knew he would regret it if he did not at least speak with Uncle Logan in person.

A small voice in his head told him that he still had time with Gracie. Mayhap some distance would help him sort out his feelings. And while she was seeking a husband, there was a good chance that he would return to the Grants before she married.

The tears on her cheeks had almost undone him. It was the reason he'd lost control and kissed her again. He couldn't allow that to keep happening. It was unfair to her.

So he'd leave. Do as he'd promised to Mac and himself. Explore his world.

This would settle his mind…wouldn't it?

He marched toward the great hall after a brutal day in the lists, wiping the grime and sweat from his face with his sleeve. Normally, he would clean up a bit before he met with his mother, but this meeting had not been planned. Braden had raced from the keep to inform him that his presence was needed in the solar.

"What do you suppose I've done now?" he'd asked his brother, Jake.

"Probably naught," he'd said with a shrug. "You know how Mama is. She tries to speak with each of us alone every so often."

Connor had grinned and waggled his brow at his brother. "Your turn is up. 'Tis your lucky day."

Finlay had yelled after him, "Dump some of that attitude before your father sees you use it with your mother. Otherwise it'll be you and your sire in the lists tomorrow."

All the way across the hillock he'd muttered to himself, "What attitude?" But he knew exactly what Finlay meant—only he did not fully understand *why* he felt this way.

He was strolling across the courtyard when a sultry voice called out to him. "When you get rid of that weight you carry on your back, I'll be waiting for you. All you need to do is say my name."

When he spun around, Peigi stood peeking out from behind one of the buildings, an inviting smile on her face.

"My thanks, Peigi, but not this eve." He turned away from her and hurried toward the steps. The lass had chased him many times before without any encouragement on his part. If he spoke to her now, she'd follow him everywhere.

As soon as he stepped into the keep, his mother bounded out of her chair by the hearth. "Oh, Jamie. I'm so pleased to see you. Come to the solar with me. I already have bread and an ale inside for you."

"Mama." He nodded as a greeting. "What is the purpose of this meeting?"

She wrapped her arm around his shoulder, leading him toward the solar. "Your sire and I discussed something we'd like to share with you. 'Tis naught to upset you. You'll see. How was your day?"

Jamie ignored her question as he followed her into the solar. As soon as he stepped inside, she pivoted to close the door behind him. So, it was to be a closed-door meeting. "Sit, have a seat near your father," she urged him.

Jamie took the proffered seat and stared at his sire, who immediately narrowed his gaze at him. "You still have that edge about you."

"What edge?" Jamie stood and backed up, wishing to put some distance between his sire and himself. While the renowned Alex Grant had slowed a bit due to the pain in his joints and bones, he could still be mighty quick when necessary.

His sire pointed to the chair, so Jamie sat again.

"The edge we've seen before that I don't like."

Jamie shrugged his shoulders. His father's words reminded him of Finlay's. Aye, he knew something was not right with him. Worse, he knew Gracie was part of it. But building a relationship with Gracie would mean he would have to stay home, give up on his chance to fulfill his promise to Mac and make his sire and uncles proud. He would have to stay put.

Then there was his other worry, the one he did not like to think about. What if he married Gracie, only to lose her in childbirth like Magnus had lost his first wife? Or to fever? Or...an accident? He'd sworn he would protect himself from that kind of pain.

"I know not what you mean," he insisted, crossing his arms in front of him and staring at the floor.

"Aye, you do. The edge you developed after Mac died. But I had to bring you to Mac's favorite place on three occasions before you would admit you were having nightmares about the man. Are you having nightmares again?"

"Papa, I'm too old for that. I recall the instance you speak about, but I was younger then. I think I would know when something specific was bothering me."

"Would you?" He could feel his parents' gazes boring into him as they waited for his response.

Aye, that had been one of the most difficult times in his life.

Mac, the Grants' stablemaster, had been one of Jamie's best friends. Jamie had spent hours talking to the man and listening to his many tales, and he'd treasured his wisdom. But his friend had never been the same after losing his wife, Alice. Jamie had seen his friend experience the very worst kind of loss, and he did not want it for himself. He would be wise to stay away from marriage. He pushed away the image of a certain blue-eyed and pink-lipped beauty. He had to.

"My apologies, Da. I do not feel myself, I'll admit, although I don't quite understand it." He stared at the floor again, but not before he caught the secretive glance exchanged between his mother and father. This did not feel like a day he needed to add anything new to his list of worries.

His sire tipped his head back, his eyebrows knitting together. It was a look Jamie had seen many times—the look Alex used to strategize against his enemies. Did his own father consider him an enemy?

He wanted to ask what was going on, what they'd decided for him, but something told him he'd best be quiet. So he waited.

And waited.

Finally, his mother asked, "Jamie, are you interested in marrying Gracie?"

Shocked that his mother had guessed what had been tormenting him for days, he formed his words carefully before he responded to her. "I'll admit that I have feelings for Gracie. As you've said, we shared a special bond as children, but I wish to travel, work for the Crown, go on an adventure…"

His father interrupted him. "Because you wish for those things or because you promised Mac?"

He gave his sire a puzzled look. "Nay, not because of Mac. I…I just feel the need to seek out my path. I think Uncle Logan can help me decide what I want to do. Mayhap I would like to work for the Crown as he and Aunt Gwyneth do."

"Is that why you sent him the message?"

"Aye. Have you heard from him?"

"Aye. He has invited you to meet with him at Uncle Aedan's and Aunt Jennie's. He'll be there on the morrow, and Molly and Tormod are coming with him."

"But we wish to be sure you are not interested in Gracie before you leave," Jamie's mother prodded. "She's a beautiful and talented young lady. She may be betrothed when you return."

The thought of Gracie betrothed to another man sickened him, but he realized it was possible. Still, he could not let it change his plans, not when this was what he had wanted for so long. "I understand. I'm just not ready for marriage. I realize many of my cousins have married, but it may not be for me."

His sire said, "The chances of you losing your wife at a young age are slim."

"Why would you say something like that, Papa?" He'd file that comment away and cling to it. Mayhap he'd need it someday.

"Just a thought. You may go to see Uncle Logan if you're sure you are still interested."

He nodded emphatically. "Aye. I'd prefer to leave as soon as possible."

"Who will you take with you?"

"Finlay and five guards."

His sire reached for Maddie's hand. "Have a safe journey."

Her smile was forced, and Jamie recognized it as the same smile she gave every time Alex left Grant land. He stood and gave her a hug, then said good-bye to his sire. At the last minute, he asked, "Mama, would you do me a favor and tell Gracie I've gone?"

"You do not wish to tell her yourself?"

"We discussed it. I told her I planned to go if Uncle Logan invited me."

His mother's forced smile grew again. "Of course, I'll tell her. Safe travels, Jamie."

"My thanks, Papa, Mama. I think this journey will help me." He smiled and then charged out of the door, almost running into Finlay.

Finlay just stared at his friend. "How did it go?"

"Get your things. We're off to Cameron land to meet Uncle Logan."

Finlay nodded. "I'll return shortly."

"Meet me at the stables." Jamie headed out the door, rushing as fast as he could. But guilt followed him. He should tell Gracie of his plans, but he knew it would be a mistake. Instead, he returned to the keep, penned a quick note and found his sister. "Kyla, I'm leaving to meet Uncle Logan."

Her face fell. "Jamie, you belong here."

"I'm glad you are certain, but I am not. Would you do me a favor and give this note to Gracie?"

Kyla gave him a puzzled look, but took the parchment. "If you feel the need to leave her a note, then mayhap you should not leave at all."

He had no idea what she meant by that, but it did not matter. He had to hurry.

Everyone would assume he was so anxious for his journey that he was in a hurry to leave, but that wasn't quite the truth.

He hurried for fear of running into Gracie. If he saw her again, he'd probably never leave Grant land.

CHAPTER EIGHT

GRACIE HAD HIDDEN IN THE learning chamber as much as possible, hoping to avoid run-ins with any of the men wishing to court her. She hated seeing the hope in their eyes, knowing that it would turn to the opposite when she rejected them.

The next was the party for the Grants. It would be her chance to meet more men, to see if she could find anyone who would turn her interest from Jamie. She scratched her head, wishing there was some way for her to escape the evening's activities. Sickness would be preferable to spending another night as the center of attention for a group of lads she did not want to marry.

Maisie, Maeve, and Morna sat on the floor playing with their fabric animals. They'd finished their letters, and their midday meal would be arriving soon, so Gracie moved over to pull the fur back from the window, shivering as the cold air burst past her. It was thrilling to feel a hint of spring in the air. How she loved the warmth of the sun on her skin and the spring flowers decorating the landscape of the Highlands, a land she would never leave. Ashlyn had traveled to Edinburgh, but Gracie had no desire to leave Grant land. This would be her home forever.

The door opened and Hildie brought in their meal—apples and mutton stew. The girls sat down to eat, and Gracie helped them get settled before returning to the window. How would she possibly get through another night with the lads, another night of Jamie being displeased with her?

Kyla flew in through the door. "Gracie, Mama is on her way and so is your mama. Something transpired in the solar. Our mamas were both there, and our das, too. I have to find out with you."

Gracie's eyes widened and she chewed on her thumbnail. "What do you think it is? You must have heard something."

"Naught. I tried to get closer without being obvious, but I could not get close enough to listen. And guess what else? Jamie left this morn. He gave me this note. He is off to Aunt Jennie's to meet with Uncle Logan. Quiet—" She held her fingers to her lips. "Here comes Mama. I can hear her footsteps on the stone."

Gracie peered at the note Jamie had left for her.

Gracie,
 I'm leaving for Aunt Jennie's to meet Uncle Logan. I hope to help you choose your husband when I return.
 Best,
 Jamie

What did that mean?

Gracie did her best to appear calm, but something had changed. She could feel it in the air. Jamie was gone. She had to choose a suitor, though her heart was not in it. Clearly, Jamie had no interest in marrying her, or he never would have left.

She did want a family, bairns of her own. Then she needed to accept Jamie's rejection and forge ahead with her plans. There had to be someone out there for her.

The door opened again, and Aunt Maddie stepped inside, followed by Gracie's mother. Their uncomfortable smiles told her something was wrong, but she quickly gave both of them a kiss on the cheek.

Aunt Maddie cleared her throat, glanced at Gracie's mother, then took a step closer. "We have some information we must share with you."

Gracie nodded, though her heart plummeted to the tips of her very toes because she knew it was not going to be good news. The pause was long enough for her legs to start trembling. Had they chosen for her? She would not believe they would do such a thing. She trusted her mother, her family, her clan.

Maddie continued. "We received two messages this morn concerning you and your wish to be married. There are two other men who are interested in marrying you, and they both plan to arrive to announce their suit in two to three days."

"The eve of the festivities?" Gracie feared asking any more questions.

Who were they? Did she know them? Probably not, as she did not know any lads outside of the clan.

Kyla wrapped her arm around Gracie's shoulder and grabbed her hand, squeezing it tight.

"Aye," Aunt Maddie said. "They will be here soon, so we must allow them entrance to the festivities. I will plan accordingly. We have discussed it and think that is the wisest course."

Caralyn said, "I know this will upset you, Gracie, but you know not what may happen. It may turn out to be someone you can love."

"But I don't want to ever leave Grant land," she said, feeling her lips tremble. "I've told you that forever, Mama."

"I know, but if you fell in love with someone, it would change everything. I never planned to live in the Highlands. I would have followed your sire anywhere. One of them is said to be quite handsome, though I've never met him," her mother said.

"Who are they?" Gracie glanced first at her mother, then her aunt, and then Kyla.

"The first is Laird Robert Chisholm and the other is the Baron of Duncrub, Gordon Crichton. Laird Chisholm lost his first wife, and he is a bit older than you. Baron Crichton is an English baron who was just awarded land in the Highlands. The baron is supposed to be a fine man." Aunt Maddie added, "I know this arrangement may not be to your liking, but we ask that you be polite. Though Duncrub is farther away than Chisholm's land, 'tis most important that we offer our Scottish hospitality to both of these men. You are not committed to either, as it would be impossible for you to accept both."

Her mother said, "I agree. 'Tis better they both come. 'Twill show them there are many lads vying for your attention. You do not have to choose either one, Gracie, but we do ask you to be polite and meet both."

Gracie felt the increasing need to heave out the window, but she would not do so in front of her mother and her aunt. "Of course. 'Twould be my pleasure to meet them both, though I hope they will wait until the evening meal." Under no circumstances did she wish to be tied up with two strange men all day long.

"I suspect the baron will not be here until late in the day, probably in three days. One never knows with the laird. But he would be pleased to speak with Alex for a time. Do not worry over much." Aunt Maddie gave her a quick squeeze and said, "Everything will be fine. You'll see."

Her mother did the same and they left.

The tears started as soon as the door closed behind her mother.

"Kyla, what shall I do? I cannot even go to Ashlyn for advice. She is too sickly with this bairn. What will I do? I wish to stay on Grant land." Her hands reached into the hair on the top of her head, scratching and kneading. What had she done?

Gracie lost control of the emotions that had started coursing through her upon hearing the news about the visitors to Clan Grant. She burst into tears, loud enough for all three girls to hear and turn to her. They stood in unison and ran over to hug their mentor. Maisie said, "What happened, my lady? Did you hurt yourself?"

Gracie, not wishing to admit the truth, came up with something that was not an outright lie. "Aye, I hurt my heart. 'Tis all, lassies. You may go back to your animals."

Maeve tugged on her skirt and held her arms up to Gracie, who picked her up and hugged her close. The lassie cradled Gracie's face in her tiny hands and gave her a kiss. "Bettew?"

Gracie sniffled and smiled. "Aye, my thanks." She set the wee one back down and Maeve hurried over to play with her friends.

Kyla whispered, "Mayhap you can get sick and not go at all."

"Nay." She swiped at her tears. "I thought of that, but I cannot lie. And I cannot believe Jamie left without saying goodbye. I wanted to wish him well. If he were still here, I could ask him what he knows of the baron and the laird."

"Jamie's been acting odd of late. Do not worry about him. I wish he had spoken to you first, but Mama said he was in a hurry and anxious to go on his adventure. I suppose that could be why he's been acting strange."

"What else could it be?"

"I know not, but I'm glad you're planning to go. 'Tis possible you could fall in love with the baron. Imagine, you as a baroness."

"I doubt that will happen. As I've said, I have no desire to leave home. I shall have to hope we do not get along." Gracie took another bite out of her poor thumbnail.

"I wish Jamie had stayed a few days more. This should help clarify one thing."

"Clarify what?" She dropped her hand to her side, listening intently to her friend.

"I've wondered if Jamie's problem is jealousy, and he does not recognize it."

"Do not be silly, Kyla. Jamie and I have not been getting along at all."

"Exactly. He's afraid of his feelings for you, so he ran away. 'Tis my belief, and I know my brother pretty well."

But Kyla, true friend that she was, had just given Gracie a morsel of hope to cling to.

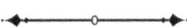

Jamie groaned. Why the devil was it taking so long to get to Cameron land? Anxious to reach their destination, he'd rushed as fast as he could without mistreating his horse.

"What the hell is your problem now, my lord pleasant?"

Jamie spun his head toward his friend, who was now riding abreast of him in the meadow. The rest of the guards were trailing them. "I do not have a problem. Do you?"

"Nay, I don't. On second thought," he said, raising a finger to his chin, "mayhap I do. I'm thinking I should have stayed with the Grants. Seems more appealing than traveling with an ornery person. The guards seem to agree with me."

"Who's ornery now? The guards have been fine."

"Who's ornery?" Finlay gave him a comical look and then glanced over both shoulders. "You are. Why do you think the guards are so far behind us? They cannot stand being around you."

"I am not ornery," Jamie barked. Hell, he knew he was being miserable, but he wasn't about to admit it to Finlay.

They were halfway through a meadow brimming with new thistles ready to burst into bloom, the tops of them showing just a touch of purple. Finlay pointed to a tall grouping off them. "You're as prickly as the sides of these new thistles. And keep your horse away from them. He'll be tossing you off his back and into a field of them. You'll be screaming as loud as the Norse at the Battle of Largs."

Jamie chose to ignore his friend. As prickly as a thistle, indeed. Where did the fool get his expressions? Thank goodness they were almost on Cameron land, the shape of Lochluin Abbey growing larger as they approached.

"Finally. I thought we'd never get here."

Finlay barked. "No one wishes to arrive more than me. Are you prickly because your belly is bellowing with hunger?"

"Stop calling me prickly. We'll settle this in my uncle's lists on the morrow. He always likes us to teach his son some skills. I'll be sure to tell him not to count on learning any skills from *you*."

Finlay slowed his horse until Jamie turned around to glare at him. "Something wrong with your horse?"

"Aye. He says I'm too close to the pricklies."

Finlay guffawed, but Jamie ignored him, riding ahead on his own. He was anxious to see Tormod. Mayhap his friend could tell him what it was like to be married. Plus he and Molly could give him the best information about what it was like working for the Scottish Crown. Uncle Logan would make light of anything difficult, as he often did. They would give him the untarnished truth.

As they came close to the gates of the Cameron keep, a group of riders came out to greet them. Once they drew close, he recognized his aunt and uncle, followed by several Cameron guards.

"Good eve to you, Aunt Jennie, Uncle Aedan. We've come for a short visit. Uncle Logan said he'd be here with Molly and Tormod. You recall my friend, Finlay?"

"Of course, I do, Jamie," Jennie said. "You're Nicol and Inga's lad, are you not?" she asked, shifting her attention to Finlay. "How is poor Inga doing?" Jennie and Aedan turned their horses around and rode on either side of them.

Finlay said, "She's not improving, but she's not worsening either."

Jamie stared at the ground, feeling a bit guilty for bickering with his friend. Finlay had every right to be ornery, yet he continued on as if all were well. He doubted he would behave half so well if Maddie were the one with the illness.

"Poor woman," Aunt Jennie said. "She is so sweet. I'm glad you and your brother are staying home with her."

As soon as they made it through the gates and dismounted, stable lads ran forward to take charge of their horses. Aunt Jennie wrapped her arms around Jamie, giving him a fierce hug, and then greeted Finlay with a hug as well, while Uncle Aedan clapped each of them on the back. "Tell me about your sire and your uncles, Jamie. I do miss my brothers so. Please tell me your sire's bones are not causing him any more troubles."

"He has his good days and his bad days, but he never allows anyone to see them. Jake taught me how to tell when he's suffering." It occurred to him that he'd never asked his aunt about her close relationship with his sire. "Aunt Jennie? Why is my sire so special to you? It seems you are closer with him than with Uncle Brodie or Uncle Robbie."

Aunt Jennie never aged, but for a few strands of gray in her hair. She looped her arm through Jamie's and led him into the great hall. "Come, we'll feed you lads and find you an ale. I swear you and Jake will be taller than Alex before you're done." She paused for a moment, considering his question, then said, "I was the youngest when we lost both of our parents, only around seven summers. Alex and Brenna were almost like parents to me, and I will admit that Alex spoiled me quite a bit. I love him dearly, as I do all my siblings. Brenna and I are both healers as our mother and grandpapa were, so that brings a special bond." She smiled up at him. "Riley and Tara are interested in healing as well."

"Are they as talented as Jennet and Brigid?"

"I love my daughters and Brigid dearly, but Jennet has a special ability. My lassies are too young. They do not have the stomach for the blood yet. Riley is ten and four, and Tara is ten summers, so even though they are older than Jennet, neither have a talent of her caliber."

Once they made it to the hall, Aedan grabbed them all ales and said, "Drink up. We have plenty for growing lads. Brin is still young at eight summers, but mayhap you'll go to the lists with him on the morrow, lads?"

"We'd love to," Jamie replied, casting Finlay a sideways glance as they settled in chairs grouped around the hearth.

Uncle Aedan caught it. "A wee challenge going on between you two?"

"Aye," Finlay replied. "We'd love to bring Brin along. He can be our impartial judge."

Jennie said, "Finlay, I cannot believe how tall you are. I remember you and Fergus when you were both less than five summers."

Finlay looked surprised. "You do?"

"Aye, your sire was fighting fever after he was injured in battle. He hadn't awakened for two days, making your mother sick with worry. But you two stayed at his side, squabbling so much that he finally awakened to tell you to stop fighting."

"Fergus and I never fight. We're too careful because of our mother. What did we squabble over at that age?"

"Hmm…" Jennie stared over Finlay's head, as if peering into the past, and said, "If I remember correctly, you were arguing over keeping still and not waking your father up. Inga was quite happy you woke him up. Your hair has darkened a touch, but 'tis still quite red. What a lovely shade."

Finlay blushed and glanced over his shoulder at the door.

Jamie spoke up, "He does not need to argue any more with his brother. He argues enough with me." Jamie grinned at his friend who snorted.

Two serving lasses brought out platters of meat pies and bread. Jamie had to admit he was starving, so they ate for a few moments in silence. Then Uncle Aedan said, "Jamie, Uncle Logan sent me a message saying he and Molly and Tormod have important information for you. They're due to arrive on the morrow as originally planned. For whatever reason, we're glad you've come for a visit."

Jamie glanced at his friend, wondering what that comment could mean. He'd expected to meet his uncle, but what new information could he be holding?

CHAPTER NINE

THE FOLLOWING MORN, JAMIE WAS awakened early by his cousin, Brin. He was lankier than many lads his age, but his sire was not as bulky as Alex Grant.

"Cousin," Brin said, shaking his shoulder, "come show me all your tricks. I must know how to beat my friends. They do not believe the Grants are so talented."

Jamie and Finlay had slept in the warrior's camp, though Aunt Jennie had pushed him to sleep inside. He sat up and wiped the sleep from his eyes. "Lad, I'm happy to help you, but I need a bit of food in my belly and a spot to pish in."

"Here. I brought you oatcakes," he said, handing one to each of them. "'Tis true that Logan Ramsay is coming? Is he as tough as they say? Or does he always beat his enemies because he's smarter than them? Because I'd rather be smarter. You have to be quick to keep from getting hurt."

Finlay sat up next to Jamie. Staring at the boy, he said, "Full of energy this morn, aren't you, sprite?"

"Your hair is really red."

Jamie jumped to his feet and laughed at his friend. "Is that what you call the stuff on Finlay's head? It sticks out everywhere, does it not?"

Brin followed them outside the camp, running along behind them as Jamie sought a bush where he could relieve himself. "You're really tall, cousin Jamie. Will you teach me some tricks to take down the big lads? They pick on me because I'm the laird's son, and because I haven't grown yet. Do you think I'll be as big as you? Next time you come, will you bring Loki with you? They say he's the best trickster of all. What do you think? Can you not help me learn how to fight?"

Having found a bush, Jamie stopped to turn to his cousin. "Brin, wait for me over there so I can pish in peace, will you not?" He pointed off to the side.

Finlay said, "Aye, you do not want to be near him, lad. You will not be telling him how big he is if you stay over there. Come with me."

Jamie picked up a stone and threw it toward Finlay, who ducked as he led Brin away from him. "Jealous, Finlay? 'Tis a sad state, jealousy."

They settled down onto a grassy knoll near the lists, and Jamie and Finlay bantered back and forth for a while as they munched on oatcakes and drank water. Brin stared at them, never taking his eyes away until they finished eating. Finally, he asked, "Can you help me, cousin?"

Jamie said, "You've come to the right cousin. I was always smaller than Jake until I hit ten and five. You see my ugly friend Finlay here?"

Brin chuckled, his hand over his mouth.

"Finlay was smaller than his brother Fergus for a long time, but now he's taller. So we can show you all the tricks we learned. We both know how to bring bigger lads down."

"You do?" The lad's face lit up and Jamie couldn't help but smile. He knew exactly how it felt to be the smaller lad.

"We do, and you're right. Being smarter is what matters. Come along. Finlay and I will show you some special maneuvers."

Nearly two hours later, Jamie noticed they had an audience. Uncle Aedan stood off to the side, his arms crossed, with a smile on his face. Jamie and Finlay had taught Brin some fighting skills, both with his hands and with his sword. The lad was a quick study. He was having the time of his life, and it showed in the way he carried himself. How well he remembered having to prove himself as the laird's son, especially since his sire was the most renowned swordsman in all the land. He would do what he could to help his cousin.

"Papa, watch this," Brin yelled, noticing his sire. "I'm going to wrestle Jamie to the ground."

Brin fought hard to bring Jamie to the ground, twisting him, tripping him, confusing him. It took him a while, but he finally managed to get the best of him, though Jamie didn't put his best effort forth. After the lad took him down, Jamie roared and jumped to his feet, picking Brin up and spinning him over his head. The lad squealed and yelled much like Kenzie did.

All Jamie could think of was that Finlay had been correct. He'd been prickly yesterday, but he'd had a smile on his face the entire time they'd worked with Brin. When he set Brin down, the lad ran over to his sire, explaining all he'd learned in the fast chatter he'd already demonstrated to him and Finlay. He was an intelligent boy, much like his sire, the book lover, and his mother, the healer.

A shout came from behind Uncle Aedan—a guard announcing that visitors had been seen near the abbey and would soon arrive. Uncle Aedan said, "Brin, take your friends off to the stream so they can wash up."

A short time later, they made their way into the hall. Molly, Tormod, and Uncle Logan were already inside. After they exchanged greetings, Brin tied Uncle Logan up with an endless stream of questions while Jamie spoke to Molly and Tormod.

"Congratulations. You two look verra happy."

Molly leaned over toward Tormod with a smile and he wrapped his arm around his wife. "Never been happier," Tormod said. "Didn't think I'd like marriage, but when you find the right one," he kissed Molly's cheek, "naught is better."

"We told your sire and your brother about your accomplishments in defeating MacNiven, but they did not quite believe us. We'll convince them yet."

"Someday soon. I promised Molly I'd take her to see all her cousins and introduce her to my family. But we have work to do first."

"Tell me about working for the Crown. Does it suit you?" Jamie asked, eager for their answer.

Molly said, "Aye, it does because we're working together. I love traveling with my husband, but I must admit I'm sad when we're away from home for long. Maggie takes it hard. She's used to it from Mama and Papa, but not from me. In fact, once we finish this assignment, we're heading home for a moon."

"What assignment are you on? May I ask?"

"We'll allow Papa to tell you," Molly said, glancing at Logan, who was still listening to Brin prattle on. "He'll wait until Brin is away."

A few moments later, Uncle Logan rustled the lad's hair, sent him off, and asked Aedan, "Mind if we use your solar, Aedan?"

"Nay, go right ahead." He led them upstairs to his solar just off the balcony. "I'll send some food up for you."

"My thanks," Uncle Logan said. Finlay, Jamie, Molly, and Tormod sat in chairs around a table in the center of the room while Uncle Logan stood at the end.

"Jamie, I take it from your note that you're interested in working for the Crown. Are you serious about this?"

"To be honest, Uncle, I don't know exactly. But I've always promised myself I'd have a bit of adventure while I was young, so I thought this could work for me."

"Finlay, what say you?"

Finlay inclined his head toward Jamie. "I'm here with him. Whatever he does, I'll go along, if you'll have me."

"I can take you both along on this assignment if you are truly interested. 'Tis not a heavy one, nor is it especially dangerous, but it'll give you a feel for what's involved. Molly and Tormod are great spies because they are mostly unrecognizable in these parts. You are known as Alex Grant's son, so there are many places I could not send you. This is a more secretive assignment than many, so it would not be a good fit for you normally, but it will do. You'll just have to learn to hide in the shadows, so to speak."

"Where are you headed?"

"Not far from here. 'Tis between Cameron's land and yours, which is why this was the perfect place to meet. We're going to pay a visit to Baron Gordon Crichton of Duncrub, though if all goes well, he'll never know it."

"I do not recognize his name," he said, furrowing his brow. "I thought we knew everyone in the Highlands."

"King Alexander awarded him some land in return for a large investment. The king is feeling more and more unrest stirring in the Highlands, so he needed the coin for future endeavors. Crichton is an unknown, other than that he's from England and is said to be quite the charmer. But he made a most unusual request that the king feels he must consider."

"I don't understand where we would fit in," Jamie said.

"We've been asked to do a character assessment. The king knows little of the baron's ways, so he wishes us to see if we can uncover aught unsavory about the man. There are rumors, but none have been proven. He needs to hear from us before he replies to the request the baron has just sent to him."

He gave Jamie a pointed look that alarmed him.

"What is the request?" Jamie asked.

"He's made a formal request for Gracie's hand in marriage. He wants your cousin to be his baroness. The baron is on his way there now to talk to her sire and your sire."

Jamie bounded out of his chair. "Absolutely not. I have to go and stop him."

Uncle Logan quirked an eyebrow at him. No one said a word.

"Gracie does not want to move off Grant land," Jamie explained as he rubbed that same spot on his neck. "She was searching for a lad to marry from our clan. That's what needs to happen. What if the king agrees to the baron's request? Uncle, you know the king. How can we stop this?"

"We?" Uncle Logan asked.

"Aye. We must stop this."

"So I am assuming you are not interested in traveling with us to the baron's keep?"

"Aye...Nay." He stared at Finlay, then shifted his gaze to Molly and Tormod. All of them looked so serious for once. He knew why. This *was* serious. Not even his sire could ignore the king's command, so if the king accepted the baron's official request, Gracie would have no choice but to do the same. "Nay, I'm going home."

Uncle Logan turned toward the others. "I'd like to speak to my nephew alone, if you don't mind."

Finlay, Tormod, and Molly all left the solar, though Molly squeezed his shoulder on her way out.

"Now, is there something you wish to tell me, lad?" Uncle Logan leaned back against the table, his arms crossed in front of him. "I've seen that look before. There seems to be more to this than a cousin helping a cousin."

Jamie floundered for words. "She's not a blood cousin."

"Absolutely true. Tell me what this is really about, Jamie. Do you wish to offer for her, or do you know someone else who does?"

Jamie felt absolutely sick inside, every part of him in turmoil. "I don't know, Uncle. But I do know this."

"What?"

"I'm going home to save Gracie from the baron."

Uncle Logan nodded, pushed up from the table, and clasped his shoulder. "Molly, Tormod, and I will go to Duncrub to see what we can discover about the new baron. On your way home, you need to give some serious thought about what Gracie means to you. 'Tis no time to play games."

Gracie dressed with care. Her aunt had brought in an ice blue gown with a silver surcoat, a beautiful garment, and then left to find Caralyn. Gracie wished she could see how she looked in the gown, but of course that was foolish. Aunt Maddie had chosen it because she thought it would look lovely with her coloring, though Gracie would have been more inclined to choose black—something to divert attention rather than attract it.

A knock landed on the door, and when Gracie bade the visitor to come in, her mother entered the room. "Gracie, you look absolutely stunning." Tears were welling her mother's eyes, and she looked away lest she start sobbing.

"My thanks, Mama."

Aunt Maddie came in behind Caralyn and stood in the doorway. Her gasp was loud enough to be heard down the passageway, and Uncle Alex soon appeared behind her.

"What are you looking at, Maddie?"

His eyes seemed to widen for an instant before they returned to normal.

Aunt Maddie clasped her hands to her breast. "My dear, I must say I agree with the minstrels. You are the most beautiful lass in the Highlands. The silver threading in the surcoat matches your hair. While I wish I could put curls in it, your hair is so long and straight and lovely to behold. Do you not agree, Alex?" Maddie twirled around to face her husband, stepping inside the door so he could join them in the room.

"Aye, Gracie is lovely." He nodded to his niece. "I do appreciate your acceptance of this situation. We will not force a marriage on you."

Gracie decided not to hide her feelings. "My thanks, Uncle Alex. I am verra nervous about this gathering, but I will do my best not to embarrass anyone."

Alex took a step back. "Lass, 'tis nonsense. You'll not embarrass us. But I did wish to let you know that I have not forgotten your wish to stay on Grant land. You understand that you'll have to leave if you become betrothed to either one of them."

Gracie's stomach flip-flopped. How she wished to beg Uncle Alex to release her from her promise to attend the gathering, but she could not. The words would just not come. She would do what was asked of her.

She always did what was asked of her.

Kyla edged her way into the chamber. "Papa, please let me through, I must see her!" Smiling indulgently, Alex stepped aside. As soon as she saw Gracie, Kyla's expression filled with wonder. "That gown, your hair, your surcoat. You are stunning. The men will all be vying for your hand after one look at you."

Gracie did all she could not to crumple to the ground at Kyla's comment. She did not want all the men vying for her hand. She only wanted one, and he was gone. While everyone chattered amiably around her, talking about the evening ahead, Gracie's mind strayed to something her mother had told her long ago.

Caralyn had said she'd never planned to live in the Highlands until she met Robbie Grant. He'd changed her mind. What if the baron was a kind and handsome man? Could she do it? Could she forget Jamie and fall in love with another?

Aye, she vowed to try her best. She squared her shoulders with a new sense of purpose, just now tuning back into the conversation in front of her.

"Alex, she will not be able to tell you after one eve if she's interested in one of them."

"Why not?"

Aunt Maddie shook her head as she folded a plaid and placed it on the end of the bed. "These things take time."

"Nay, they do not have to." He smiled at Aunt Maddie, a crooked smile that was unusual for her uncle. "It did not take me long."

Aunt Maddie's hands went to her hips, and she turned to give him her full attention. "Alex Grant, do you not recall how timid I was around you? Or how you always yelled at me when we first met? Mayhap *you* had made up your mind, but you frightened the devil out of me. Do not rush the lass, please."

Kyla blurted out, "Papa, give Gracie a chance. Mayhap her perfect man will not be here this eve."

"Her perfect man? I do not know a perfect man. Where would I find one, Kyla?" Uncle Alex chuckled at his daughter. "Is that what you want? A perfect man?"

"Papa! Stop teasing me, Papa. This is serious."

Gracie's head jerked back and forth. She took two steps toward the door as four of the people she adored most bickered about her future. This was wrong. She slid out of the open door, then closed it behind her before heading down the corridor. Their voices were still volleying in her chamber, one trying to outdo the next. She made it to the staircase before she realized the huge mistake she was making.

The great hall was full of admirers, and they waited for her alone. The hush that fell across the hall told her so. She stood at the top of the stairs, gathering her courage and strength, and then started down the steps.

CHAPTER TEN

THE FIRST PERSON TO GREET Gracie at the bottom of the stairs was Uncle Brodie. He took her arm and escorted her over to meet Laird Chisholm.

"Grace," Uncle Brodie said, using her proper name, "I'd like to introduce you to one of our neighboring lairds, Robert Chisholm."

Laird Chisholm bowed to her and said, "Greetings to you, my lady."

"I am no…" She could feel Uncle Brodie's fingers squeezing hers, so she didn't finish explaining that she was not officially a lady at all, that she was just one of the clan. Laird Chisholm had kind eyes and a warm smile. He was quite a bit older in age than she'd expected, probably thirty summers or even thirty and five. He had a full head of brushed hair and a full beard, both speckled with gray.

She cast a quick glance at her uncle before she whispered, "I am pleased to make your acquaintance, Laird Chisholm." As soon as he looked away, she glanced over his shoulder, hoping to see the baron, but she did not see anyone who appeared to be of nobility behind the laird. She had to admit it was sheer curiosity on her part to see what the baron looked like. She hadn't seen many who could claim to be of English nobility.

He held his arm out to her. "My lord, if you do not mind, I would request to take the lass outside for a stroll while we chat a bit? 'Tis still light out. I promise to take good care of her."

Uncle Brodie searched the hall, though she was not quite sure why, but then he nodded. "For a few moments only, Laird Chisholm. I do not wish to tarnish the lass's reputation." Perhaps her uncle had also noticed that everyone in the hall was now focused on the three of them.

Gracie took the laird's arm and walked out of the door and down the steps of the keep with him, wondering where on earth he would take her. She had thought Uncle Brodie would deny his request, but he had not. And while she did not wish to be out here with this laird, she had promised to give the visitors a chance.

"I believe 'tis a lovely spring day, Grace. What think you?"

"I agree. 'Tis most lovely."

"Tell me, have you had much experience with lads? Have you been proposed to before?"

She was not sure what he searched for, but she answered him honestly. "Nay."

"I know not if you have been informed, but I lost my dear wife over a year ago. I do have one son at home, but I hear you are wonderful with bairns." He led her into a corner away from the courtyard and her clansmen. "Pardon me for being so forward," he said, turning her to face him, "but I have heard there are others coming to announce their suit, and I wish to find out whether we would make a good match before I am pushed off to the side." He cradled her face in his hands and kissed her.

It was a soft kiss, a nice kiss, but it fell totally flat for her. There were no sparks, no butterflies, no desire for this to continue. Was it because he'd caught her off guard? Or simply because he wasn't Jamie?

A growl erupted behind her, followed by a loud bellow. "Laird!"

Laird Chisholm ended the kiss and spun around in time to see Jamie barreling directly at them. Jamie grabbed Gracie and shoved her behind him.

Gracie was so surprised to see him that all she could say was, "Jamie?" Where had he come from? Finlay was not far behind him.

"What the devil is wrong with you?" the laird shouted. "Are you not one of the laird's sons? Brodie Grant gave us his blessing for this wee jaunt outside. Your actions are inappropriate, and I will speak to your sire about this." The cords on his neck stood out as he bared his teeth at Jamie.

Jamie's voice came out in a deep tone that almost frightened Gracie. "As her cousin, 'tis always my job to protect the lass against untoward advances, and the way your hands were trailing over her was far more inappropriate than my behavior. I will escort her back inside the hall."

Jamie gave her a rough shove to put her in front of him as they moved toward the keep. She tripped over her gown and he caught her, holding her upright. "Jamie, please slow down."

He whispered in her ear. "Mayhap you think you're doing what's expected of you, but my sire would not want you to allow a near stranger to corner you and take advantage of you."

His hand gripped her upper arm tightly as they headed toward the stairs, but at the last minute he moved her over behind the armory. "Jamie, you're hurting me," she said.

"Forgive me for hurting you," he said, loosening his grip and waving at Finlay to go inside, "but I just returned from Cameron land, and I found you out here in that man's arms. What say you about this?" The line of his jaw told her how upset he was.

"Your uncle introduced us and approved of our stroll." She felt near tears. "How was I to know what he had planned? And why have you come back so quickly?"

She could see the fury in his gaze calm just a bit. Unexpectedly, he hauled her in close to him, wrapping his arms around her, encouraging her to rest her chin on his shoulder. "My apologies, but something came over me when I saw his hands on you. I promise to be better, and I did not mean to hurt you. You know I would never intentionally hurt you, do you not?"

"You're forgiven, but how will I know who is right for me if I do not kiss them? Is that not a good way to tell? I would not have allowed anything else, but I think it's helpful." She pushed away from him. It was as much as she could bear to say to him. She wanted to mention their kisses—to tell him that they'd moved her in a way that no other man had or probably could—but he'd already rejected her. He had to come to her. "Why are you here?"

"I learned some things that made me come back."

"What?" She wrapped her arms around her waist to warm herself against the chill of the night air just starting to settle around them.

"'Tis of no importance now. That laird had no right to maul you." He rubbed a spot on his neck, something he'd taken to doing recently, his lips pinched together in a tight line.

"Maul me? I hardly think…"

"He would have mauled you had I not interrupted him." He briefly closed his eyes, and when he opened them again, he looked at her with such hunger she gasped.

He stood a couple of paces away from her. They stared at each other for the longest time, and Gracie loved every moment of it, her body responding to him with a heat she could not comprehend. She could almost feel his emotions, his feelings for her. Had he come back because of her? His anger had indeed been born of jealousy, and she could see that this would be a difficult eve for him, just as it would have been difficult for her to watch him with another lass.

His head dropped and his boot rubbed something on the ground, making a clicking noise that was the only thing she heard. When he lifted his gaze to hers again, she tried to tell him with her eyes how much she loved him, that she wanted him and him alone, that all he had to do was say the word and she would put an end to this night. All he had to do was give her some indication that he felt the same, something...anything...

But the words he said were the last she wanted to hear. "Forgive me, I'll not carry on in that manner again. You have the right to kiss whomever you choose. But do not expect me to stop watching out for you. If you need me, I'll be there."

And she wished to kick him, slap him, shove him, yell at him.

Instead she did what she should do. She always did what she should do, what was expected of her. Swiping a tear from her eye, she whispered, "My thanks. I'll return to the hall to see my other suitors, as your parents and my parents have requested."

The dreaded silence settled between them again.

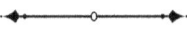

If he'd just slit his own throat, it would have been less painful.

When he'd first set eyes on Gracie, he'd actually stopped breathing. Had he ever seen her look so beautiful? The blue and silver gown she wore was so striking that his mind had stopped working properly at the sight of her.

There were no words to describe Gracie's beauty. The minstrels were all correct. He could imagine the tales they would spin after seeing her tonight. Her hair shone like a diamond, mesmerizing him. He'd spent many a day wondering what she would look like standing in the middle of a forest at night in the nude, her thick silky strands adorning her luscious curves. In his mind, she was a goddess or the most brilliant of the faeries. She deserved to be protected. He hated the thought of the lads swarming on her, but they needed to return to the hall.

Holding the door open for her, he offered her his arm. He would treat her as she should be treated—like royalty. A smile spread across her face as she gazed up at him, and all he wished to do was scoop her into his arms and take her upstairs into his chamber and make slow passionate love to her all night long.

His thoughts were brought to an abrupt halt by her sire's approach. "Gracie, why do I not escort you around the hall for a bit? I admit 'tis a surprise to see you here, Jamie, but why do you not get something to drink?"

Just like that, he was excused from her side, but when he glanced at his sire, Alex waved him toward the solar. He was undoubtedly looking for an explanation about Jamie's travels and his abrupt return.

Once they were both inside, Jamie fell into the chair in front of his sire's desk. His shoulders slumping as he rubbed his throat again. Hellfire, but the memory of that sword at his throat had popped up again.

His sire took his time settling behind the desk. "I did not expect to see you here. Did you see Uncle Logan?"

"Aye." He was quiet for a moment, considering how best to describe the situation. His father expected information to be brief and to the point.

"And?"

He lifted his gaze to his sire's. "Uncle Logan informed me that Baron Crichton of Duncrub has petitioned the king for Gracie's hand, and he, Molly, and Tormod are going to assess the baron's holdings, see what they can learn about him before the king agrees."

"Did Logan invite you to join them?"

"Aye." He dropped his gaze to stare at his hands again. Had he done the right thing in returning here? Should he have stayed with his uncle? "I decided to come home."

"Why?"

"Because you know Gracie does not wish to leave the Grants. I needed to let you and Uncle Robbie know of the baron's official request." Full of nervous energy, he jumped to his feet and began pacing about the chamber. "But on my return, I see her with another, Laird Chisholm. How many have asked for her hand? And the baron made an official request to the king."

"Did you tell Gracie?"

"Nay." He spun on his heel and headed in the opposite direction. "Has Laird Chisholm made an official request for her hand, too? Are there two sharks seeking her hand?"

"Chisholm has only spoken to me about Gracie. Word traveled to him and he wished to see if they suit. We must offer hospitality to him as our neighbor, and I know not what he thinks of Gracie."

"Don't you think two men after Gracie is too much?"

"Nay. She has more choices. Why did you not tell her about Baron Crichton? She is expecting him, but she knows not that he has petitioned the king for her hand."

"Because I did not wish to upset her. You know how she feels. When will Baron Crichton of Duncrub arrive? Or is the baron here? I'd like to meet him. I thought it was him outside…"

"Outside?"

He stopped, gripping the back of the chair in front of him. "Outside. I believe Laird Chisholm was the one mauling Gracie."

"Mauling her?"

He could see he had his father's attention. "Aye, he had his hands all over her. I had to stop him before he went any further."

"Jamie, you need to get control of your emotions," his sire said, giving him a sharp look. "This is Gracie's choice, not yours. We'll tell her about the baron's request on the morrow. He has not arrived yet, but when he does, I will discuss the issue with him. I would appreciate it if you would do your best not to offend any of our guests. Can you manage that?"

With a heavy sigh, he replied, "Aye."

His sire rose and circled the desk, then reached out and clapped a hand on his shoulder, stopping him from pacing. "She's stronger than you think, Jamie. Allow her to use her own judgment. I applaud your efforts to protect your cousin, but she has me and her sire and her uncle to watch over her. Go have something to eat. We'll talk on the morrow."

Jamie nodded to him before leaving the solar. His cousin. He was tired of hearing her referred to in that way. But his sire was correct, he needed to give her more credit.

She'd stood up to him and spoken her mind, and he was proud of her for that. Gone was the wee lass he'd needed to protect because she couldn't watch out for herself. After his mother had reminded him of that long-ago day in the stables, more memories of their youth had popped into his mind. Gracie giggling, Gracie rolling down a hill, Gracie throwing leaves in the air and letting them fall on her head. He'd watched her in awe, and kept everyone and every critter away from her.

It had been his job to protect her. But who had given him that job?

He could not recall.

Once her family had moved to the loch, he had not seen her as much. True, they'd visited at clan gatherings, but he'd been too busy in the lists, talking about battles and wars, to think about her. Then she had moved to the keep to take care of the bairns, and he had suddenly found himself going to the great hall just to talk to her. Stealing glimpses of her beautiful smile. Playing with her and the bairns. Spending time with Gracie had become the brightest part of his day.

Everything had run afoul when she'd gotten the notion of marriage into her mind. Now someone had petitioned for her hand and the situation was spiraling out of control. He had no idea what to do about it.

All he knew was that there was an unshakable bond between them. But a new fear had cropped up in his mind. A baron wanted her as his wife. She had become a pawn, a bargaining tool for their king. What would King Alexander say if Jamie requested her hand?

He'd probably refuse. He'd gain no coin from Jamie marrying Gracie. Jamie was the second son of a laird, which meant he had naught to offer but his heart.

He wouldn't be surprised if Gracie met the baron and decided she would love to be a baroness.

He stood back and listened to all the greetings the lads made to her as her sire led her around the hall.

Sean was first. "My lady, you are stunning as usual. I hope we can spend some time together later."

Fergus was next. "Lady Grace, you are…I mean…you look…" He turned a deep shade of red to match his hair before he managed to spit out, "beautiful."

Ned followed, "Lady Grace, I hope you will allow me the opportunity to dance with you this eve. I would like to get to know you better. You are the prettiest lass here."

Jamie did his best to hide his smirk at the stream of compliments and stumbling sentences. As Uncle Robbie escorted Gracie to the dais, he tipped his head to the table directly in front of it. This was where Jamie was to sit, and after he took his seat, Finlay joined him.

His friend whispered, "You'll have a verra busy night protecting that."

Jamie glared at him.

"Och, aye," Finlay said, his eyes gleaming. "Tell me she's not the most beautiful one here and I'll tell you how bad your vision is."

Jamie didn't respond, instead keeping his eye on all that transpired.

His gaze took in everything at once, but something bothered him. "Where's the baron? I know everyone else in the hall. I cannot believe we arrived here ahead of him."

"He has not appeared yet. You're right in keeping an eye out for him. He is your greatest competition."

Jamie glowered at him again.

"Och, aye. You're not interested in Gracie at all because she's—" and this part he drew out as slow as possible, "—your...cousin...of course. Cousins never marry, even if they are not blood cousins. Never. You need to find a new excuse."

"Enough. Enough or I'll tie you to the back of a horse and send it flying into a thicket of nettles."

Finlay hid his smirk and rolled his eyes. "Hit my mark. Enough... said."

The door flew open then and a hush traveled through the crowd as the new arrival appeared in the entranceway. He was every bit as handsome as the rumors had said.

The devil himself had just barged his way between Jamie and Gracie.

CHAPTER ELEVEN

G RACIE HEARD THE DOOR OPEN and chose to ignore it. What she could not ignore was the hush that had settled over the crowd. Gracie lifted her gaze and gasped. It was the baron. She did not need to ask anyone. He was dressed in a dark blue brat, and the guard who accompanied him removed his outer garment to reveal a yellow leine with a belt and a shorter *ionar* underneath made of dark blue wool. His trews were gray. His gaze crossed the hall, pinning on her. Aunt Maddie and Uncle Alex started to rise, no doubt intent on greeting him, but the baron moved toward the dais himself. He found his way to Gracie in no time at all.

Now that he was standing directly in front of her, Gracie's breath caught at the sight of him. His brown hair, long enough to curl at his collar, was carefully combed, and he was strikingly handsome. When he took her hand in his, she noticed he wore a sapphire ring set in silver. He bowed slightly to her and kissed her knuckles with just a wisp of a touch. Then he stood in front of her, a smile breaking out on his face.

"You can only be Lady Grace. I am Baron Crichton of Duncrub. It pleases me to finally make your acquaintance. Your reputation is legendary in these parts, and quite accurate, if I do say so myself. It seems you and I are of the same line of thought. Your blue and silver will look heavenly next to my dark blue and gray. That is as it should be with a married couple." His brown eyes bore into hers. It was almost a bit too intense, but everything about him set her on edge. She just had to determine if it was a good edge or a bad edge. Would her mother consider him bold or just rude for greeting her first?

Fortunately, her mother and father came to her rescue, appearing on either side of the baron, making small talk as they moved him toward the open seat next to Uncle Alex. His gaze did not leave Gracie's until the last possible moment.

She heard him say, "I'd prefer to be seated next to the lady, if you please." He'd pointed to Gracie, but Uncle Alex said, "In my castle, you'll speak to me first."

The baron recovered quickly and replied, "My apologies, Laird Grant. I would of course be pleased to talk to you now and get to know the lady later. I plan to be here for a day or two, so I'm sure we shall have plenty of time to get to know each other. Now, my first question is how soon can we marry?"

Her eyes widened in shock, so she turned away and her mother, who had taken the seat next to hers, squeezed her hand. She whirled around to face Caralyn, shaking her head ever so slightly in denial. "Please, nay. I am not ready to decide."

"Allow Uncle Alex to handle him. Clearly, the baron is a man accustomed to getting whatever he wants. But he has not met Alexander Grant yet. Ignore the baron for now and eat your meal. I think it shall be a long night."

Once the meal was over, Gracie made a point of finding her way over to Fergus first. There would be no dancing tonight, just mingling and minstrels to entertain everyone. She stood next to Fergus for as long as she dared, feeling safe in his presence, but they had little to talk about.

Fergus said, "Have you made your…mind…or your decision…or have you chosen anyone yet?"

"Nay, Fergus. I have not, but I hope matters will be settled soon." Truth was, she wanted naught more than to quit this charade and hope that Jamie would come around. She'd seen the evidence of his feelings on more than one occasion.

"I'd be a fine husband for you. I work hard as a warrior, and we could live here or at Castle Curanta with Loki, if you'd prefer. I'll do whatever you like."

"My thanks, Fergus. You are verra sweet. I agree, you would make any lass a fine husband."

She could tell by the expression on Fergus's face that they were no longer alone. Jamie had been watching from a distance, so there was a possibility it was him, but she doubted it. A booming voice came from behind her.

"My turn, laddie. Step away and allow us the opportunity to speak."

She was quite certain it was the baron, but she did not wish to turn around. A mixture of fear and excitement spread through her. True, she wanted Jamie, but could a lass not enjoy the attentions of a handsome baron for a wee bit?

Fergus pivoted and departed in a hurry, and the next thing she knew, a warm hand had grabbed hers and was leading her over to a table in the corner. He turned around and gave her his best smile.

"I would like some time to get to know you, my lady. Come along with me to this table where we may speak in private."

Gracie did not say anything, just nodded in agreement and then searched the crowd around them. She noticed Laird Chisholm was speaking with her sire, but she could not find Jamie. She needed to know that he was doing as he'd promised—that he was watching over her. There. He stood a short distance away, and while he was indeed watching them, he made no movement toward them. His arms were crossed and the rest of his body was in a warrior's stance. His facial expression was quite serious, but it couldn't have been any worse than hers. For some reason, she was paralyzed in fear.

Rather than stopping at the table, the baron managed to maneuver her toward a passageway off the hall. It led to her uncle Brodie's tower, which was well lit with torches, but the passageway itself was darker than she would have liked. Still, she was doing what was expected of her, was she not? She smiled at the baron. "Forgive me, but you are the first baron I have met. How should I address you?"

"How refreshing that you choose to ask instead of risking a mistake. I am pleased with that quality. You may call me Baron Crichton. If we become more familiar, my given name is Gordon, but that would be premature at this point. Do you not agree?"

"Of course, Baron Crichton."

"An agreeable, beautiful woman. Just what I have been searching for." He reached up and ran a finger down her cheekbone. "You are quite elegant, a true beauty. The noble blood in you is so obvious. Regal, just as a baroness should be."

He gave her a tender kiss, short but sweet—a kiss that confused her because it was nice. As nice as Jamie's? Nay, nothing could be, but she still felt something.

"How do you feel about becoming a baroness, running my household, traveling to Edinburgh to see our king? I'll see that you have several maids to take care of you. You'll give me the finest sons and the loveliest daughters. Your every desire will be met."

Gracie did not know how to answer him, because she suddenly felt uncertain. She'd sworn never to leave Grant land, but if Jamie was not interested, then should she marry another? She did want her own bairns.

Suppose the worst thing possible happened. Suppose Jamie fell in love with someone else, married someone from afar who would move here. Would she be able to watch him with another? The prospect of becoming a baroness was more enticing than that. If Jamie changed his mind, she would reconsider, but what if he did not? No one else had interested her at all, but this man was different, mysterious.

A voice interrupted them. "Gracie, is he bothering you?" Jamie came down the passageway toward them.

The baron turned to address Jamie. "Nay, I am not bothering the lady. Take your leave."

"I asked the lady, not you. Gracie?"

"And I am giving you a direct order."

"I do not take orders from you." With each comment, Jamie took a step closer.

The baron pulled out his small sword, and the swish of the blade against its sheath brought two of his guards into the passageway. "Who are you?"

"I am her cousin, and 'tis my duty to ensure she is treated with respect. Is he treating you respectfully, Gracie?"

She gave a quick nod, not wishing to anger the baron, pleading with her gaze for Jamie to back down. Something told her this would not end well at all.

"Of course I am treating her with respect. She will be my baroness, and as such, deserves your respect as well. You will address her as Lady Grace, not Gracie." He gave an odd sound after he stated her childhood name. "Do I also detect a touch of jealousy?"

"Do not be ridiculous, but I will protect her reputation."

"I think you want more of her than her reputation, and I mean to put an end to it." His sword, which had been down at his side, was now raised, and the baron stood in a fighting stance.

Gracie's heart started beating doubly fast, as if it might jump out of her chest. Jamie drew his own sword as the baron's minions approached with their weapons raised. "You're on Grant land, so drop your sword unless you wish to start a clan war. We did not invite your suit, and now you may consider it rejected. Take yourself back to Duncrub, Baron. You're no longer welcome."

"I'll stay as long as I wish."

"Gracie, step back. I do not want you hurt."

"Jamie," she whispered, "three to one. Please do not…" She knew her words had not been heard and would not be heeded. The tension in the passageway was strong enough for all to feel. What if he was hurt? What if he was killed? She couldn't bear it.

"Nay, three to three." Her uncle Brodie and his son Braden appeared out of the tower room, swords drawn.

"Stand down, all of you." Uncle Alex's booming voice echoed down the passageway. Gracie leaned against the wall, trying to make herself as small as possible.

The baron was not about to give up so easily. "This fool is interfering, Grant. I am simply attempting to get to know your niece better. His actions are inappropriate."

Alex Grant's muscular body, still larger than any in the clan, blocked almost the entire passageway. His sword was drawn, and he still had a reputation as the best swordsman in all the land. No one made a move to anger him. "You are inappropriate, Baron Crichton, by drawing your sword in my hall in front of a woman of my clan. Drop your weapon and leave my land. Take your guards with you. You are no longer welcome here."

The baron lowered his sword, but did not sheath it. "Laird Grant, I request the lady's hand in marriage, respectfully. I ask that her sire accompany her to my keep so we may become better acquainted without the presence of so many interfering suitors, including her cousin here."

Jamie barked, "I am not a suitor."

"I will take my men and depart on friendly terms if you agree to bring her to my land, escorted by any men you choose except this one." His sword made a quick lashing in Jamie's direction.

"That one is my son, and I'll do as I see fit. If you wish to do battle, it will be you and me in the lists, Baron."

While Alex waited for the baron's response, Gracie could hear the panting in the room, each of the men ready to fight at the slightest provocation. She could see Kyla had arrived at the end of the passageway along with Gracie's mother and father.

The baron paused, his gaze taking in all in the passageway, then nodded to his men. "We shall take our leave, but I have already petitioned the court for Lady Grace's hand in marriage, and I expect you to bring her to my land within half a sennight. If not, I shall bring an army of men to retrieve her myself." He sheathed his sword, then gave Gracie a short bow. "Until then, my lady."

Gracie must have heard him wrong. Petitioned the court? Did that mean what she thought it did? Had the baron asked the king for her hand in marriage? Her heart pounded loud enough to be heard by others, she feared. She attempted to lock her legs so the trembling brought on by the argument would stop.

If the baron had in truth made such a petition, her destiny would be sealed once the king agreed.

No one moved until the baron was out the door. In a low voice, Alex asked, "What provoked him, Jamie?"

"I did. I did not like that he brought her down a dark passageway, so I came to investigate." He gave Gracie a furtive glance. "'Twas a hunch—my intuition told me not to trust the man."

Alex turned to Gracie.

"Was the baron inappropriate with you?"

Gracie did not know what to say. If she said aye, the issue with the baron would be over. But did she want it to be over? Her world had always been small and simple since she'd joined the Grants, but now it seemed as if every decision she made would have an enormous impact.

"Papa, why are you putting her through this?" Jamie pressed. "Leave her be. She does not wish to leave our clan. Marrying the baron would require her to go."

The words were kind and caring, but he did not even look at her as he said it.

"You came here to tell us that the baron has petitioned the king for her hand," Alex said, his voice loud and sonorous. "You know that if the king orders the marriage, refusing him would be considered an act of treason. Torrian went through this."

Her hands shook as she reached up to brush a stray hair from her face. Dear Lord, she was doomed. She wished to tear down the passageway screaming loud enough for all to hear. She wanted no part of any of this. The only thought in her mind was that she wished to return to the safety and tranquility of the loch, her parents' home. It had been a mistake to want more.

"Can you not petition the king to refuse him?" Jamie asked, his cheeks turning red. "I do not think they suit each other. Grandmama said that we should all have a say in our marriages. Uncle Robbie may be Gracie's stepsire, but she is still a Grant."

Gracie held her breath, waiting to hear Uncle Alex's response.

"This seems to be more about what you want than about what Gracie wants."

Jamie threw his arms up in the air. "I do not know what you expect me to do, Papa. You taught me to protect the innocent, but now you've changed your mind."

"I do not think Gracie is an innocent. She's a woman grown."

Jamie's expression changed from one of anger to one of acquiescence. He bowed to Gracie. "Forgive me. I'll not intrude on your life again." He spun on his heel and stalked away without saying another word to his sire.

A moment later, Alex shouted after his son, "Jamie, in the stables at high sun on the morrow. Be there, or I'll come and find you." He said it without looking at him.

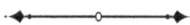

Gracie lay across her bed, sobbing in her gown. Her mother had attempted to talk to her three times, but she could not stop the tears long enough to listen.

Jamie did not love her. He'd walked away after saying he'd never intrude on her life again. It was obvious he didn't care if she was forced to marry the baron—at least not enough to offer for her himself.

Her heart felt like it was being split into pieces. She wanted nothing to do with the pompous baron. He'd intrigued her at first, but after the scene in the passageway, she had doubts about his character. Still, she feared he'd get his way with the king.

What was she to do?

Laird Chisholm had left as soon as he found out that the baron had gone to the king to ask for her hand. The others, Sean, Fergus, and Ned, had each nodded to her and said they were sorry in so many words.

This entire fiasco had ended without her having a choice at all. She would be forced to marry the baron, who, handsome as he was, had threatened her family.

Aunt Maddie came into the chamber and sat down in a chair near the hearth, turning it to face Gracie. "Gracie, when you are able to discuss this, we must."

She did her best to stop her hitching breaths. When she finally managed it, she sat up, used a linen square to swipe at her swollen eyes, and said, "As you wish, Aunt Maddie."

Her mother and Kyla sat on the bed with her. Ashlyn was still too sick to leave her cottage, though Gracie needed to speak to her more than anyone. She wiped her eyes again, waiting for her aunt's news.

"The baron has not changed his plans. As you know, he formally requested your hand in marriage by petitioning the king. He is still requesting that you come to his lands."

"When must I leave?" She couldn't stop fresh tears from falling down her cheeks.

"I ask for your feelings. Are you interested in the baron?"

"Nay," she bawled. "He made me uncomfortable, but what if the king says I must marry him?"

Her mother said, "Why do you not sleep on it tonight, and let us know on the morrow."

She forced her voice to calm because she had finally come up with the perfect solution. There was one way she could save herself from a forced marriage. "Nay, I do not need to sleep on it. I know what I'd like to do, and I will not change my mind."

Aunt Maddie, her mother, and Kyla all stared at her, waiting to hear her response.

"I wish to be a nun. I'd like to go to Uncle Aedan's, Lochluin Abbey.

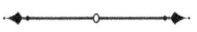

The festivities in the hall had come to a halt as soon as the baron left. Jamie couldn't stop thinking about the bastard. Then there was the small matter that he would have to face his sire on the morrow. He'd begged a few men to go to the lists with him since it was a full moon, and a few had obliged him. He needed to get Gracie out of his mind.

That was easier said than done. After his confrontation with the baron, he'd looked at her face, and the fear he had seen there haunted him. How could he explain that to his sire? His life was a mess. He'd refused his chance to go off with Uncle Logan, and though Finlay was of a mind that his uncle would give him another chance, the prospect was suddenly not so appealing.

Jamie dropped his sword and fell to the ground, exhausted. The four men around him applauded him, hooting at his skills.

Finlay said, "I think you killed the baron for sure, this time."

Finlay's friend, James, said, "Aye, the baron's dead for sure." He stood up and walked away, waving his hand at Jamie. "I've enjoyed the show, but I have better things to do, Jamie."

Once James left, Jake said, "Jamie, you need to stop. You'll not be any stronger on the morrow. You've worked yourself into a frenzy today in the lists. The baron's already gone. You'll gain naught from working yourself into the ground."

Connor, leaning back on his elbows and chewing on a blade of grass, said, "You think he's still fighting the baron? I think he's fighting Da."

Jake shook his head. "Nay, he's not. He's fighting the baron, but you should stop, Jamie. Once you go past a certain point, you'll not be able to function tomorrow unless your life is threatened, not if Da's the one sparring with you. Only the baron would be able to draw any fight out of you."

Connor swung his head around to stare at his brother, Jake. "Da scares me as soon as he pulls his sword out. Always has. How can you say another would make him dafter?"

"Trust me, you'll know it when it happens to you."

"Nay, Jake." Connor spat the grass off to the side. "Da is enough to frighten the devil out of anyone. Do you not recall the stories of how Da killed a man in front of all the clan with a wound in his thigh?"

"Aye, I do. Da wanted to tear that man limb from limb for what he did to our mama. 'Tis why he beat him so easily."

Finlay choked. "Easily? 'Tis not what your uncles say. He dropped to the floor once he stepped inside the keep. Your da drained every ounce of strength he had, all of his energy aimed at one man."

"Never mind. Jamie, stop now so you have some strength left to face Da in the stables. I'll be there for you, if Da allows it," said Jake.

Jamie panted, "He'll not allow any of you. 'Tis between Da and me."

Connor whispered, "I swear I never want to meet Da in the stables or the lists again. Never."

Jake laughed and patted his shoulder. "Da tries to make us stronger. I'm going home to my wife. Aline's waited long enough. I'll be looking for you on the morrow, Jamie, just keep some calm about you and you'll do fine."

"Jamie, you sleeping in the warrior's camp?" Finlay asked, standing up and moving to Jamie's side.

"Nay. I'm going to the keep. Connor and I have a chamber for the night. Had to give mine up for guests, though I'm too tired to see if Laird Chisholm is there or not." He lied. True, he planned to sleep in the same large chamber as Connor, but the reason he wished to return to the keep tonight was to find out how Gracie had fared. He hadn't seen her since he'd left the passageway. He needed to find her so he could try to explain why he'd done what he had.

And he had to know if she had any feelings for the baron. He hoped she'd seen his true character, but he did offer her the title of baroness. Wiping the sweat from his brow, he said, "You ready, Connor? I'm off to sleep."

"Sure, I'll go, unless I get a better offer on the way." Connor winked and waved at Finlay as they headed their separate ways.

Jamie was so wrapped up in his own thoughts that they didn't speak on the way to the keep. He couldn't stop thinking about how he'd messed up again, both with Gracie and with his sire.

Royally.

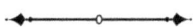

Once everyone had left, Gracie did her best to wash her face. She had one person she needed to speak to before she made her final decision about the abbey.

There was nothing left to lose. She would find Jamie and offer herself to him. If he refused to court her, then she would ask to leave for the abbey on the morrow, before the baron could come for her. There would be no clan war over her betrothal.

She dressed in the trews Ashlyn had given her long ago, then plaited her hair and tied it up. Wrapping a plaid over her head and around her shoulders, she snuck down the staircase, hoping to avoid notice. Jamie would be in the warriors' camp. She'd have to find someone to locate him for her.

Moving as quickly as she could, she was passing the stables when a strange sound echoed through the night. It sounded like a lad in pain. She heard a woman's voice, but the sound was different, strangled and panting.

Her eyes widened as soon as she realized what the lovers were doing in the stables. Mortified by the sounds she'd heard, she hurried to get away from the couple's grunting, but something stopped her in her tracks.

The woman's voice was Peigi's, and she heard what she called out next very clearly. "Jamie, Jamie, ohhhh, Jamie."

Gracie stood still, her feet frozen to the spot.

She turned around in a slow circle, no longer wishing to speak to Jamie.

Apparently, he was quite busy.

CHAPTER TWELVE

J AMIE STRODE TOWARD THE STABLES, tipping his head back to
check the sun. He hadn't found Gracie last night, so he'd vowed to
find her sometime later today. If he survived this meeting with his sire,
he'd find her right away and explain his foolishness to her. He'd go with
her if she had to go to the baron's land—of course he would. Staying
behind was just unacceptable. What the hell had he been thinking?

His sire's voice called out to him as soon as he entered the stable.
Jamie sighed. From the sound of his da's voice, he knew exactly where
he was—Mac's stall.

That's what he'd called it for as long as he could remember. Mac
had chosen a stall for himself. He'd had a storage closet built into it so
he could keep all his tools there for when he groomed the horses. He
always kept sweet treats for the wee ones and the horses in his special
closet. It was a place where Jamie had spent a great deal of time as a lad.

"Why here, Papa?" He noticed all the stable lads were gone, not a
good sign.

His father stood from the bale of hay where he'd been seated. "Why
not? You are acting like a horse's arse, just as you did shortly after Mac
passed on. Do you not recall?"

Jamie did not want to look at his sire. That time had been so painful
for him, but he had not let himself cry. Instead, he'd become so furious
with the world, he'd sniped at each and every person who crossed his
path.

"Aye, I recall. But I was young, Papa. Every time I came here 'twas
painful for me. Why mention it now? No one has died."

"Your mother and I believe the way you're acting now is exactly the same way you were acting then."

"So your plan is to fight me until I start crying? If I recall, 'twas what happened the first time. You swung your sword at me until I was so upset that I cried and cried. I was a lad then. You'll not be able to make me cry now. I tell you, the two situations have naught to do with each other."

"I think they do," his sire's voice came out in a whisper, and he stood there as he always did—calm and controlled.

Telling Jamie what he thought.

Telling Jamie what to do.

Telling Jamie how to run his life.

Jamie did not care to listen any longer.

His sire narrowed his gaze at his son and lifted his chin, spinning his sword with his hand, acting like he knew everything. "I think 'tis exactly the same."

And Jamie's temper blew. "I do not, and I'm tired of everyone telling me what to do, where to go. The bastard deserved to be thrown off our land, putting his hands all over Gracie."

His sire just leveled him with a look.

He'd never known anyone who could control his temper like his father could. Alex could be furious and one would never know it, but Jamie had learned the subtle signs that meant he was close to losing his temper. He'd see that wee tic in his sire's jaw and he'd nod to Jake, telling him to start running.

That tic hadn't started yet.

"You and Mama taught me that a Highlander should protect women. I protected Gracie against Sean and Chisholm and the baron just as you raised me to do. Why was I wrong?" He could feel his voice growing louder, but he did not care. It felt good to yell at his father. "Did you ever consider that mayhap I did not *want* to protect her, that it was our clan's code of honor that made me go after the baron?"

The tic in his sire's jaw started to wiggle. It did not matter. He could not stop now.

"The way the men all circled her, you should have assigned her a team of protectors. Mayhap had three guards follow her everywhere. The lass draws men like bees to a honeycomb—all of them flitting around her, trying to sniff her, trying to lick her, trying to…"

"Get your arse outside and draw your sword, lad."

Jamie stared at his father, at the tic of his jaw, at his narrowed gaze, another bad sign.

But he didn't stop, plowing ahead without any thought of the repercussions. The anger had grown in him over the past weeks, peaking last night. "They wished to stick their cock in her like she was a common wench, a whore..." he growled.

His sire's voice bellowed through the rafters. "Get your arse outside and draw your weapon, lad, or it'll be my fists."

Jamie hollered back, "Suits me. Kick my arse any way you want. Mayhap I'll kick yours." He stalked outside, took his shirt off, and grabbed his sword.

His sire came at him with a roar, his blade poised over his head, waiting for Jamie to ready himself. Once they were far enough from the building, Jamie charged toward his sire, forcing the confrontation. He would hold back nothing. Metal clashed against metal, and though Jamie's muscles begged for mercy, he would not stop. He could not. He swung and swung, stopping his father's advances. Out of the corner of his eye, he saw Jake and Connor, but they stayed back. This was between him and his sire.

He'd had enough. He could take no more of watching those bastards flitting around his Gracie. *His* Gracie! Aye, he was supposed to protect her, but he'd failed.

He swung his sword from the side, hoping to catch his sire off-guard, but Alex was faster, and he swung with a force that knocked him on his arse.

He hadn't protected her as he ought to have. Those bastards had touched her.

He jumped up and ran straight at his father with his sword, and again his father knocked him on his arse.

Laird Chisholm had kissed her. *Kissed his Gracie.*

Jumping to his feet, he spun in a circle and brought his sword down on his father's weapon so hard that sparks flew.

Sean had kissed her...*his Gracie.*

He swung again and his father knocked his weapon out of his hands. He grabbed it quick and ran at him again, but he knocked him away.

The bastard baron had *kissed his Gracie!*

His sire stood in front of him, heaving, his sword down in front of him. "Jamie, this is no different than before. You couldn't handle losing Mac. Can you not see what's bothering you?"

"Nay. Naught is bothering me. Draw your weapon, Papa."

His father lifted his sword again, but with a different attitude. "Can you not see what you're doing? You're deliberately keeping your distance from the lass. She'll not hurt you like Mac did." His father let up a touch, though he continued a light parry while they talked.

"Aye, she could," he said, choking on the words. "You've lost loved ones before, I know that, but have you watched them die in front of you? Da, a bolt of lightning shot down out of the sky and sucked the life right out of him, and there was nothing I could do but *watch*. I'll never put myself in such a position again."

"What happened to Mac was a terrible accident, but it wasn't a common one. We did not raise you to be afraid of life, Jamie. Stop hiding from it."

"I held him in my hands, Da. As soon as I touched him, I knew he was dead. Women die in childbirth, from the fever. What if…" He couldn't even say it. The thought of Gracie dying made him ill.

They continued to move and spar, but Jamie said naught. He told himself that the water around his eyes was only sweat, but part of him knew better. He'd never forget that night. Never forget seeing someone alive one moment and dead the next.

His sire's voice came again. "You need to knock that wall down, lad. If you do not, I'll do what I can to knock it down for you. You need Gracie in your life and you know it. You're afraid you're losing her. 'Tis why you are fighting everything and everyone around you."

Jamie spun in a circle and attempted to knock the sword out of his sire's hands, but his father did something new, twisting his sword in such a way that Jamie lost his grip. The weapon flew out of his hands, and his sire flipped him onto his back, putting his foot on his chest.

He stared up at Alex, shocked that his sire had beaten him so easily.

"Now, son, you're going to listen to me and I do not wish to hear a word from you." His voice fell to a whisper, low enough so no one else could hear them. "You lost to me because your emotions are ripping you apart, both your mind and your heart. You couldn't handle losing Mac, and you are about to lose another person you love, Gracie, and you cannot handle that either. I came out here to knock some sense into you, hopefully, and help you realize that your heart belongs to that wee lassie you loved many moons ago. Her smile might melt a thousand men's hearts, but her heart belongs to you. Now you have to be smart enough to accept that truth and offer for her. If you do not, you will lose her, and she'll be gone forever. You cannot spend your whole life being afraid to love. You must trust your own heart.

"Now, I have a letter that was written a long while ago, and it belongs to you. I set it in Mac's cupboard. When you've finished reading it, come see me at the door to the stables. We'll see if we cannot come up with a plan to end this foolishness."

His sire picked up his sword and strode into the stables, leaving him flat on his back. He stared at the sky for a long time, not moving, thinking about all his sire had said.

Was he right? Did Gracie truly love him? Jamie had to admit to having strong feelings for her, stronger every day, but he'd done his best to bury them. Fear had stopped him, fear of losing her, fear of her not reciprocating his feelings, fear of not being good enough, fear of too many things.

After he mulled it over for a while, he stood up and walked back toward the stables. Jake stood a good distance away, but Jamie waved him away. This was something he needed to do alone. He sheathed his sword and moved into Mac's stall. There in the cupboard sat a folded piece of parchment.

His hand shook at the sudden surety that this was a note from his beloved Mac. He opened it and began to read:

Jamie,
I had your mother pen this letter before I got to be too old to think clearly. I miss you, wee bean.

Jamie smiled at the term. He had no doubt that Mac had dictated this note to him. He had not called him wee bean in front of many.

I know you'll be upset when I go. You're young and well, so you do not understand death. But I will go willingly when my time comes so I can be with my Alice again.
I know you've told me about all the things you wish to do in your lifetime, but I wish to tell you something different. 'Tis not what's out there that is the most important, but what's at home. I know you dream of traveling and exploring, of being a hero like your da, all the things young lads wish to do.
Mayhap it sounds simple, but my advice is to find your lass. Naught will make you happier than the love of a sweet lass. You are too young to believe me now, but one day I hope you will believe me. I know she's out there for you, but your

heart will tell you when it's time. I fought loving my Alice, my sweet flower, but marrying her was the best thing I've ever done. Our life together made me happiest of all.

Find your flower. Follow your heart and do not fight your feelings as I did. I almost missed the greatest gift in my life.

Be a good lad now. Someday we'll meet again.

Mac

Jamie folded the parchment and tucked it into his sporran.

He needed to find his flower, Gracie.

His father stood with his arms crossed, right where he'd said he would be. None of the stable lads had returned yet, probably at his sire's request.

"Did you read the note, Papa?"

"I did."

"What do you think?"

"It does not matter what I think. What do you think?"

"I think he has a good point." Jamie stared at the ground in front of him, unsure of what to say to his sire.

His sire, not one to overuse words, said, "I agree."

"Do you think Gracie is my flower?"

"I do." His father clasped his shoulder. His sire stared up at the sky, a strange look crossed his face—an expression of almost…delight. "Stablemasters are special."

"They are?"

"Aye. If 'twere not for Mac and my stablemaster before him, Old Hugh, I never would have found and married your mother."

The thought shocked him. "Truly?"

"Aye. I would not have enjoyed my life without her. She means as much to me as Alice did to Mac. Listen to the old men of the world, Jamie."

"Did Jake go through this with Aline?"

His sire shook his head. "Jake sees what's right in front of him, but does not pay attention to what's around him. All he saw was Aline; he did not care about the circumstances that brought her to us. You see everything around you, but not what's right in front of you."

"Gracie's right in front of me."

"Aye."

"Does it matter that we're cousins?" he asked. "I worried 'twas wrong." He glanced at his sire, hoping he would approve of what he wished to do. Men that underestimated Alex Grant were foolish. He couldn't believe the battle he'd just had with his sire.

"Nay. She's not a blood cousin. I don't think Gracie sees you as a cousin."

Jamie thought that was a good sign. He did not want Gracie to see him as a cousin at all. He thought about each of the kisses they'd shared. She'd never pushed him away the way she'd pushed against Sean. She'd looked extremely uncomfortable with Laird Chisholm. Was it his imagination or had she fit him just perfectly? She'd never pushed away from him but instead found the perfect way to melt into him, her softness something he suddenly craved. "I need to find her, talk to her. Do you think Uncle Robbie would accept my request for her hand?"

"Aye. But I would suggest courting her. You need to talk to Gracie first."

His father's tone had changed to one of encouragement, the rough edge he'd had before their swordplay now gone. He'd been crude about Gracie, said horrible things, all signs of his jealousy. For some unknown reason, it all started to make sense to him. His attitude had been all about her, though he wouldn't admit it to many.

"You and Mama will support me?"

"Aye." His sire smiled, sheathing his sword.

"I need to find Gracie, then talk to Uncle Robbie and Aunt Caralyn."

His father nodded before he glanced up at the sky. "That could be a problem."

"Why?"

"Because Gracie decided she wished to go to the baron's this morn. They left at dawn."

CHAPTER THIRTEEN

A FTER OVERHEARING JAMIE AND PEIGI in the stables, Gracie had run aimlessly, thoughtlessly, before returning to the keep and asking to speak with Aunt Maddie. Then she'd packed her things and headed for Ashlyn's cottage.

Once there, she barged in without knocking.

Magnus flew out of the bed chamber, ready to attack whoever had broken into his home, but he rubbed his eyes in confusion when his faithful deerhounds, Mada and Sim, raced over to greet the visitor.

"Gracie?" Magnus asked. "Is aught wrong? 'Tis the middle of the night, is it not?"

Ashlyn stuck her head around the corner of the doorway, then stepped into the room as soon as she realized it was Gracie. "What is it? Mama? Robbie? One of the lads?"

Gracie shook her head as she pulled a chair out from the table and flopped into it. "Nay. I needed to come see you before I leave."

"Leave? Where are you going? What happened with the baron?"

"I'm going to the baron's holding. He's offered for me, and I wish to go. I was going to become a nun, but then I...I..." Gracie burst into tears and lowered her head to the table, burying her face in her crossed arms.

Ashlyn took the seat next to her. "What? You cannot go to the baron's. You cannot become a nun either. You promised me, remember? I changed my mind about going back to Edinburgh because I recalled the promise we made to each other that we'd never leave Grant land. If you go to the baron's, he might keep you. What has happened?"

Gracie picked her head up from her arms, but it only made her bawl louder. She could not stop the sobs. "Jamie..." She flopped her head back down into her arms.

"Jamie?" Magnus asked in bafflement. "What does he have to do with this? I thought your suitors were Ned, Sean, and Fergus, and then the laird and then the baron. What happened with Jamie?"

She picked her head up and stared at both of them, wiping her tears. In a small voice, she said, "I love Jamie. I do not want anyone else. I only want Jamie, and I wish to stay here." She hiccupped as she waited for her sister to speak.

"You love Jamie?" Ashlyn asked. "Aye, he's a fine choice, so tell me again why you're going to the baron's."

"Because Jamie does not want me, he wants Peigi." She kept her head up, crossing her legs in the chair.

Magnus looked at Ashlyn and said, "I think I'm in the middle of a nightmare. Pinch me and awaken me, would you please, wife?"

"Nay, 'tis all true," Gracie moaned. "Jamie loves Peigi." She knew the last sentence came out in a wail, but she just could not stop herself.

Magnus chuckled. "Gracie, pardon me for disagreeing, but Jamie does not love Peigi. I think Jake would have told me if his twin had his eye on someone."

"He loves Peigi. I heard them. 'Tis why I'm leaving. I cannot bear to watch them together."

Ashlyn asked, "What do you mean you heard them?"

"I heard them. In the stables. I heard, you know, the sounds," she said, her cheeks growing hot. "Grunting and panting and..."

Ashlyn smirked, then covered her mouth, but Magnus guffawed.

"Stop. 'Tis not funny."

"Sorry, Gracie, but you heard Jamie and Peigi having relations in the stables? When did this happen?" Ashlyn hid her smile and reached for Gracie's hand.

"About an hour ago. I went outside the keep to find Jamie, to tell him how I feel, but I overheard them in one of the stalls."

Magnus's face lost its smile. "Gracie, Jamie does not love Peigi. In fact, he tries to stay away from her because he knows how she is. She is unreasonable about her desire for Jamie."

Ashlyn glanced at her husband. "Aye, but husband, that does not mean he may not have had a quick...you understand what I'm saying."

"I understand, but I'm telling you that I don't believe it. She would be the last lass he would search out to satisfy his needs, if you'll pardon me for speaking bluntly, Gracie."

"Are you sure it was Peigi and Jamie?" Ashlyn asked. "Did you see them?"

"Nay, but I'm sure it was Peigi's voice. And she called out his name two or three times." She covered her ears as the memory washed over her. "*Jamie, Jamie, oh, Jamie.* I can hardly remember how many times, I was so shocked. I ran. I ran and ran, and while I was running, I decided to accept the baron's suit. I give up. I thought to become a nun, but why should I give up having bairns and a family of my own simply because he does not want me?"

"I see you're upset, sister, but do not make a mistake because you are angry at Jamie. You cannot ruin your life because of what you think he did."

"But I do not know the baron. Mayhap he is not the man I fear him to be. He ordered Uncle Alex to send me to Duncrub so we can get to know each other better."

Magnus sat down in front of Gracie and took her hand in his. "Gracie, I've known Jamie all his life, and I'm telling you Jamie Grant was not with Peigi. I'd swear to it on my mother's Bible."

Gracie sniffled as she thought about what Magnus said. Could he be right? Did it matter?

Ashlyn brushed the hair back from her face. "Look at you, you're a mess and you're still beautiful."

"And look where it's gotten me," she said softly. "The lads all see my beauty, but they do not see what's underneath. None of them want *me*." She paused. "I'm sorry that you lost your sire, Ashlyn, but at least you remember him. My sire did not even care to know me. Does that not say something?"

Magnus whispered, "I do not know the circumstances, but if your sire's never met you, then he knows not what he's missing."

"Ashlyn," she said, finally ready to voice the fear she'd carried for her entire life, "do you think it's possible that my sire is truly Malcolm? Could that be why all these bad things are happening to me? Mayhap I'm of bad blood."

Ashlyn hugged her sister. "Gracie, nay. Mama said your sire was someone she only saw a couple of times. Do not fret over it. You are a wonderful person, no matter who your sire is."

Magnus added, "You are a treasure and any lad would be lucky to have you for a wife, lass."

"Jamie does not think so."

"Gracie, how long have you been in love with Jamie?" Ashlyn whispered.

She lifted her chin as the tears began to fall again. "My feelings for him changed when I moved to the keep. They grew stronger." She paused and then said, "I cannot force him to love me."

"Have you told Jamie how you feel?"

Gracie shook her head, staring at the table. "Nay. I was going to find him earlier when...when I heard Peigi in the barn."

"Then find him today and tell him. You only need wait until dawn."

"Nay. I've already spoken with Aunt Maddie and Mama. I told them of my decision. We are to leave for the baron's land at dawn. Mama and Papa and Kyla. We'll visit him and see what happens." She lifted her gaze to Ashlyn's. "I'll miss you, Ash."

"Gracie, please talk to Jamie before you leave. He needs to know."

Gracie pushed her chair back from the table. "Nay, I am finished with Jamie."

Now she'd done it. She'd told the biggest lie ever, and God would hate her for it.

They left at daybreak. Uncle Alex had stopped her and whispered, "Are you sure about this, lass? We shall support you however you wish, but please be careful with the baron. Neither your uncles nor I know him well, and he appears to have a temper. He's not had the land for long. The king has not sent a message to me yet, and when he does, I can refuse."

"My thanks, Uncle Alex, but I must find my own way."

"A word of warning to you. You may see Molly and Tormod there, or Uncle Logan. Do not speak to them until they speak to you. I know not what capacity they will show themselves in, but the king has ordered them to investigate the baron."

Robbie said, "They'll let us know what they need from us, if anything."

The baron had left one of his fancy carts for traveling, leaving instructions that the future baroness was to travel in it within a sennight. "Gracie, you and Kyla and your mother can ride in the cart. You look exhausted, and your mother slept little. See if you can sleep a wee bit." He'd filled it with furs and then chose his warriors, none of whom had been among her suitors.

They arrived at the baron's home before nightfall. The baron rushed out to greet her, but she had claimed to be plagued with a terrible ache in her head from the journey, which was not far from the truth. He allowed her to go to retire to her chamber with Kyla.

He'd also given her a serious command, his tone brooking no argument. He expected her in his great hall in the morn, headache or not.

She'd have to do what was necessary soon. Until then, she'd sleep.

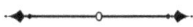

"Papa, why did you not tell me this before?" Jamie thought his head would explode. He'd finally come to terms with his feelings for Gracie, and she'd left for the baron's.

"You were being belligerent. You needed to accept your own feelings before you spoke with Gracie."

"True, but now I must go after her. When did she leave? I must ready my horse."

"Jamie, hold."

"Nay, Papa. I must leave at once. I need to tell her about Mac. Gracie deserves to know why I've been such a fool." He paused and scrubbed a hand over his face. "Did I tell you that I spoke with Molly and Tormod? They are verra happy, but somehow, their life did not seem like the life for me. They talked about being alone, away from their clan. I'd like to travel on occasion, but I wouldn't wish to be away from home all the time. Da, I must go to Gracie." He pulled away from his sire, intent on his mission, but Alex tugged him back.

"Not right now. She's not ready to listen to you, lad. When I spoke with her last, she was verra upset. Now, I do not know exactly what transpired between the two of you last night, but in less than a sennight, the lass changed from wishing to find a man to marry and stay on Grant land to wishing to become a nun, then early this morn she decided she'd accept the baron's invitation to see if they suit. That would require her to live at Duncrub, not here."

"What are you trying to say?"

"Something must have happened between last night and this morn to change the lass's mind. Do you know what that might be?"

Jamie hung his head. Damn, but this was all his fault. "The last time I saw her was when I walked away last eve. You were there. Was that enough to change her mind? I lost all sense of reason when I saw the baron's hands on her."

"Something else happened. I do not have a problem with you finding Finlay and chasing after the lass. You can go along as a Grant guard—Robbie will be glad to have you there—but you need to find out what else happened to change her mind."

"I'll ask Kyla." He started to push past his sire, but his father shoved at his chest, preventing him from leaving.

"Nay, Kyla went with her. Uncle Robbie, Aunt Caralyn, Gracie, and Kyla left with a score of guards. I wanted Gracie to have a companion, and Ashlyn is in no condition to travel."

"Ashlyn. I'll go see Ashlyn. She might know."

"That would be a wise choice." Alex waved to one of the stable lads outside, giving him instructions to saddle Jamie's horse.

"Jamie, I'll also caution you not to be headstrong. Just because you've come to grips with your feelings does not mean Gracie has done the same. Your mother thinks she's verra confused. Tread carefully with her." He paused. "You know, when I first decided that I wished to marry your mother, she wanted naught to do with me."

"Mama? Why not?" Jamie was stunned by this confession. His parents had the best marriage ever.

"I cannot tell you that, but all she did was run away from me. She had to work everything through in her own mind, on her own schedule. 'Tis why I'm advising you to act with care."

"I will." He was standing in front of the stables waiting for his horse when he noticed a horse headed straight for them. There was a sinking feeling in his chest when he recognized the lone rider. "I hope naught has happened to Ashlyn."

His sire glanced off into the distance. "Who is it? 'Tis too far for me to tell."

"Magnus, and he's headed toward us. He's not smiling either."

"Are you certain?" His sire watched the lad's approach, squinting.

"Aye." He waved to his brother's best friend. At the same time, he saw his brother striding toward the stables.

"Are you two all right?" Jake called out. "May I join you? I wish to see why Magnus is not smiling."

His sire waved him over. Jake stared at his friend as the horse galloped toward them. "What the hell?" he said, rubbing his jaw. "Magnus is always smiling when he's on his horse."

Magnus reached them and dismounted.

"Ashlyn?" Alex asked at once, voicing the worry all of them shared.

"Nay, she's fine, my laird."

"Problem?"

Magnus nodded. "I came to speak with Jamie."

Jamie waited to hear more, trying to be patient though it felt as if his heart had risen into his throat.

"Gracie. 'Tis about Gracie."

Jamie asked, "You've seen her?"

"Aye. She came by to speak with Ashlyn before she left. She was verra upset."

Alex tipped his head toward Jamie in a silent "I told you so."

"Why?"

Magnus frowned, then glanced at their laird. "I'm not sure if 'tis proper for me to say here. Jamie, can we not talk in private? With all due respect, my laird."

"Speak, Magnus," Alex said.

"Aye, just say whatever it is." Jake nodded to his friend.

"All right." Magnus cleared his throat as he turned toward Jamie. "Gracie says she has feelings for you. She left the keep in the middle of the night in the hopes of talking with you, but instead she found something else…" He paused and glanced from Jake to his laird.

"What?" Jake asked. "Just say it."

"Forgive me, my laird. I speak because I've been instructed to. Gracie heard a certain lass in the stables calling Jamie's name…"

"What?" Jamie glared at Magnus.

Jake snorted and covered his mouth.

"What? Och, hellfire, 'twas not me. I went in early with Connor. I was going to seek Gracie out, but I could not find her and I fell asleep."

His sire quirked his brow at him in a silent question.

"Papa, 'twas not me."

"Who was the lass?" Jake said.

"Peigi."

This time, Jake laughed so hard he choked. "Jamie and Peigi?"

"Hellfire, nay," Jamie snarled. "She's made no mystery of her interest, but it is not, and has never been, returned."

His sire said, "Does anyone know who the lass usually spends her time with?"

Magnus replied, "I've seen her with James and Ned."

Jake lost it completely then, and a guffaw broke free from him.

"Jake…" his sire said, though there was a grin on his face, too. Magnus's smile had also returned. What did they find so funny about this situation? It was a disaster.

"Sorry, Papa, but James said she likes to call him Jamie when they're…"

"Got it, Jake."

Jake muffled the rest of his words, controlling his laughter. But he allowed himself one more jest. "She thinks James is you. In her head… when she's… She does want you, Jamie."

Jamie closed his eyes, envisioning exactly what had taken place. "Gracie walked by the stables and heard Peigi yell my name, so she thinks 'twas me in there with her."

"Exactly," Magnus said.

"Papa, Connor will vouch for me."

"It's not me you must convince. I think you and Finlay are headed to Duncrub."

CHAPTER FOURTEEN

GRACIE SAT UP IN THE huge bed covered with pillows and warm furs, at first confused but then recalling all that had happened the previous day. It was dawn, and while the baron had allowed her to retire early last eve, accepting her complaint of a headache, she'd have to face him today in his great hall. Kyla opened her eyes to stare at her.

"Now will you tell me?" she asked.

"Tell you what?" Gracie played with the coverlet on the bed so she would not have to meet her friend's gaze.

"You carry such a burden that I can see it in your eyes, but you keep telling me naught is wrong. What is it, Gracie?"

Gracie sighed so forcefully, it might have blown the covers off the bed if she'd aimed correctly. It was time for her to be honest with Kyla. "It's your brother."

"What did Jamie do now? I heard him say he didn't want to be your protector anymore, but I think 'twas too painful for him. He did not like seeing you with other lads."

Gracie stared at Kyla, wishing there was some truth to that. "I love Jamie, or rather, I did."

"Truly? You love my brother? But why did you not tell me, or *him*?"

She could feel tears burning behind her eyes again. "Because." She shrugged her shoulders.

Kyla continued to stare at her.

"Because I did not know if he felt the same way. I did not wish to embarrass myself. For a while I thought he might be interested in me, but then he left for Cameron land."

"I told you he was confused. I thought all along he had feelings for you. The situation with Mac was so devastating for him. He was running away. Gracie, you must tell me everything."

There was a quiet knock on the door just before it opened.

"Yes," Gracie said tentatively, exchanging a glance with Kyla.

A servant opened the door and stuck her head through the crack. "May I help you, my lady? The baron sent me to see if there's aught you need."

Gracie almost shook her head in refusal, but then thought for a moment. Mayhap she could delay her trip to the hall. "Would it be possible for a bath? I feel dirty from my trip yesterday."

The maid entered, closed the door, and bowed to her. "Of course, my lady. I will send a bath up shortly and advise the baron."

Kyla added, "Please wait a quarter of an hour before you send the bath up. And we would like some porridge with it, please."

"Of course, my lady." The maid nodded and disappeared, closing the door behind her.

Gracie giggled. "You act as though you've had your own maid for years now."

Kyla shrugged her shoulders. "I thought I'd try." She laughed. "It worked, did it not? Now tell me the rest of your story."

Gracie nodded. It felt good to talk about her feelings so openly. For much too long, she had held them all inside. "I started to feel differently about Jamie when I moved to the keep. He's so charming with everyone, especially the wee lassies, and seeing that playful side of him changed something in me. I love being around him, and I love his smile, and…"

Gracie got up from the bed and paced in a small circle, her hands behind her back, trying to decide how best to explain. "You recall when I said I liked the kisses of someone after the first party?"

"Aye." Kyla clapped her hands together. "Jamie? 'Twas not Sean at all, was it? Then why are you not together? I do not understand this at all."

"Aye, 'twas Jamie, but he said it was wrong of him to kiss me, and I believed that he truly regretted it. Then he said he would not intrude in my life any more, and…"

"And? Go on before the maid returns."

"And then there was Peigi." She told Kyla about the disaster at the stables, about what Magnus had said, and how she'd decided to leave.

"I must think on it all," she said. "Even if I'm wrong about Peigi,

Jamie has had plenty of chances to declare his interest. I was so hoping he would court me that first eve of festivities. He kissed me that night, but then he immediately told me he shouldn't have. And then he left."

Kyla's eyes widened. "Who else have you told? Who knows?"

"I have only told Ashlyn and Magnus. Please do not mention Jamie's name to my mother and sire. Mayhap 'tis best for us to be apart."

"But I agree with Magnus. I do not see Jamie with Peigi. I think my brother's confused. 'Tis obvious he does not like seeing you with other men. Do not marry the baron until you talk to Jamie. Please?"

"I came here to get to know him better. Aye, he has a bit of a temper, but at least he knows what he wants. I would not be far from Grant land." She heaved a sigh. "Besides, he's petitioned the king for my hand. If Jamie does not want me, then the baron could be my only choice. Mayhap I will not *have* a choice."

"He is dreamy looking. But imagine if you married Jamie. We'd be sisters!" Kyla laughed. Their conversation was cut short by the return of the maid.

"My lady, Baron Crichton said to take your time. He'll see you mid-day in the hall. He sent some fruit and flowers for you."

That suited her just fine. She had an important decision to make. Should she be honest with Jamie? Or should she move on and try to forget how much she loved him?

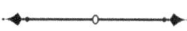

Jamie came upon Finlay fighting in the lists with his brother Fergus. He waited for them to finish, then nodded to Finlay. "Come. I'm leaving the keep, and I need someone to travel with me." Once they stepped away from Fergus, he said, "I need to speak with you alone."

Finlay took his plaid and wiped the sweat from his face and neck. "And may I ask where we are going?"

"Aye. We're headed to Duncrub, and my sire wants you to travel with me."

"I must check with my sire, make sure Mama has not gotten worse."

Jamie nodded, not wanting to take that away from him. Nicol, Finlay's sire, had been Uncle Brodie's best friend for years. The two of them had fought together in the Battle of Largs. Nicol had been near death before, but he had always survived his injuries. Now Finlay's mother, Inga, had a growth in her belly that Caralyn and Jennie had been unable to treat. On her last visit, Jennie had given everyone the sad news: Inga did not have much longer. He would not force his friend to leave if his mother was close to death.

As soon as Finlay returned, Jamie asked after his mother. "She is well enough?"

Finlay said, "Aye. She's having a good day. She says spring is making her feel good. Now why are we off to Duncrub?"

"Gracie and Kyla have gone to Duncrub."

"To Baron Crichton? Are they daft?"

"Gracie has decided to give him a chance. Actually, I think she's running from me." Loathe to admit it, he dared speak the truth to his trusted best friend.

"And why would a nice lass like Gracie run from you?" Finlay's gaze narrowed as he came closer to Jamie, searching for as much information as possible.

Jamie knew it was time to tell all, or at least most of it. "Because I was a fool and didn't let her know how I feel. Now I'm going to find her and tell her."

"And that's the only reason we're riding after her?"

Jamie said, "Nay, but 'tis the only reason you need to know."

Finlay crossed his arms. "I'll not go into a near battle with you unless you tell me all. I know your ways, Jamie Grant. You'll drag me into the middle of it, then tell me all after 'tis too late."

Jamie could tell his friend was serious by his stance. He thought of Finlay's situation with his mother and decided he deserved to know exactly what had transpired, as much as he hated to admit the worst of it. "All right. She heard Peigi in the stables last eve, and she thinks Peigi was with me."

Finlay's face lit up. "Truly? You and Peigi?"

"Nay, I was not with her. I left with Connor, you'll recall."

"Aye, but I know not where you went from there."

"Enough. Will you go with me or not?"

Finlay laughed. "Would not miss this for all the coin in your sire's coffers. I'll gather my things. Finally, you are making sense."

"What do you mean by that?" Jamie scowled at his friend as he strode back toward the stables, Finlay beside him.

"You've finally accepted that you and Gracie belong together."

"Get your things," he said, shaking his head. "We leave within the hour."

Finlay laughed and ran off to talk to his brother.

Why the devil had he been the last one to figure this out? His mother, his sire, and Finlay had all known. Why hadn't he and Gracie known?

He'd ask her as soon as he saw her. No more hiding anything.

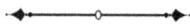

Gracie made her way down the broad staircase, Kyla trailing her. Her mother sat near the hearth while her father paced the chamber. The baron's great hall was only half the size of the Grant hall, but everything inside was tastefully done. The careful needlework on the tablecloths, tapestries, and seat cushions spoke to many hours of labor. Many of the dishes were gold, and the hall was festooned with fresh spring flowers in silver containers. The walls held a multitude of weapons, probably from the baron's ancestors, though many did not appear to be as old as the Grant weapons.

Baron Crichton stood at the base of the staircase with his hand outstretched, awaiting her arrival. "My dear, you are lovely in the color of the forest, and your hair is stunning."

She'd allowed his maid to plait her hair with ribbons interwoven in the back. "My thanks. Your hall is verra nice, especially the fresh flowers and rushes."

"I had them picked and arranged for you, my lady. And pardon my poor memory, but who is your friend?"

"This is Kyla, my laird's daughter."

"Kyla," he bowed to her, "you are exquisite in your dark beauty. Welcome to Duncrub."

Kyla tipped her head. "Many thanks, Baron."

"May I give you a small tour before we share our midday meal?"

"Aye. I'd like to greet my parents first." Caralyn and Robbie had come up behind the baron. She gave them each a hug and explained, "The baron has offered a tour of his bailey. Do you mind, Mama?"

Her mother said, "Nay. Kyla may stay and chat with us. Go ahead and enjoy."

They headed out the door, and Gracie was surprised to see how all of his needs were anticipated. The door was held for them, someone brought them their brats, and everyone stepped back when they saw him coming.

She heard numerous greetings, all to "my lady" or "Lady Grace."

Clearly he had informed his staff of her attendance. Once they stepped into the middle of the courtyard, the baron pointed off into the distance. "One of the things I am proudest of is the hill to the north of my land. 'Tis a most beautiful view in the fall, when the leaves change, and in winter, when snow crests the land. It makes for a grand entrance to the castle. Do you not agree? Did you notice it when you arrived?"

"Nay, but I see how lovely it is now. You have every reason to be proud of your land."

As he escorted her around his property, she noticed a difference between his clanmates and hers. In the Grant bailey, everyone would stop to chat with the laird if he walked past. Here, they continued with their tasks. Only a few people spoke to them. All the buildings were well kept, and the fields beyond the castle were carefully tended, but there was no gaiety.

"As my wife, this will all be yours," he whispered. "You'll be my new baroness soon, with maids and servants to tend to all your needs, and with me to love and spoil you."

Gracie glanced around at the place. It was truly impressive, but his words did not have the intended effect. He'd thought to excite her, but he'd only made her long for her home.

She did her best to placate the baron, whose manners were impeccable here on his own land, quite different from the other night. They made their way back inside for the midday meal, and he escorted her to the dais. The fare was pleasant, and she was surprised to see that her parents seemed to enjoy the baron's company.

After the meal, the baron stood and held his hand out to her. "If you would be so inclined, I would love to go riding with you, Lady Grace. This is a most lovely afternoon, and I'd like to take you to the top of my favorite hill."

They rode out to the hill, surrounded by guards, and the look on his face was like the blue sky after the clouds pull away. He was so proud of his land, his accomplishments. When they reached the top of the hill, they turned their horses around to face his castle.

"What a magnificent view, Baron."

He sighed and moved his horse closer to hers, reaching for her hand. "Yes, it is. I love to come up here to admire my land. The mountains covered in pines make the perfect backdrop for the castle with its tower peaks."

"I love the loch off in the distance. 'Tis calm and serene today."

"And that does not happen often. Usually there's a Scottish wind blowing up in the hills." He squeezed her hand. "Just think. This will be all yours. Ours. I must ask you if you'll agree to the marriage now that you've seen my home. I'm sure we would make beautiful heirs for this land. I'd be proud to call you my wife. We need not wait for our king's order of marriage. We could plan everything now. What say you?"

Gracie turned frantic. She'd thought there would be more time to get to know him, to consider the possibility of joining with someone other than Jamie. "Baron, your land is lovely, but I'd like a bit more time. I've only just arrived…"

"Of course, I am too quick with my excitement. It's just that I'm so fortunate to have found you. You are my equal in so many ways. Please think on it."

She gazed into his eyes. Could she do it? The day had been almost heavenly. He'd seen to her every need; had been most polite to her, Kyla, and her parents; and had never attempted to take advantage of her. The baron was a handsome man, an imposing image on his horse, and he'd give her bairns. But could she marry another man and be content?

A figure on horseback crossed her peripheral vision, and she started. The baron swung around, and when he caught sight of the approaching horseman, he sent his guards out after him. Who was it? Another horse followed the first. The baron's guards rounded up the visitors and led them in the baron's direction. He had arranged his horse in front of Gracie, but she peeked to see if she recognized the riders.

Jamie.

Jamie and Finlay.

As soon as they drew closer, Jamie yelled, "Do not agree, Gracie. We must talk."

The baron's mood shifted to cold fury. "Leave my land. You are not welcome here. Whatever your goals are, they are not in her best interest. My men will escort you and your friend off my land."

Jamie said, "Baron, I came to see my uncle Robbie. He is here, is he not? I have a message for him from my sire." His gaze bored into Gracie, sending a chill traveling down her spine. But as the guards led him closer, that chill transformed into a wave of heat. Just the sight of Jamie Grant sent her heart aflame. He was so ruggedly handsome as he sat his horse, even with the fury in his gaze.

"You are not welcome here, even to deliver your message. Go now or

I'll take you and yours prisoners."

Gracie gasped at his declaration. What kind of man was the baron?

CHAPTER FIFTEEN

JAMIE WAS READY TO TEAR the baron apart, limb by limb. He'd been so calm on the way here, focused on what he needed to do and say, but that had changed the instant they'd come over the hill and set eyes on the baron and Gracie.

Something about their stance had convinced him they were discussing marriage.

What would he do if Gracie agreed to marry the baron? He'd have to put a stop to the wedding. Better to end it all now. If he could just get inside and speak to her, he'd explain everything, apologize for his foolishness.

Tell her he loved her.

The baron's guards had escorted them back to the edge of his land and waited for them to depart. He and Finlay sat on a log in a clearing, not far from where they'd been unceremoniously kicked out.

"I'm going back."

"Aye, go back. They'll throw you in the dungeon."

"Nay, they'll not see me."

"Aye, you are just a wee lad, nearly invisible. I can see 'twould be an easy task." Finlay threw the rabbit bones he's been chewing on over his shoulder.

Jamie, who had no stomach for food, was pacing the clearing. "Must you always be sarcastic? Can you not help me with this? I thought you wished to see me with Gracie? Is that not what you've been pushing me toward for a while now?"

Finlay held up his hands in surrender. "All right. You've made your point." He found a tree to lean on and crossed his arms. "I'll help you."

"My thanks. What are your thoughts?"

"First, you do belong with Gracie. You always have, but…"

"But?"

"I think she's confused. He's a baron, and an attractive one, and I'm quite sure I heard him tell her she would be a baroness." He shrugged his shoulders. "Many a lass would have her head turned by the promise of such a title. Gracie's not the sort, but you can hardly blame her for considering his offer. She wishes to marry, and you walked away from her."

"Aye, but we could marry."

"Could you? Are you sure about that? You've only just realized how you feel about her. You need to be certain before you ruin her chances at becoming a baroness. I did not see her settling down with my brother or Sean or Ned, but the baron…? Mayhap."

"Aye, I'm sure of how I feel about her. But I need to speak with her first. She's mighty angry with me."

"Agreed. So we need to find a way for you to sneak into her chamber so you can talk with her. Kyla is with her, which will be to your benefit. We can count on her help. Finding out which chamber she is in should not be too difficult."

Jamie nodded. "During the evening meal, I'll send one of our guards over the back curtain wall so he can find another Grant guard to tell him where the lasses are sleeping. Then I'll find a way into her chamber later this eve."

Before Finlay could respond, one of the Grant guards hurried toward them through the trees. "You have a visitor, Jamie. Logan Ramsay."

Jamie and Finlay both jumped off the log, staring through the trees. Finlay said, "Good. We need someone with an objective view of the situation."

Jamie glowered at his friend. "I'm objective."

"Hellfire, you're not."

Uncle Logan rode into view and dismounted, Molly and Tormod fast behind him. They were far enough off Crichton land to remain undiscovered.

"You're just now arriving?" Jamie asked. "Why so late?"

"Nay. We've been all around the inside of the keep, and we've spoken with his men," Logan said. "We just discovered you were here." He sat down on the log and waved his hand for the rest to join him. "Guards," he said, addressing the men who'd come with Jamie and Finlay, "Keep watch around us. Make sure the baron's men do not come too near."

"So?" Jamie prodded. "What have you found out? I don't like the man and I'm quite sure he was just discussing marriage with her."

Uncle Logan gave him a pointed look. "What's your purpose? Why are you and Finlay here?"

Jamie explained the best he could without going into all of his foolishness. "I'm here to offer her marriage. I need to talk to her before she does something foolish."

No one looked surprised to hear it.

"I'm glad you've finally seen reason," his uncle said, "but for now you'll stay away. Here's why. Molly uncovered something about the baron you'll be interested in." He nodded for her to take over.

"The baron was married in England and his wife died mysteriously," Molly said. "The only other thing I learned was that the baron wants heirs, and his wife of four summers never carried. I cannot find anyone who'll admit to more than that."

Tormod added, "His guards say he can be violent at his worst, but it doesn't happen often. It builds in him, and when he releases it, 'tis harsh. They gave me no examples."

"If he's desperate for heirs, he could have found a way to eliminate his wife without any recourse," Uncle Logan said. "She had no family. We're trying to find out more."

"Then Finlay and I will assist you, but I must see Gracie first." Jamie stood, indicating he was ready to leave. "Or mayhap I'll get her out of there now. Whether he's daft or just a cold-hearted murderer, I do not like Gracie inside the keep with that man."

"Sit down," Logan snapped. "You're not going. The baron knows who you are, and if we heard correctly, he already sent you off his land. This is not a man you wish to anger when the woman you love is at his mercy. You need to leave this to us for now."

Jamie moved closer to his uncle because he wasn't ready to yield. "Why? I need to find Gracie and get her out of there. What if she's to be his next victim. We must move with haste. She'll come with me."

Uncle Logan ran his hand down his face, a frustrated expression on his face. "Shite, lads in love are enough to make me to lose my temper." He glared at Jamie again. "Are you listening this time? We need proof for the king. A nobleman of our country requested Gracie's hand. If she's available and there's no good reason for the king to refuse, the marriage will take place. If the king chooses, he can order the marriage and you will have no say."

Jamie bellowed, "I love her and she loves me. 'Tis all the king needs to know."

Uncle Logan threw his arms up in the air and shifted to look at Molly and Tormod. "Did I not tell you he was daft? Our king does not care about the word 'love.' Your grandmother did, your mother does, your aunt may, my wife certainly does, but the King of the Scots? Nay! Love is not considered a…what was that word again, Finlay?"

"Good," Finlay replied before covering his mouth with the back of his hand to hide his smirk.

Uncle Logan threw his arms up in the air again. "*Good* reason. My thanks, Finlay. I'm telling you, from my experience, which runs a little longer than yours, nephew, there's something else behind this man's sudden wish to marry Gracie. He's not after Gracie, but her name. We have to find out why. If we discover he's a traitor, then he'll never bother her or any other Scottish lass again. He'll be forced to go running back to England. You must give us time to discover what's rotten in him. Are you following me, Jamie Grant?"

Jamie rolled his eyes and said, "Aye, but you need to be watching her carefully. What if he's worse than you imagined? Who will suffer but Gracie? I do not like this, Uncle Logan."

"Molly, Tormod, and I are leaving, and I promise to keep watch over Gracie. Do not forget her sire is with her and some Grant guards. The baron will not do anything foolish with all those witnesses. But we must find a good reason to remove her from his castle," Logan said, rising to his feet. "We'll meet you back here just past midnight. You are not to step foot on his land. Understood?"

Jamie mumbled, "Aye." Though his beloved uncle was daft if he thought Jamie could sit here and wait while he went inside the castle.

"I did not hear you, nephew." Uncle Logan took a couple of steps toward him.

"Aye!" Jamie yelled. Damn, could the man read his thoughts?

"Good. Finlay, see that he follows my instructions. We'll regroup later this eve."

As soon as they were gone, Jamie turned to Finlay and said, "This changes naught. I must sneak into her chamber tonight and you'll help me. We'll both be back before Uncle Logan knows we're gone. We only have to wait until dark."

Finlay closed his eyes and shook his head. "You are the most stubborn man I've ever met."

"You'll go?" He waited for his friend's answer. If he had to, he'd go alone, but he'd prefer to have Finlay by his side. Who knew what he would find inside?

"Aye. I must follow and assist where I can. Otherwise, who knows what'll happen to you?"

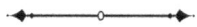

Gordon Crichton paced in his solar, his second, Simon de La Porte, watching him.

"You have nothing to offer?" the baron asked. "This should have been a simple task. The great Alexander Grant is past his prime. His coffers are rich and ready to be taken. Your friend MacNiven told you so many times. Now that he is gone, it is our time to attack Grant. But I did not expect to have to go this far into the Highlands. There are too many savages here. If I see his son again, I'll twist his neck with my bare hands."

Simon waited until the baron stopped his rant. "I'll give you my opinion when you are ready." He was of medium height, but all muscle, and kept his hair dark tied back with a leather thong. A deep scar crossed his right cheek, something the baron had asked him about a few times, but de La Porte only glared at him, refusing to explain its origin.

"Go ahead. Tell me your drivel."

De La Porte's left hand twitched and he snorted. "Drivel is it? First I'd advise you not to try to kill Grant's son with your bare hands because he's twice your size and solid muscle. He'll kill you easily unless you have a dagger to put in his heart before he can draw the mighty sword at his side."

"Continue. What should we do next? I have not heard from the king. Alexander promised to find me a young bride. I told him which one I wanted, and I've heard nothing. Why is he delaying his decision? A messenger should have arrived long ago."

Simon leaned back in his chair, tipping it on its back legs. "I say forget Alexander. You have the girl here. Find a priest and marry her. Who will stop you? You need to marry a Grant to get closer to your goal." He set the legs of the chair down with a thump, reaching for an apple in the center of the table.

"Her sire is here and he's no small man either." The baron pulled a small sword down from the wall, running his finger across its edge, his hand jerking when he finally drew blood.

De La Porte chewed on the fruit, juice running down his chin "They have how many guards to ours? We can manage the three people who came along with her."

"You cannot kill them or you'll bring all the savages down upon us by morn. We need time to gather our forces, attack on our terms, not theirs." He returned the sword to the wall, sucking the blood from his wound.

"True, I did not suggest killing them. We could easily distract her mother. She's a healer."

"Then do it. Find the priest, bring him to the hall and arrange the rest. Tell him he'll be performing a wedding. I wish to be married before dawn. I do not care what time of the night it is, he must perform the ceremony before daybreak."

CHAPTER SIXTEEN

THEY HAD FINISHED THE EVENING meal, but the baron had not joined them. Gracie's heart had been in turmoil all afternoon.

She knew not what to do.

The baron had promised to give her everything she could ever want. The only problem was the one thing she wanted wasn't part of that—Jamie Grant. No matter how much she tried, she could not change her heart.

Her heart belonged to Jamie. He'd been in the forest, and the baron had sent him away. She had to admit her hope had blossomed as soon as she'd seen him. Why had he come? She needed to speak with him, but how?

Her mother reached out and touched her cheek. "You realize that if you choose the baron, you will be moving away from Grant land, away from us, from your brothers and your sister, your niece or nephew?"

Tears welled in her eyes as she thought about what her alternatives were. She gave a furtive glance around her before she whispered, "I saw Jamie in the forest. The baron sent him away. Why would he come?"

Silence settled over the group. Gracie wondered what they were thinking, but she did not have much time to wonder. The baron arrived, kissed her hand, and said, "Would you and your parents join me in my solar, if you please?"

Kyla looked confused, but then said, "I'll go to our chamber, Uncle Robbie."

They followed him into the solar and arranged themselves around the table, the baron taking the seat next to Gracie.

Taking her hand, he gave them all a huge smile and said, "I've decided to make this announcement with your parents here. I'd like to ask for Lady Grace's hand in marriage. I would like for us to marry before the morrow if you are agreeable." He glanced at her parents and squeezed her hand.

Gracie's throat felt as if it had collapsed in on itself. How could this have happened so quickly? Her mother and father looked at her for guidance, but she could not speak.

Her mother started, "Baron Crichton, this has been a lovely visit. I know my daughter has enjoyed it, but your question comes as a surprise to us."

The tone of the baron's voice changed. "And why would this surprise you, my lady? You knew my intent when I invited her here. I have many Grants as witnesses."

Her mother looked to her sire for guidance. "We all understood your intent, Baron," Robbie amended, "but Gracie has not been here for long. 'Twas a quick decision is what my wife meant, I believe."

The baron's manner relaxed. "Aye, 'tis true. It did not take long for me to see that we are a perfect match. Your daughter will make a lovely baroness. Lady Grace Crichton of Duncrub."

Gracie had such a lump in her throat, she could not think of anything to say. "Forgive me, Baron Crichton, but I need more time. To marry this night? 'Tis most impossible."

A look crossed his face that she didn't like, one that told her he usually got what he wanted. Gracie made a bold decision. Not this night. Not any night.

Her mother assisted her. "Why, Baron, Gracie…"

"Lady Grace." He gave her mother a smug smile.

Gracie shifted her gaze to her parents to gauge their response. Robbie squared his shoulders, his gaze cool but determined, and said, "You will speak to my wife with respect, Baron Crichton, or not at all."

Gracie's mother reached over to grab his hand. "Lady Grace does not have a proper gown to wear for a wedding. Becoming a baroness is something special, something all your nearby neighbors should be allowed to celebrate along with you. There is no time to prepare for a wedding. Why, your cook would not be able to handle such a hasty ceremony."

Gracie's sire said, "What about a priest?"

"Oh, I have a priest available to me at all times."

"Baron, I thank you for your hospitality, but we will be going home. If you wish to have further correspondence with our daughter, you will do it through me." Robbie Grant stood just as the door burst open and a pale serving girl appeared in the opening.

"Forgive me, my lord, but there's been a terrible accident and Cook is bleeding terribly. 'Tis coming out in spurts."

Caralyn jumped out of her chair and said, "I'll go with you."

Robbie followed her, but when Gracie attempted to follow them, the baron stopped her. "What is your answer, Lady Grace? 'Tis your choice, not your parents'." He kissed each knuckle on her hand. "Please say yes and become my wife this night."

Gracie did not need to consider her answer. "Nay."

She charged out of the solar and ran to her chamber. Then she closed the door behind her and threw herself into Kyla's arms.

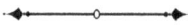

Jamie picked his way up a back staircase and crept down a passageway. He counted the doorways carefully, hoping Kyla had gotten the message to listen for a tap on the door.

With his back to the wall, he reached over and knocked three times on a door and waited until the door cracked open a touch. Kyla's face peeked out at him, her eyes wide. He made a gesture for her to step outside so he could step in.

He whispered to his sister, "Knock if I need to get out." She nodded and stepped out of the chamber. Once his eyes adjusted to the gloom, he found Gracie standing near the window dressed in her night rail. He muffled the groan that fought to escape him at the sight of her. Everything had changed. It was as if the conversation with his sire and the letter from Mac had freed him to see his feelings for Gracie for what they were.

"Jamie?" She rushed over to his side. "Why are you here? The baron will be furious. You must leave immediately."

"Nay, not until I've said what I need to say." He paused for a moment and reached for her hands. "You're cold."

"I was near the window, thinking…"

He tugged her closer, wrapping his hands around hers. "Gracie, please just listen for a moment."

She nodded, looking every bit the angel. Her blue eyes seemed darker than usual, but they were still filled with the warmth and the concern that made her Gracie.

"First, I must clear something up. Magnus told me what you heard outside of the stables. Gracie, 'twas not me. I've never been with Peigi, and I will never be with her. The lad she is seeing is named James, and she must call him Jamie. Above everything, I need you to believe that."

She gazed into his eyes and whispered, "I believe you."

"My thanks. I came to take my role back, to be your protector, but I must be honest with you—'tis not all that I want. I cannot tolerate knowing you're here to see another man, to consider marrying him. Gracie, we belong together. I've always felt better, happier, when you're around. When we were younger, 'twas a friendly desire, but now that we're both grown, I want you by my side. You and no other. 'Tis torture to watch you with the baron."

Gracie smiled and leaned her head down on his shoulder. Her soft curves melted into him and he closed his eyes, taking in her sweet scent, knowing he needed as much control as he could muster.

"Gracie, I love you. You're my flower."

"What?" She gave him a puzzled look.

Smiling, he said, "I'll explain another time, but you smell as sweet as ever tonight. What is that scent?"

"Lavender. Aunt Celestina gave it to me. Jamie, do you know how I've longed for you to say such words?" she said softly, running her hands down his chest in a caress that threatened to overtake his control.

He wrapped his arms around her, pulling her close and kissing the top of her head. "I've fought my feelings for you, feelings that have grown ever since you moved to the keep. Until I left to meet Uncle Logan, I didn't realize how much I had come to depend on seeing you each day. Gracie—" He paused, then pulled away enough to stare into her eyes. "I never want to spend another day apart from you. Everything that happened with Mac confused me. I knew I needed something, and I thought traveling with Uncle Logan would make me happy, but what I truly wanted was *you*. I…it's hard to say this, but after Mac died, I've been afraid of losing the people I love. I've kept running away instead." He ran his hand through his hair and hung his head. "I'm mucking this up. I love you. Will you marry me when we return to Grant land?"

She lifted her head from his shoulder and gazed into his eyes, her fingers moving up to caress his bottom lip. Such a simple touch, yet he felt his knees shake, his groin tighten. "Aye, I love you, Jamie Grant. I'll love you forever, and naught would make me happier than to be your wife. I worried you would never think of me in such a way, especially after you said that you regretted kissing me."

"I never regretted kissing you," Jamie insisted. He hated to think he'd made her feel unwanted, especially when the opposite was true. "I loved every moment of it. 'Twas what helped me realize we belong together. I felt I took advantage of you, but 'struth is I could not stop myself from kissing your luscious lips." He leaned down and captured her lips with his, tasting her sweetness when she opened her mouth to him. He ended the kiss abruptly. "I must go. Uncle Logan and Molly and Tormod are here, and my uncle made me promise to stay away until he had the information he needed to convince the king to reject the baron's request."

"Nay, take me with you, Jamie. I do not trust the baron. He wanted me to marry him this eve, but I refused. My mother was called to tend to an injury, and my parents have not returned. Kyla and I are worried."

"I cannot," he said, reaching out to stroke her cheek. "I promised Uncle Logan. He'll peel the skin from my legs slowly if he finds out I'm here. I trust him to handle the situation."

"What is he trying to do?"

He touched his forehead to hers. "I know this is difficult, but he knows how we feel about each other, and he's on our side. He knows the only way to end this with the king is to uncover something bad about the baron."

"He thinks he can prove the baron has a questionable character?"

"He does. Once he finds what he needs, he'll find me and let me know. I'm sure he'll contact your sire and get you out of here." He kissed her forehead and stepped back, but she clung to his arms.

"Nay, do not leave me. Please, Jamie?"

"I must. Trust that we'll be back for you. I will tell Uncle Logan about your parents and he will search them out. Stay here in this room. One more day. We shall marry soon and all this will be behind us. I'll come for you on the morrow. I'll be just off his land watching and waiting."

"Promise?"

"Aye. Promise." As he kissed her lips again, a soft knock came at the door. "I must go."

He disappeared into the night, making sure no one saw him. A sense of calm settled over him. He and Gracie were going to marry, and nothing would stop them.

CHAPTER SEVENTEEN

JAMIE CLIMBED ON HIS HORSE and flicked the reins, leading the way off Crichton's land. He had a bad feeling about the baron, but he had to stay the course and stick with the plan he'd made with Gracie. One more day.

Once they reached the point where they could slow their horses, Finlay pulled abreast of him. "Did it happen the way you'd hoped?"

"Aye, I asked her to marry me and she said she would. We will marry when we return to Grant land." His gut had settled a bit since leaving her, but until they were together on Grant land, he would not rest.

"Did you learn when they'll be leaving?"

"Probably on the morrow. The baron asked for Gracie's hand and she said nay." Every time he thought about how close he'd come to losing her, he wished to spew his insides off to the side of his horse.

"Why are they not leaving now?"

"Because Aunt Caralyn was called away to assist with a serious injury. Uncle Robbie went with her. Probably not wise for them to travel at night. 'Tis best to wait until the morrow."

"I do not like the sounds of that, Grant," Finlay said, turning in his saddle to get a better look at Jamie. "We should find your uncle Logan."

"I doubt we'll find him. He's probably inside. When he tries to hide, believe me that you'll not find him." He didn't have a good feeling about the situation either, but he'd promised his uncle not to go after Gracie. After countermanding that promise once, he didn't want to break it again. Besides, Gracie loved him. She'd agreed to marry him.

What more did he need?

He needed to know she was safe.

"He said he would return in the middle of the night," Finlay said. "'Tis not far off."

"Aye," Jamie replied. "We'll go back to the spot where we met before. We'll update him, and if we need to go back and get them, we will."

When they dismounted and settled the horses, Finlay clasped his shoulder. "Gracie said aye. Did you have to convince her? Did she turn you down the first time?" Finlay waggled his brow at him. Even in the dark he could tell.

"Nay. She feels the same way I do." The thought sent a surge of warmth through him.

"Did you tell her about Mac? Explain why you've been hesitating about marriage?"

Jamie shook his head. "There wasn't enough time. I promised to tell her later." He moved over to the log, repeating that horrible night of Mac's death in his mind for the thousandth time. He'd gone to help Mac with two of the horses who'd gotten out of the stables in the storm. He'd thought if Mac could calm one down, he could calm the other.

Mac had run up the hill ahead of him. He'd almost reached the horse when the bolt of lightning came out of nowhere. The bolt had been so powerful that the ground had shaken enough to knock Jamie over. It had hit Mac directly, throwing him up into the air.

He'd run to his dear friend, but the old man was dead by the time he reached his side. No matter how he shook him and called his name, he did not awaken. Aunt Caralyn had told him there was naught he could do. By the time his sire had found him lying across Mac's body, the rain was pelting them in buckets. He hadn't even noticed. Alex had picked him up, peeling his fingers from Mac's plaid, and then carried him back to the keep.

The incident had been many years ago, but the memory lived fresh in his mind and in his heart. That memory had built a wall around his heart, warning him not to let anyone get too close.

He knew Gracie threatened to tear that wall down, but he could not allow himself to miss out on what was important. Now that he'd found his flower, he'd marry her. He'd never been more certain of anything.

One more day.

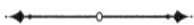

It was almost dark when Gracie dared to step outside of her chamber. She'd sworn she would never leave until her parents returned, but Kyla had left a short time ago in search of them, and she had not returned. What if something had happened to her? She had to at least follow her path to make sure she had not fallen down the staircase or something worse.

She left to find her friend.

She hadn't gone far down the passageway when laughter filled her ears. There was no humor to it. "I knew you'd have to come out eventually."

The baron leaned against the stone wall of the passageway, his gaze narrowed and an unhappy expression on his face. She decided speaking would get her nowhere, so she said nothing.

"Apparently, your parents did not do their job properly. When a member of the nobility tells you to do something, you do it. We are getting married, and we're marrying tonight. I have your parents tied up," he gave her a smirk, "so you'll not be seeing them for a while. Your friend too. You and I are alone, and I think it's time for a wedding."

She shook her head and tried to walk around him.

"Nay? You have a lot to learn, my dear. You are a mere woman, and your word does not matter. The priest is waiting for us, and you will march down the stairs and into my solar and be agreeable." He grabbed her arm and hauled her close to him. "You will marry me."

"Nay, I will not." She would marry her love, Jamie Grant, not this awful man.

There was a look of sick fury in his eyes, but before she could run from him, he wrapped his arm around her back and hastened her down the hallway. "We shall see."

He opened a door to a chamber and pushed her in ahead of him. Gracie was surprised to see that it was a bed chamber. She whirled around to stare at him as he closed the door behind them. "Baron, this is not proper. This is…"

"Cease your prattle. You know naught of proper behavior, and no one will come to rescue you, even if you scream."

"Baron, my apologies. I did not intend to hurt you, and I had not formally accepted your suit, so there is naught lost on your part. We shall leave on the morrow and never see each other again."

The man circled her slowly, running his finger down her neck and dropping it lower as he continued his perusal. When he reached her breasts, she swatted at his hand, knocking it out of the way.

His voice came out in a deep snarl. "Don't you dare try to correct anything I do."

She did her best to calm the panic building inside her, to still the trembling of her limbs, but she could not. When she tried to dash toward the door, he caught her and shoved her back.

"You'll stay here and pay me for playing with my affections."

"You do not love me. 'Tis quite clear. Please let me go." She knew that to be true. No one who cared for her would ever treat her this way.

"Nay, I do not." He began to circle her again, his hand touching her in inappropriate places. "But only innocent fools believe love is a precondition for marriage. You'll give me your maidenhead. Then you'll be ruined. And if I recall Scottish law, you'll be forced to marry me. No one would allow you to walk away from me. Not even your sire."

His next move was so quick, it took her completely by surprise. He lifted her up and tossed her on the bed. Before she could process what was happening, his hands were ripping off her night rail and her shift. Something snapped inside her when she felt his hand on her bare leg, touching her private area. She wriggled and screamed, but he slapped her twice. He fumbled with his trews, and tears sprang to her eyes as she realized what was happening.

He was going to steal her maidenhead, and then he was going to force her to marry him. She fought and clawed, eventually biting his shoulder, but he only laughed and said, "You want it rough, you'll have it rough."

He punched her in the side of her head, enough for her to almost lose consciousness, but she didn't. She clung to the only thing she could think of.

"Jamie! Help me, Jamie!'

The baron panted, and his hand fumbled down with his trews again, scratching her skin, and suddenly she recalled something.

Jamie's advice. What had he said? Kick him in his bollocks. But there was no way she would have the opportunity to kick him there. His arm came up across her shoulders, pinning her to the bed as he loomed over her, a smile on his face. "I'll have you now, bitch."

Jamie had said kick him, hit him, anything that would stop him for long enough to get away. Punch him. Her right hand was free, so she tried to punch him, but he caught her arm as she swung it. Her left hand brushed his hard member through the cloth as she struggled to free herself.

She'd taken care of her brother's as bairns, so she knew the male anatomy. She took a guess and grabbed the material below and squeezed and twisted as hard as she could.

And it did just what she'd needed to do. He rolled to the side, screaming in pain, and let go of her.

She ran to the door and down the passageway, totally disoriented, but she found herself at a back staircase. Looking down, she realized most of her gown was gone, but she was still wearing her shift. When she managed to push open the door to the outside, she finally started sobbing... and the only word she could get out was "Jamie."

So frightened she could not make any sense of her surroundings, she slipped and fell into the mud, only then noticing the steady rain all around her. She had no idea where she was due to the darkness, but suddenly a bolt of lightning shot across the sky, showing her the way. The courtyard was near deserted and the gates were still open, so she ran through them, ignoring the guards who yelled at her.

She ran toward that hill the baron loved so much, oblivious to the thunderstorm that raged around her, lighting the sky up enough to show her the way. To the hill, that was the only way she knew to get out. She ran toward it, screaming and holding her arms up toward the sky. "Jamie!" she cried out at the top of her lungs.

CHAPTER EIGHTEEN

J AMIE JUMPED ON HIS HORSE at about the same time the rain
started.

"What the hell, Grant?" Finlay shouted. "What are you doing?"

"Gracie's in trouble. I'm going back. Finlay, I have to go alone. I can
just feel it."

His friend gave him a long, measuring look before nodding. "I'll wait
for your uncle and follow you. Someone has to tell him where you are.
He should be here at any moment."

"If I'm not back in two hours, tell him to come after me. There's a
cave just over there. Keep the guards here with you."

Something had happened, and he could swear Gracie had called out to
him. Jamie couldn't explain how he knew, he just did. Riding through
the rain, he cursed when he saw the first flash of lightning. Nature was
planning to test him again. Another thunderstorm in the dark of night
to taunt him, tease him, tell him to go back into the cave where it was
safe.

But he couldn't leave, not if Gracie was in danger. Another two flashes
of lightning followed by increasingly loud rumbles of thunder told him
the storm drew near. The hill was not far ahead of him—and the sight
of it reminded him a little too well of another night, another hill.

After Mac's death, people had said the old stable hand had made a big
mistake going up on a hill in the storm. Legend had it that the higher
you were in the mountains, the more likely you were to get hit because
the mountains brought you closer to the storm.

He did not wish to go up the hill, but it stood between him and Gracie. Once he came to it, he dismounted, trying to come up with a plan. A flash of lightning seemed to hit a tree on the far side of the keep. He tugged his horse over to a line of bushes, wrapping the reins around a branch in such a way to keep his horse there. Aye, his horse was not happy, but he refused to risk the beast's life by taking him to the top of the hill.

Memories of the horses and Mac played over and over again in his mind.

After the next flash of lightning, he heard something. He listened closely—they were a woman's cries, *her* cries—and then saw her.

Gracie. She was running up the hill in a terrified state. She appeared to be only in her shift. What the devil? What could have happened...

Then it hit him.

"Nay!"

He raced as fast as he could toward Gracie. "Nay, Gracie, not the top of the hill!" She continued up the hill, her legs churning as fast as he'd ever seen them go.

Jamie's heart sent him up the hill, his blood pulsating through his body at a pace that frightened him. "Gracie, nay." How could he get her to hear him in this storm? He had to stop her.

The worst possible scenario played out in front of him. The lightning could hit her and take her away, just like it had done with Mac. Aye, he'd gone and fallen in love with her, and now she sat in that place, that dreaded place, so close to his heart, waiting to hurt him, ready to rip his heart out with a single bolt of lightning.

Just one second could change his entire life.

"Nay, I love you, Gracie. Do not go to the top of the hill. Go back." He ran and ran, bellowing as if his own life depended on it.

It did.

"Nay, go back. I'll not lose you. I'll never survive losing you." He continued on because something had dawned on him.

She was such a part of him that he'd never survive without her. He'd rather go with her. She reached the top of the hill and finally saw him when another bolt lit up the sky.

"Jamie, Jamie!"

He ran straight toward her, his arms held out to her. She threw herself into them, sobbing and crying

"Gracie, what happened? Where are your clothes?" She mumbled incoherently and he could see the fine tremors in her body. He grabbed her hands and forced her to look at him. "What happened?"

"The baron. Tried to…tried to." Her breath caught and she almost heaved. "Hold me, Jamie. Please?"

"I'll not let him touch you again. Ever. I love you." He wrapped his arms around her and held her tight, trying to give her his warmth to stop her trembling.

"I love you," Gracie cried. "Take me home."

"I will. I shouldn't have left you. I'm sorry. Forgive me."

A loud crack rent the air, and branches fell from a nearby tree as if they were small twigs. Jamie scooped Gracie into his arms and ran down the hill, praying they would not get hit. He lifted her onto his horse and climbed up behind her. She sat facing him and held him so tight that he feared they would fall off the horse together.

They had not gone far when he felt her trembling change to shivering. The damp cold air was more than she could handle. He needed to get her warm. Once he was sure they were off the baron's property, he found a small ravine protected by a low stone ledge. Dismounting, he carried her over to the ravine, leading the horse behind him. The entire ravine was nearly dry because of the direction it faced.

The huge stone wall had enough of an indentation to provide shelter from the wind. He left Gracie shivering under the ledge and went back to his horse to grab his saddle bag. There was a dry plaid inside, and he brought it back to Gracie.

"Jamie, I'm cold."

"I know, love. We'll fix that. Hold your arms up so I can get your shift off."

"But Jamie, I'll have naught on."

"Sweetings, it does not matter, we're going to marry. I must get you warm." She helped him remove her sodden shift, but her lips had turned a dusky shade he did not like, and he feared it would not be enough to wrap her in the plaid. He doffed his own clothes and enfolded her in his arms before securing the dry plaid around them both. He laid her down between his body and the stone wall, making sure she had the thick cloth underneath her.

She snuggled into him. "Jamie, you're so warm."

"Tell me where you're hurt."

"I got away. I did what you told me to do and I got away." Her head was tucked into the crook of his neck.

"I think you are bruised. He hit you? I'm glad you got away. I'm so proud of you for fighting him. You have no broken bones, sweeting?"

"Naught is broken, but I do not wish to talk about it now. Please? I wish to forget it happened."

Her voice trailed off, and as much as he wished to know everything, he gave in to her. It could wait until the morrow.

"We'll do whatever you wish." He could feel her trembling slow and found himself in a situation that he did not wish to explain. Her curves fit him perfectly, and he'd turned hard the moment her shivering had ended.

"Jamie, why did you come back for me?"

"I cannot explain it, but you called to me. I heard you. I knew you were in trouble so I came back." He cupped her face and kissed her forehead, each cheek, her nose, and her lips. "I adore you. We belong together, and I'm sorry it took so long for me to figure that out. Gracie, I promise you he'll never hurt you again. I love you."

"Aye. I've waited a long time to hear those words, and I love hearing them."

His lips descended on hers and he did his best to show her how much he loved her, moving his mouth over hers until they both gasped for air.

"Make love to me, Jamie."

"Here? In the cold? On the stone?"

"I only feel you. Aye. Make love to me."

He could not think straight after hearing those words. "Gracie, you have no idea how much every fiber of my being aches to make you mine. You are so beautiful, and you have the warmest heart of anyone I know, but are you certain you don't wish to wait…"

"Shush." She cupped his face and tugged him down to her, kissing him with a passion he'd had no idea existed inside her, but he wanted more.

He kissed her cheeks, her lips, her neck, every part of her he could get to as she ran her fingers through the wet strands of his hair. She smelled of the rain and the outdoors with an extra dose of sweetness.

He brought his mouth down from her neck to her breast, flicking her nipple with his tongue until it hardened into a point. He did the same for the other and she gripped his hair as a low whimpering sound started in the back of her throat.

"Gracie, this will hurt the first time, but never again. I promise you. I'll wait until the pain subsides."

"I do not care, Jamie. I want you, I want you inside me and everywhere. Just make me yours. I cannot wait any longer."

His hand crept down to the vee between her legs, teasing her at the spot that he knew would please her most. He softened his touch, rubbing the tiny mound until she squirmed and wiggled against him.

"Jamie? Tell me what's happening. What are you doing?"

"Trust me, love. I will take care of you."

He entered her with his finger, groaning at the wetness he found, proof that she wanted him as much as he wanted her. He moved over her and grasped her hips, teasing her entrance until she spread her legs wide for him.

"Jamie?"

He thrust inside of her, breaking through her barrier with one push, then stilled.

Her voice whispered in his ear, "Jamie, it hurts."

"I know. The pain will end soon. Allow me to hold you until it does." He kissed her lips. "Trust me?"

"Aye. 'Tis a wee bit better."

"I promise I'll not move until you tell me 'tis gone."

She wiggled underneath him.

Groaning, he said, "Please do not do that until you are ready. 'Tis hard for me to hold still."

He gazed into her eyes, and he saw the trust she had for him, the love. Why had he never noticed it before? "I love you, Gracie. We'll marry as soon as we return to Grant land."

"I love you, too. I think 'tis better. Try to move slowly for me."

He groaned and said, "You feel so good, you have no idea how wonderful it is to be inside you."

She pulled her hips back so they almost came apart, then arched toward him, taking him deeply inside of her. He groaned, "You are better?"

She gave him her answer by moving the same way three more times, plunging him in and out, picking up the rhythm, taking him deeper, doing her best to rub against him in just the right place.

He picked up her rhythm and took over, moving hard and fast, just the way she had. Her eyes were heavily lidded, and he did aught he could to bring her to the edge before he exploded, reaching down at the last minute to rub the spot between them. She screamed his name, shuddering beneath him as her orgasm consumed her. Her muscles clamped down on him and he climaxed, shooting his seed into her raging heat, her thighs tightening on him as he pumped into her, wanting to make this orgasm last forever for both of them.

When he could finally speak, he hovered above her on his elbows, kissing her face softly in several places.

"You're mine, Gracie. No one will ever come between us again."

The last remnants of the wall inside him crumbled, and he gave her his heart.

CHAPTER NINETEEN

AFTER HE HELD HER IN his arms for a few moments, he whispered, "I would love to stay as we are, but I do not think 'tis wise. We
know not where the baron and his men are. I wish to find Uncle Logan
and Finlay, if we can. I'll step out to wet my cloth so I can clean us both
before we go."

He released her—instantly missing her sweet warmth—and stepped
outside into the pouring rain. After letting the cool water wash over
his skin, he wet the small cloth he kept in his sporran and returned to
clean her.

Gracie tried to cover her body, but he stopped her. "Gracie, I love
you, and I do not want you to ever hide from me. Every inch of you is
beautiful."

She did as he asked, her eyes watching him as he spread her legs to
wash the blood from between them. His hand froze before he finished,
and he reached up to turn her face from one side to the other. He'd
noticed the cut on her temple before, but there were many other small
cuts and bruises, and the wound on her head was swollen enough that
she winced when he cleaned it.

"He did all of this to you? I only noticed the one on your face before."

She nodded, looking into his eyes, and her finger moved to his chin as
he knelt beside her and finished washing her. "Please do not do something foolish. I know you would go back and right the wrong that he
has done, but I beg you to take me home instead. I do not care to ever
think on it again, and mayhap all would be best that way."

He nodded as he placed a tender kiss on each of her wounds, so gentle her eyes teared up. He said, "I promise you he will pay, though I will not seek him out now. 'Tis best to get you home." He did not speak what he knew to be true. He would kill the baron.

"Did you see your parents after I spoke to you?"

"Nay. I know not where they are. Kyla, either. But the baron said he'd had them tied up. We have to find out what happened to them, see that they are safe."

"I know. I left Finlay and our guards at a cave. Uncle Logan, Molly, and Tormod were to meet us there. Mayhap they know something about them. If not, we'll go back." He kissed her forehead. "Do not worry."

"Do not make me see the baron again. Please?"

"Hush, you'll not see him again. I promise to keep you safe."

He helped her don her shift, then wrapped the one dry plaid over her. She had no cloak, no gown or surcoat. The thought of where they were, of what the baron had tried to do to his love, threatened to put him in a killing rage, so he tried not to think on it. "I'll keep you warm. Once we mount my horse, I'll wrap my plaid around you so I can give you my heat as we ride."

Jamie was surprised by how cold it was once they mounted the horse and broke out of the ravine. He wrapped his plaid around Gracie as he had promised, hoping it would be enough to keep her warm. Though he briefly considered seating her behind him so he could block the wind, he worried she might fall off the horse if she fell asleep.

As if sensing his thoughts, Gracie gave a wee yawn and said, "Jamie, I'm sleepy."

"Go to sleep," he said, stroking her hair. "I promise to take care of you."

She closed her eyes and fell asleep almost instantly. Despite the danger that lay ahead of them and the anger that tightened his gut whenever he thought of the baron, Jamie felt at peace. He and Gracie were meant to be together, of that he had no doubt. Making love to her had exceeded his greatest expectations. She was a passionate, loving woman whom he would be proud to call his wife. He'd see them married as soon as possible.

Up ahead, he noticed a group of riders headed their way. They were not far from the cave where he'd left Finlay, so he prayed they were Grant guards. It would be hard, though not impossible, to fight with Gracie mounted in front of them.

He breathed a sigh of relief as soon as he recognized his cousin Loki.

Wee Kenzie was mounted in front of him, and Finlay rode at their side.

"Where the devil have you been, Grant?" Finlay's deep voice carried across the valley to him.

"Busy." He stopped his horse between Finlay and Loki. Gracie stirred in front of them.

Loki's features tightened. "All makes sense now."

"Of what do you speak?"

"Och, I'm looking at Gracie's face."

Gracie stirred and picked her head up, smiling when she realized who was talking.

"Papa," Kenzie whispered, his eyes as big as coins, "look at Gracie's bruises. Who would hurt her so? 'Tis dark, but I think her face is blue and purple and black."

Loki jerked his head toward Jamie, placing the question to his cousin.

"Baron Crichton attacked her. Tried to force her to accept his proposal."

Gracie turned her head into Jamie's shoulder, hiding her embarrassment over the situation.

"Gracie, you have naught to hide. He was in the wrong, not you." He lifted her chin to keep her from looking down. His love had no reason to be ashamed.

"We'll get him for you, Gracie," Kenzie yelled. "I'll hit him with my slinger, right between his eyes. Mayhap in one eye." He swung his arms out in a practice shot.

Jamie asked, "Why are you here, Loki?"

"As soon as Uncle Robbie got Caralyn and Kyla home, he called half the Grant warriors out to find Gracie. They've been searching furiously for you, but the baron is eager to find Gracie too. We need to get you home."

"My parents and Kyla are safe and unhurt?" Gracie asked.

"They are fine. It took Uncle Robbie a while to get his wrists free, but then he had to locate his sword before he could get them away from there. The baron had departed with many of his men so he had an easy time once he found his weapon. One of the serving maids told him Gracie had escaped."

"Uncle Logan headed to Grant land with Molly and Tormod, searching for you in a different direction. We're to meet him there. We'll get you home and put this behind us," Finlay said.

"Mayhap not," Loki replied, turning his horse around. "This attack on Gracie and the insult the baron has leveled on the Grants could start a clan war. We cannot afford to waste any time."

Jamie pulled on his horse's reins and took off at a gallop.

"Hang on, Gracie. I'll not slow until we hit Grant land."

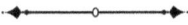

When they finally arrived, Gracie's head was pounding so hard she feared it would split open. The blow to her temple throbbed, and the reality of all that had transpired clouded her mind. How could she get it all to go away? No matter how she tried, memories of the baron would not leave her.

They hadn't encountered any other guards, but Loki knew the forests well enough to steer them away from the main path. Right before they left the densest part of the forest, Jamie had rearranged their plaids to hide her state of undress.

Once they were inside the gates, people ran from the hall to greet them at the stables. Fortunately, since it was nearly dawn, not many of their clan members were there. Gracie was relieved to see her parents at the front of the group, Ashlyn and Kyla behind them. Jamie handed Gracie down to her sire. "Be careful, she's sore."

Robbie took one look at her and asked, "Did the baron do that to you?"

Gracie whispered, "Aye."

Her mother reached out to wrap her arms around her, but she pulled back. "Please, Mama. My head pains me terribly."

Her mother glanced at her temple. "Hellfire, did the lout take his fist to you? That bruise is enormous."

Gracie couldn't stop the tears. She nodded. "He hit me." She reached for Jamie again to keep from falling.

Her sire's face turned dark as he glanced at Jamie. "Get her to her chamber and meet me in the solar." She saw Ashlyn's face and Kyla's, and part of her wanted to call out to them, but her head felt too addled.

Gracie held onto Jamie with an iron grip, afraid that if she let go the baron would appear and pull her back. She tripped over a rock, so Jamie scooped her up and carried her up the steps to the great hall. The others trailed in behind them.

He took her straight to her chamber and settled her carefully on the bed, doing the best he could not to jar her head. How she loved him.

He was so gentle with her.

She held a death grip on his biceps—he could not leave, not now—but he whispered into her ear, "Do not worry. You are home. He'll not get to you here. I must go downstairs and talk to my sire in the solar. Your mama can bathe you and find some clean clothes for you." He kissed her forehead and pivoted to leave. Gracie almost moaned for him to come back, but she saw her mother and sister and Kyla by the door. She would not be left alone.

"Where are her clothes, Jamie?" her mama asked, her voice barely above a whisper. "She wears your plaid and her shift is torn."

"She was wearing only her torn shift when I came upon her running up the baron's hill in the storm. She has not told me all yet. She didn't wish to talk about it. Mayhap she'll tell you." He squeezed her hand, nodded to Ashlyn and Kyla, and then left the room.

Gracie tried to smile at the three women she adored most.

Her mother whispered, "Gracie? Do you wish to tell us what happened?"

She sat up in the bed. "You've no need to worry...I'm fine. Jamie came along and saved me. I do not know where I would have gone if I had not seen him. You see, I ran without thinking. I never do that. I never go anywhere unless I have a plan, but I did this time. I went the wrong way, ran down a dark staircase, and then I was outside. It was raining and storming, and then the wind came up. Lightning lit the way so I knew where to go. 'Twas almost a blessing."

She continued, trying to explain everything exactly the way it had happened, barely taking a breath. "You know I always do as I'm told, even when I would rather not. When I was a lassie, I thought I had to be a good all the time so you and Papa would never leave me. I feared Malcolm would come back and steal me if I was bad. But you and Papa stayed, so I always do what I'm supposed to do." She looked at her mother. "Mama, I could not give the baron what he wanted."

Her mother rushed forward and wrapped her arms around her shoulders and said, "You did the right thing, Gracie..."

But Gracie pulled away because she wasn't finished. She smashed the bed with her fists, and something surged inside of her, something forceful and ugly, that made her pick up the goblet beside the bed and throw it against the wall. She felt tears course down her cheeks as she continued. "The baron thought he could force me to marry him if he took my maidenhead. I pushed him away, but he was stronger than me. I tried to bite him, to scratch him, to fight him. He was so angry when I hurt him, and he hit me and hit me.

"Jamie told me what to do if anyone ever tried to force himself on me. He told me there was one place where I could hit any man if I needed to run away. He was right—it worked almost perfectly." She stared at the ceiling, scowling. "I couldn't kick him because he was holding my legs down. He…he rubbed himself, and I felt him against my leg. It was disgusting…he was disgusting because…and I tried to kick him, but I couldn't, so I squeezed something as hard as I could, and he…"

Her mother was stroking her hair now, keeping her down on the bed when something inside her wanted to jump up, to fight. "You need not worry about this anymore. You did the right thing. I am so verra proud of you, and Papa will be, too. Here. I'm going to send Kyla downstairs to fetch a big tub of water for you. Would you like to wash yourself now? Why don't we scrub your skin?"

"Aye," she said softly, feeling that wild thing inside her calm. "That would be lovely."

Caralyn nodded at Kyla and she ran out the door. "Aye, wash me everywhere he touched me," Gracie heard herself say. The memory of his violence, of his unwanted hands all over her, struck her again. Suddenly, she could not take it anymore. She stared at her mother, who had always loved her unconditionally, no matter what, and it was as if the world had given her permission to release her pain.

"Mama, the baron…" She burst into tears and started to sob, gut-wrenching sobs that came from her toes. How she hated the baron for treating her that way. Her mother held her on one side and her sister held her on the other, and she sobbed and sobbed into her mother's shoulder.

Once she could speak again, she said, "I got away and Jamie came for me."

She was still crying when Kyla came back. Finally, after she'd cried more tears than she'd thought possible, she wiped her cheeks and said, "I would appreciate that bath if it would not be too much trouble. I'd like to wash my hair, too."

When she undressed, her mother and sister both gasped when they saw the bruises on her body.

"Oh, Gracie," Ashlyn said. "I'm so sorry."

She lifted her chin and replied, "I'll be fine, do not worry. Jamie loves me. We're getting married."

CHAPTER TWENTY

JAMIE PACED INSIDE HIS SIRE'S solar, waiting for him to enter. He'd hardly noticed the night had passed and the day was breaking. As soon as Alex sat down, he said, "Speak, and do not leave anything out."

Jamie glanced about the room, finally registering the presence of the others who were there with him. His father, Uncle Logan, Uncle Brodie, Uncle Robbie, Jake, Connor, Molly, Tormod, and Finlay.

Jamie gave his side of the story, explaining the condition in which he'd found Gracie and what little he knew about the attack.

His sire's hand came up to stop him. "This all took place during a thunderstorm?"

"Aye."

Uncle Robbie said, "And 'twas a horrific storm."

"What happened after Gracie ran up the hill?"

"I could see she was terrified and daft at the same time, so I had to go after her."

"You ran up the hill? In the middle of a bad thunderstorm?"

Jamie nodded. He knew what was passing through his sire's mind—Mac and his death. "Aye, 'twas not my best judgment, but I could not leave her up there, could I? I could not watch another person I love be brought down by a bolt of lightning. I had to get her off that hill."

His sire nodded. "Well done, son."

When Jamie finished with his side of the tale, his sire turned to look at Robbie. "And what was the baron doing when all of this took place?"

"I do not know. At the baron's bidding, the servants pretended the cook had been injured. Caralyn and I were tied up in the kitchens for a time, and Kyla was thrown in there with us. When I was finally able to free myself and find my weapon, I almost tore the great hall apart, but all we could determine was that the baron had gone off to chase after someone. One of the maids told us Gracie had escaped and he went after her. So we took our leave immediately."

Finlay asked, "Do you think the baron will make it this far? Will he attack?"

Alex nodded. "If he still wants Gracie, he'll be here. If not, we'll find him. I will not ignore this deliberate attack on one of our clan."

Uncle Logan crossed his arms and glowered at Jamie, "Did I not ask you to stay away until we returned?"

"Aye, but I needed to speak to her. I needed her to know how I felt. Had I not, she could have accepted the baron's proposal." Jamie would not apologize for the way he'd handled things.

"And did you speak with her?" his sire asked.

"Aye, and she agreed to marry me. We intend to wed as soon as possible. I left the keep with the intention of speaking with Uncle Logan, but I should have taken her with me. If I had, none of this would have happened."

"We will not look backward," Alex declared. "Logan, what did the three of you discover about the baron?"

Uncle Logan gave the floor to Tormod, who stood and said, "The baron is after your coffers, laird. There's no easy way to say this, so I'll just out with it. He thinks you're old and weak and ripe for defeat."

"Gracie was used as a way for him to get closer to you and claim your land," Molly added. "He wished to gain your trust before planning his attack. His second is Simon de La Porte from England."

"He failed," Alex said with a smile. "Well done, all. The question now is whether we should go on the offensive or wait for him to come to us. I'd as soon attack the bastard now, but first I'd like your input, Logan and Robbie. Tell me what else you know."

Logan said, "The last I heard, he was planning to wait for the king's acceptance of his marriage bid. If you refused, it would be his prompt to attack. I decided to come here to warn you before going to the king. I knew naught of the attack on Gracie. Something, possibly Gracie's rejection, moved his plans forward."

"He probably has around two hundred guards, way below our number," Tormod said, "but many seem well trained."

Logan added, "I've heard of de La Porte. Do not trust him."

Alex looked around at all of them. "We must all be on our guard. Jake and Jamie, talk to our men. Prepare them for possible battle. If naught develops by the morrow, I'll send a slew of guards to his land. I suspect we shall know the situation within a day."

Jamie cleared his throat. "I have one more request. Uncle Robbie, I'd like to formally ask for Gracie's hand in marriage. I'm sorry for my mistakes, but I believe we'll do well together."

Uncle Robbie smirked, but he did not say anything for a few moments, an eternity in Jamie's mind. He finally walked over to clasp his shoulder. "Aye, 'twould please Caralyn and I to have you as a son. But you better hurry, lad."

He glanced at his sire, who nodded.

"The baron's on his way."

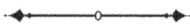

Gracie plaited her hair in the anticipation of going to the great hall. She'd slept almost a day away, and it was time for her to talk to her family. Jamie had come to see her, but he hadn't been able to stay because they were preparing for battle. His last words had set her heart afire. "My sweet, your sire and my sire gave us our blessing to marry when this is all over. I cannot wait to have you in my arms every day."

She'd kissed him on the lips and whispered, "You have my heart. Whenever 'tis possible, I'm yours."

She hadn't seen him since. Kyla had stopped in several times, but Ashlyn had gone home again because she was uncomfortable. Magnus would take good care of her.

The door banged open, and Kyla and Caralyn rushed inside, both pale. "You must come with us to the parapets," Gracie's mother said.

"Why?" She did not like the looks on their faces.

Kyla took her hand and said, "We have no time to waste, just come." She tugged her down the passageway and up the long staircase to the parapets. Once outside, they ran around the curtain wall until they reached the front, where they had a good view of the gates. Some of the guards who waited in the crenellations with their bows pushed them out of the way.

The sight sent a wave of panic through Gracie. "There are so many." A sea of warriors sat on their horses in the meadow, the Baron of Duncrub's flag waving above them in the breeze. Uncle Alex took his time getting out there, making their enemy wait as he often did. Her sire, Uncle Brodie, Jake, and Jamie already sat on their horses in front of the gates, and a score of Grant guards waited behind them and off to the side of the field.

"Will we be able to hear? What do you think he wants?" Kyla whispered.

Gracie said, with as much conviction as she could muster, "He cannot want me unless he wishes to tie me to a whipping post and give me forty lashes in front of his clan." She chewed on her thumbnail as she stared out over the land. The sight of the baron, even from a distance, sickened her. "We might be able to hear. There's no wind."

Alex moved to the front of the Grants, and the guards all moved aside for their laird.

"Da looks bigger than everyone," Kyla said. "Still...it frightens me when he goes to battle. What would I do if I ever lost him? The baron thinks he's weak."

Gracie reached down to clasp Kyla's hand in hers, giving it a squeeze. "He's the strongest laird in all the land. Everyone knows that but the baron."

Uncle Alex roared loud enough for all to hear. "State your business. You're not welcome on my land."

"I'll be quick, Grant," the baron bellowed back, his voice sickeningly familiar. "I want your niece, Grace. We arranged for our betrothal before the mighty storm hit us. She became frightened and ran away. I want her back."

"You gave my niece bruises on her face and neck. She'll go nowhere with you."

"I'll not leave until I get her."

Gracie could almost see the fire in the baron's eyes. She saw Jamie's horse prance a bit, and fear clutched her heart, but Jake grabbed the mare's reins and shot his brother a quieting look.

"You did not hear me, Crichton. You'll not get her. And you will have to get past my sword to get to her."

"You have twenty-four hours to send her out. If she's not here by then, we will attack and kill as many of your clan as we can, including your women and children. I have a priest who will marry us as soon as she leaves your gate. Think on it, Grant. You may have many men, but I have two hundred more warriors coming."

"You have no right to the lass, so leave now."

"Och," the baron chuckled. "You are wrong about that. I took her maidenhead. She belongs to me. The king will grant my request as soon as my expert examines her. Twenty-four hours."

Gracie turned around and ran all the way back to the doorway, down the staircase, and into her room. Now what was she to do? The vile man had lied about her. Jamie was the one who'd taken her maidenhead, but if she were examined, the doctor would say it was gone.

She would lose no matter what.

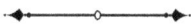

An hour later, Jamie's sire stepped outside of the solar and said to Loki and Kenzie, "Your sole assignment is to be sure no one is close enough to eavesdrop on our conversation."

Kenzie snapped his shoulders back and lifted his chin, "Aye, my laird." He crossed his arms to give everyone a glare in the hall. "Move along, move along."

Jamie didn't know what was about to take place, but he had a good guess. There were only a few called to the meeting, and he was standing next to Jake against the back wall of the solar. Their mother was sitting in a chair next to their father's, and Gracie and her parents were seated on the opposite side of the chamber. His heart broke for the inquisition she was about to endure, but he'd thought it might come to this. His sire needed to know exactly what had taken place at Duncrub.

Once Alex stepped back inside and closed the door, Gracie started to tremble. How Jamie wished he could stand behind her to give her strength to get through this, but his sire had set him away from her. The expression on her face reminded him of the look he'd seen on men about to head into battle—afraid, but also a wee bit sick.

"Papa, I'd like to speak first, if I may," Jamie said. He was not going to stand back and watch her go through this. He'd put an end to the inquisition by confessing what he'd done.

"Jamie," his sire barked. "You'll have your chance. Until then, you are forbidden. I ask the questions. Understand?"

Jamie nodded and stepped back. There would be no changing his father's mind at this point.

Jamie's sire broke the silence. "Gracie, I hate to ask you this question, but I must. Did you lose your maidenhead at Duncrub?"

The question was like a blow to his chest. His sire had asked the question in exactly the wrong way.

"Papa!"

"One more word, Jamie, and I'll remove you."

Jamie cursed inwardly and closed his eyes to gain strength.

Several minutes passed without any response from Gracie. Jamie almost crossed the room to her, but Caralyn turned to her daughter and whispered, "Gracie, did the baron take your maidenhead? You must answer Uncle Alex."

She shook her head and whispered her response to her mother before turning toward Alex and repeating it. "Nay, the baron did not take my maidenhead."

Quick witted as always, Jamie's sire asked, "May I ask why it took you so long to answer my question, but only a second to answer your mother's?" In a softer voice, he said, "I have to ask, lass. This could be war."

Jamie could not tolerate the inquisition any longer. He crossed the room to stand behind her chair and said, "Because I took her maidenhead, not the baron. We agreed to marry."

Gracie's head fell into her hands, but a second later she stood up next to him and clasped his hand.

Alex's gaze never wavered. "Gracie?"

In a voice that came out much stronger than he had expected, she replied, "I gave my maidenhead to Jamie. He offered marriage and I accepted."

Alex nodded, then shifted his attention to Jake. "Fetch Father MacKenny, Jake. Tell him and him only that we are about to have a wedding here in my solar."

Once Jake left, Alex came around the desk and stood in front of the two of them. "Gracie, forgive me, but I was forced to ask those questions. We welcome you into our family as a daughter as much as we welcomed you as a niece." He gave her a brief hug and turned to Maddie, who had also risen to join them.

"Gracie, you know we adore you," Jamie's mother said. "You and Jamie will have a wonderful life together, I am sure on it."

After she and Maddie hugged, Gracie turned to her parents. "Mama, Papa, do you forgive me?" Her voice quavered as she said it, and a ball of tension formed in Jamie's gut.

Gracie's father embraced her, kissing her forehead, and the tension eased. "There is naught to forgive. Jamie has already asked for your hand in marriage, and you both have our unwavering support."

Father MacKenny came in and greeted everyone. A moment later, Finlay knocked on the door and was bidden to enter. "Your pardon, my laird. The baron is approaching the castle."

"Father," Alex said, "you need to marry them quickly."

Father MacKenny nodded. Grasping their entwined hands, wrist to wrist, he wrapped the Grant plaid over them. This was really happening, and instead of being afraid, as a part of him had feared he would be, Jamie felt at peace.

Alex whispered, "My apologies to all in this room, but Father, you have two minutes to say the words 'You are now husband and wife.'"

Two minutes later, Jamie kissed Gracie and she smiled up at him. But there was no time to enjoy their happiness. Their smiles changed to frowns when an urgent knock landed on the door.

Uncle Brodie shouted, "The baron is on his way to the gates, with many more guards behind him, Laird."

They were married, and now Jamie was headed for battle. How ironic that all the adventure and excitement he'd been searching for was about to arrive, and he wished to take Gracie and lead her away. A lump formed in his throat as he looked at the ones he loved, realizing their lives could all be in danger.

His sire said, "Brodie, mount every warrior available. Prepare to attack. Surround the fools."

This battle was at home. This was not at all what he'd wanted.

CHAPTER TWENTY-ONE

E VERYONE MOVED AT ONCE. GRACIE turned to Jamie and said, "This battle is over me. I should never have gone to Duncrub."

Uncle Alex, who stood at the door to the solar, ready to leave, turned to her and said, "This has little to do with you, lass. If this battle were about you, he would send his army of warriors home the moment he learns you are married, but he will not. 'Tis about more than a maidenhead. You are a pawn in a dangerous game the baron is playing. The man longs to show his strength to all. Do not take any guilt on your shoulders. He would have found another reason to attack us before too long. Jamie, I know you are newly married, but I expect you in the second line."

Jamie nodded and held the door for Jake, who patted his shoulder and kissed Gracie's cheek before following their sire out the door. Aunt Maddie and her mother went up the staircase, probably to check on the bairns.

Moments later, they were alone. "Must you go?" Gracie cried. "Please stay here with me."

He cocooned her face in his hands and touched his forehead to hers. "I must go, for my honor, for Grant honor, but most of all, for your honor. We must put a stop to the baron and his lies." He kissed her deeply, but pulled away before she was ready. "I love you."

"Where should I go? I must be somewhere so I can see what transpires. You will be down there, and so will my sire, my uncles, and my cousins. What if someone is hurt?"

"Gracie," he said softly, reaching up to cup her cheek, "my sire has the reputation he does because he makes sure our warriors are prepared at all times. He was expecting the baron would attack, and many of our warriors are stationed outside of our land, ready to charge the baron's men from behind. Our scouts have told my sire exactly what to expect. Do not worry overmuch. Find your mother and my mother and Aunt Celestina. They will show you where to go."

She kissed him quickly and whispered, "I love you. Please be careful."

Jamie left and Gracie felt as if she'd just lost a part of her. When she stepped into the great hall—much, much too empty—she heard her name and turned to the staircase. Her mother descended the steps with Maddie, Kyla, Eliza, and the three bairns. Maddie said, "Come, we'll sit by the hearth. One of the guards will let us know what transpires."

Gracie looked at Jamie's mother. She was still a beautiful woman with many strands of silver throughout her golden hair, but her features were stiff with tension. "They'll keep us updated?"

"Aye, and hopefully the baron will accept Alex's explanation and be on his way, though I'm not sure that Alex believes this to be true. I must admit I am a wee bit worried about what will happen if they stay."

"Are you?"

"Aye, because I know Alex is worried."

The thought of anything frightening Jamie's sire, their powerful laird, terrified her. Gracie said a quick prayer for God to protect their clan. She could not handle it if anyone was hurt.

She'd feel it was all her fault, no matter what Uncle Alex had said.

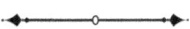

Jamie rode his horse to the left of his sire, and slightly behind him. The laird was always in the center, flanked by Uncle Robbie on one side, and Uncle Brodie on the other. Uncle Logan had been placed in charge of the warriors in the periphery so was not with them. Alex's sons rode behind him—Jake on one end, Jamie on the other, and Connor in the center—but their cousins Roddy and Braden rode between them. This was done to ensure that two of the laird's heirs could not be taken out in one swing. Magnus was behind Jake, and Finlay sat behind Jamie, their primary job to protect the laird's heirs.

A sea of warriors in the Grant plaid fanned out behind them including Tormod.

Jamie had seen the archers in the curtain wall. He'd bet his cousins Molly and Ashlyn were among them, sickness and all for Ashlyn, because they were both so powerful and true. Wee Kenzie was perched on the wall with his slinger.

The baron came forward as far as the Grant warriors allowed him, riding side by side with another man, probably Simon de La Porte. He guided his horse to a stop in front of Jamie's sire. "Where is Gracie?"

"Gracie, who is married to my son, Jamie, is inside where I told her to stay. She'll not be going anywhere with you."

"That's either a lie or they were just married," the man said, his eyes practically glowing with fury. "I told you I took her maidenhead. You'd allow your pup to marry a wench? She gave it freely to me."

Anger burned Jamie from the inside out, but he soothed himself with the thought that the baron would pay. It was only a matter of when.

"You have the tongue of a viper, and you disrespect my daughter-in-law," Alex bellowed. "Take your men from my land or prepare to do battle, Crichton."

He knew his sire's tactics. The baron would never make it off their land in one piece. Alex was only acting reticent about the attack because he wanted the baron to believe he'd been right to think the Grants weak.

By the time he realized how wrong he was, it would be too late.

No one moved for several moments. Jamie took the time to size up their opponents. He noted that some looked young, though that meant little enough on a battlefield. He knew wee Kenzie could be deadly with his sling, and he was just a laddie. A moment later, the baron let out his war whoop. He swung his sword arm over his head as he rode straight for Jamie's sire.

Alex fought him off, giving his own war whoop to signal to the Grant warriors that the battle had begun.

The field erupted into chaos and death.

Jamie moved in next to Uncle Brodie, keeping an eye on his sire as he blocked blows and made them, but Alex did not need anyone's help—he sent the baron back easily, though two other warriors rode in to take his place. Jake forged ahead as he usually did, mounting his attack from in front of his sire but off to his right.

The sound of swords clashing echoed across the Highlands. The reverberation was so deafening that Jamie could not hear aught else. His knees controlled his steed as his weapon caught one rider in the belly, then another in the arm. Men's screams rent the air as arrows flew overhead. He fought and fought, fueled by thoughts of the baron and Gracie—he wanted to be the one to kill the man who'd attacked his wife—yet trying to keep his emotions in check.

The baron had backed up after the initial onslaught, showing his true spirit. Jamie decided to make his way in that direction. He would knock that smirk off the baron's face.

As the battle raged on, he noticed the number of red plaids now outnumbered the number of green plaids. He attempted to search the injured for Grants, but it was almost impossible because warriors were still coming at them from many directions. Bodies were strewn all over the ground, and horses fell and rolled in the skirmish, some getting up and wandering off.

Jamie's sword arm, aching and tired, continued to strike and defend, but something caught him from the corner of his eye—his sire tumbling off his horse.

The man who'd dealt Alex a blow was preparing to strike him again, but Jamie rode hard toward them and took the man out. His war whoop came next, followed by the words they'd always dreaded to hear, "Protect your laird!"

Immediately men on horseback surrounded his sire, who still lay on the ground, blood darkening his plaid. His eyes were open, but he appeared dazed. He'd never thought to see the time his sire would be beaten on the battlefield, the man had appeared invincible to all. Yet here he was flat on the ground, unable to protect himself. He prayed his eyes deceived him and his sire would get up soon.

There was no sign of Jake either. Magnus, Connor, Braden, and Roddy had all joined him in the circle around his sire, but where the hell was Jake? When he finally set eyes on his brother, he saw he was far ahead of them, still fighting like a fierce warrior. He had no idea their sire was down.

Jamie yelled again, "Protect your laird!" Two more rode in hard to join them, and the weight on Jamie's shoulders eased a slight bit. He could protect his sire from further damage until the conflict ended. The number of green plaids were dwindling, so the battle would end sooner rather than later. Then he saw something that took his breath away and stole what was left of his composure.

Gracie on horseback. Gracie was riding hard off into the forest, far away from the battle. But why? What had possessed her to leave the safety of the keep?

Jamie's composure left him. Did he chase after Gracie and leave his sire undefended? There was no one around to take his place in the circle. He swung his sword again and took two more bastards down. From his position, he could see a sea of red plaids streaming toward the baron's men from behind—Uncle Logan's warriors.

They would help end this.

"Gracie! What are you doing?" Frantic, he called out to Finlay, "Finlay, cover my sire. I must go after Gracie."

Finlay answered his call immediately.

The worst of all happened. The baron had also seen Gracie leave and charged after her. Jamie tried again to get his brother back, but he was too far away to see or hear what was happening. Two Grant warriors came up from the back of the field, so he bellowed. "Here. Protect your laird." Three had filled the spaces, so he galloped after Gracie as fast as he could.

Gracie was still ahead of both of them, but the melee slowed her. She stopped once to cover her head with her arms, screaming for them to end the battle. Jamie knew the precise moment when the baron realized he would catch her because an evil grin crossed the man's face. He moved toward Gracie at about the same pace Jamie was moving—slow but persistent. There were too many warriors between him and Gracie and the baron.

Jamie yelled again. "Kill him. Take the baron out." No one could hear him over all the screams. He glanced back at his sire again. The blood stain at his midsection continued to grow and his eyes were now squeezed shut. "Da, fight, do you hear me? Fight, stay alert."

What the hell was he to do? All of a sudden, all the faces around him seemed to blend together. Dirt and sweat and spit and blood flew everywhere. He was losing the ability to distinguish between the enemy and his brethren. A shock of bright hair popped out against the others, and he saw the baron was now only a short distance from his bride.

Jamie lost all control. He kneed his horse and headed straight for the baron, swinging his sword arm over his head. The strike did not land, which threw Jamie's balance off and gave the baron a chance to flee toward Gracie. Horror overtook Jamie as he watched the baron ride hard in her direction.

His sire's words rang out in his mind. *Take your emotions out of it, Jamie. You'll not best your enemy if you allow your emotions to overtake your reason.*

Then, a miracle happened. A horse appeared out of the dust, cutting the baron off from behind, forcing him to slow enough for Jamie to catch him. Tormod. His friend had given him the chance he needed.

Forcing Gracie out of his mind, Jamie slashed his sword at the baron again. The bastard locked gazes with him, smiling that hideous grin.

Jamie swung at him, but the baron easily blocked his blow. They parried a few more times before the baron struck at his lowest point with words.

"She's a whore, Grant. You married a whore, and I liked her."

Jamie ignored him, knowing the feint for what it was. He would not be distracted. He faked a swing at the man, who immediately raised his sword to block it, then changed his direction at the last instant and buried his sword in the baron's belly, a death blow for sure. Tormod struck him with another blow from behind.

The baron dropped his sword and grabbed his belly, and Jamie pulled his sword out, wiping his blade across the man's legs just before he fell to the ground. Jamie took a moment to gather his strength, searching his immediate area for any more warriors in green. Mayhap they'd leave now that their baron was dead.

But it wasn't to be. The man who'd rode in with the baron, probably Simon de La Porte, barked orders at the remaining guards. Four warriors came toward Jamie and Tormod, but they managed to fight them off together. Tormod did battle from one side while Jamie attacked from the other, slicing bellies and flesh everywhere they could. Men fell to their right and to their left.

A voice came from atop of one of the towers. "Kill them all, Tormod! That's my brother."

Lyall. His brother was standing watch on the parapets, and he'd seen Tormod fighting like a man set on fire.

Uncle Logan and four more Grant warriors joined them, and together they fought off the last few green-clad warriors around them. When Jamie glanced at his brother in the front lines, he saw that Jake was still holding strong, fighting two of the green-clad men at once.

Moments later, the few remaining enemy warriors fled the scene, Simon de La Porte with them.

Jamie immediately searched the area for any sign of Gracie. There was none. He'd lost sight of her when he'd met with the baron, but she could not have gone far. Perhaps she was hiding in the trees.

His breathing still ragged, Jamie rode back to the circle of protectors surrounding his sire.

"Where's Gracie?" he asked.

No one answered.

"She was just here on horseback." He searched the grounds for light hair, but there was no sign of her.

Jake came up behind him. "Nice battle with the baron. Great way to put an end to this ruckus. Why is everyone in a circle?" He pointed toward the spot where their sire lay, clearly still unaware of what had happened.

"Da took a sword to his belly," Jamie said bluntly, wiping his sleeve across his face to get the blood off.

Jake stunned, asked, "What? Da? But he's...where is he?" He jumped off his horse and raced to the circle, pushing everyone aside as Jamie shouted to him.

Jamie followed. "He was bleeding heavily when I last saw him. He couldn't get up, but I saw his eyes open and close."

He dismounted and pushed his way into the circle. Uncle Brodie was already kneeling beside Alex, whose eyes remained closed.

"Papa?" Jamie leaned closer to him, searching for any signs of life. His heart was beating hard in his chest, yet his limbs felt almost numb, and he could not find any beats of life in his arm or his wrist. His face was so pale, that alone frightened him. Jamie's mind clouded again as he tried to reason through all that had transpired.

This could not be happening. Could not. He should be going after Gracie, but she'd probably run off to hide. The threat had lessened now that the baron was dead and his men were gone. Loki rode up from the outside, staring down at Alex with a strange look on his face. "Loki, see if you can find Gracie. She was on horseback headed west."

Loki simply nodded and rode off.

Jamie grabbed his sire's arm and shook it, attempting to get a reaction. Alex's eyes fluttered open and then shut again. "Papa!" Jamie lifted his head and shouted, "Someone bring Aunt Caralyn."

"Robbie's already gone for her," Uncle Brodie said. "He's barely alive."

Connor moved next to Jake. "Papa?"

Jamie put his hand up on his sire's neck, searching for a sign that he still lived. "I feel it. He's still alive. Papa!"

Alex's eyes opened and he glanced at Jamie. "My thanks," he said in a weak voice, "your actions saved me. Take me inside...Maddie."

"He's alive. I heard him, Jamie. He'll come back." Connor's voice was full of hope.

Jamie wished he had the same hope inside him right now.

Caralyn arrived moments later on foot, Maddie by her side. Jamie bolted up before they reached the circle, hoping to lessen the pain of what his mother was about to see. He grasped her shoulder. "Mama, remember how strong Da is."

"Is he dead? He looks dead… Nay, Alex, please, nay…our time is not done yet." Maddie's fist went into her mouth and tears streamed down her cheeks. "Help me, Jamie, Jake. My knees. Help me get down, I must be close to him, please, please." Jake came over to help console his mother.

Jamie did as she asked as more and more people gathered around. Magnus had stepped away from their group to give instructions on cleaning the area up, gathering the dead, and looking for wounded men. There was a dampened mood, and many of the warriors surrounded their fallen laird at a distance. Some had even dropped to their knees to pray.

"Alex?" Maddie brushed his long locks away from his face and kissed his forehead. "Alex, come back to me, please." Her voice had broken into sobs. Jamie watched as his sire reached for her hand and squeezed it, though it was obvious he had no strength.

"Fine…, Maddie. I'll be fine. Do not…worry." His eyes closed again.

Jake asked, "Aunt Caralyn?"

She looked at Uncle Robbie and Uncle Brodie and shook her head. "I…'tis naught I can… Healing a belly wound is beyond my abilities. I'm sorry."

Maddie screamed and rested her head on her husband's chest.

Jamie whispered, "How long before he's dead?"

"Not long," Caralyn said. "Mayhap a day."

CHAPTER TWENTY-TWO

JAMIE BELLOWED, "GET THE CART."

"Nay, Jamie," Jake said. "We can get him in a large blanket and carry him into the keep. 'Twill be less jarring."

Loki arrived on his horse, dismounting not far from them. "Uncle Alex? Is he dead?"

Kenzie, who was trailing behind his sire, burst into tears. "Uncle Alex! Nay!"

"Nay, he's not dead. Did you find Gracie?" Jamie asked.

"She's not out there. Mayhap she returned to the keep after you killed the baron. She was not far when you went at him in the middle of the fray."

"Get the cart, Finlay, Braden. Jake, I'm taking him to Aunt Jennie."

"What? It will take almost a day to get there. Aunt Caralyn says he'll be dead by then. Why put him through it? Leave him here so he can be with Mama." Jake's rapid pacing indicated his level of tension over their father's condition. His brother rarely showed emotion, much like their sire. The pacing meant he was close to the edge.

His mother was flat on the ground, her head cradled on his sire's shoulder. She was no longer sobbing, but tears still coursed down her cheeks as she moved her hand lovingly back and forth across his chest. His sire's eyes remained shut, but he was still breathing.

"We're taking him to Aunt Jennie's. 'Tis the only chance he has."

Uncle Brodie nodded, but Uncle Robbie said, "Leave him here. He's near death now. Let him go in peace. He'll die a hero's death. I cannot see putting him through the pain of riding in that cart."

"I'm taking him," Jamie replied, "My sword goes with me, so do not try to stop me. Someone find Gracie for me, please."

Jake pursed his lips and dipped his head, then lifted his gaze to Jamie's, a piercing look in his eyes. "Take him. Connor and I will stay here. Take Mama." He clasped Connor's shoulder, who stood off to the side in shock, and left. "We'll find Gracie."

His mother reached for Jamie's hand, so he gave it to her. He pulled her up to standing, wondering what it was she wanted to say to him. If she tried to stop him, he didn't know what he'd do… Nay, he would not give in, he couldn't. She was not thinking clearly.

She reached up and cupped Jamie's cheek. "Take him to Aunt Jennie. I'll get my things. Your father is a fighter, and we'll not give up either. I'll bring more furs, and his head will rest on me. I'll keep him from jarring, keep him warm." She kissed Jamie's other cheek and hurried toward the keep.

No one said a word as she walked away.

As soon as she left, Uncle Logan came out of nowhere and said to Jamie, "Take him to Jennie and do not slow. I'm heading out to get my two fastest messengers to Brenna and Jennie. Brenna will meet you there. Godspeed, Jamie." He disappeared before Jamie could say anything.

They were on the road less than an hour later. Jamie was still worried about Gracie, but he'd forced himself not to think about his wife. If he did, he'd be forced to leave his father and go after her. Before leaving, he had sent the best team he could assemble to search for his wife—her parents, Loki, Kenzie, and Finlay. At the last minute, Kyla had attempted to join Jamie's group, but he'd shaken his head. He could not worry about Kyla and his parents. He'd tipped his head and yelled out, "Finlay. She goes with you."

Their best horses drew the cart, and Jamie rode in the front, marking the fastest route and helping steer the cart away from the uneven portions of the path.

Moving his sire into the cart was one of the most difficult things he'd ever done. Jake, Jamie, Finlay, Braden, and Roddy had hefted him onto a large blanket they'd used to transfer him. His sire was a bear still, more muscle than anything else, and the five of them had strained to move him smoothly.

His sire's eyes had popped open at one point, but they'd locked on Jamie's and closed—a silent message that he trusted him. That one move had almost unmanned him. Never had he expected his sire to be anything but larger than life.

They moved with two score of Grant guards for protection, as Jamie had vowed that he would allow nothing to slow their journey.

He glanced back at his mother, who was holding his sire the best she could, her mouth moving in silent prayers.

Jake, Connor, Celestina and Brodie had stayed back to see that the men's minor wounds were taken care of and to continue to guard the castle should any louts still be swooping through the area. A score of warriors were trailing the group who'd gone off in search of Gracie, and they had instructions to head to Aunt Jennie's once they found her.

They'd find her. They had to.

They'd only been married a day.

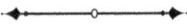

Gracie had run to the curtain wall as soon as she heard the war whoops. Others had tried to stop her, but she'd fought her way past them.

This battle was all her fault.

She was leaning over the wall when she saw the sword plunge into Alex's lower belly. Jamie had seen his sire go down, thankfully, and protected his sire from another blow. But that didn't change the fact that the famous laird of Clan Grant, Laird Alexander Grant, renowned as the greatest swordsman in all the land, sibling to four, father to six, and uncle to many, had been unseated and was now hurt badly enough that he was lying vulnerable in the middle of the scuffle.

Jamie had yelled for the other warriors to fall in to protect him, but Gracie became frantic. All of a sudden, she had the need to get away. It was as if a cloud had dropped over her. She could not handle watching her loved ones get hurt or die, especially not when it was her fault. The sounds that echoed through the air were devastating to her.

She had to get away. Bad blood. Her bad blood, probably from Malcolm, had struck a mighty blow on the Grants as soon as she had become part of the family. The heavens were telling her she did not belong.

She'd accept the decree and leave.

She raced down the staircase, and out through the front doors, barely slowing as she ran to the stables. Every stall was empty except for one. The stable lads were gone, probably watching the fight and grabbing stray horses, so there was no one to help her.

Or stop her.

She mounted the horse and rode out through the gates and headed straight for the trees, the only way she knew to get off Grant land. She ignored everyone as she traveled, did her best not to look at the death and destruction everywhere around her, sucking her into its vortex of evil. She'd never heard such awful sounds in her life. Each blow echoed in her own belly, each scream brought a squeal from her throat. She did her best to move toward the forest, but the warriors around her prevented her from getting close.

How she wished she could do something to end this before anyone else in the clan got hurt. She'd do anything to stop this clash, this battle that had been fought for her. It was all her fault. Had she never shown an interest in the baron, never gone to his castle, would this truly have happened? Despite her uncle's assurances, she doubted it.

Then her husband rode straight for the baron. She could see the fury in his eyes when he caught her gaze, but he quickly regained control, taking his emotion out of the battle. Her horse panicked and headed toward far edge of the forest. It was a struggle to control and calm the beast, and when she finally managed it, she found herself far away from the battle. She was surprised at who she found outside the battle zone, away from the chaos and death.

After seeing Alex Grant's condition up close, she said the one thing that came to the forefront of her mind. "This is all my fault. I have bad blood in me. Look at all that has happened in the last few days. Will you take me away from here? I never wish to step foot on Grant land again."

After a thoughtful pause, the man had agreed with a smile, and she'd gone with him.

Gracie had left behind everything she loved.

Even her husband.

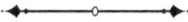

As soon as Jamie arrived inside the Cameron gates, Aunt Jennie flew out to Alex's side, oblivious to everyone but Alex and Maddie in the cart. Alex and Jennie held a special relationship, and they were all witnesses to it.

"Alex. Please, Alex. Wake up, open your eyes for me." She jiggled his shoulder but he did not move. "Alex!"

"Maddie, how long has he been like this? When was the last time he opened his eyes?"

"It has been a couple of hours. I tried to keep him awake, Jennie, but he kept falling asleep."

"Alex," she shouted in his face. "You listen to me. You shall not give up. Do you hear me?" She poked her finger into his chest, tears beginning to clog her voice. "'Tis too early for you, you need to stay here. You have not even met your first grandson yet. How could you think about leaving all of us? Your lads still need you and so do your lassies. Do you not want to meet your grandson, the future laird of your clan?"

She gave a few curt instructions to those around her to get him into the keep. Jamie helped his mother out of the cart.

"Alex, I'm warning you. *Wake up.*"

He stirred and opened his eyes. "Mayhap I'd prefer a grandlassie first."

Jennie laughed and kissed his cheek. "I love you, Alex. Do not go, please? Aye, you may have a granddaughter if the heavens abide your wishes."

They used another large blanket to get Alex inside, though he was too pale to Jamie's liking. At least they had made it. He'd had been petrified he would die on the journey here.

Aunt Jennie could save him, he had faith in her.

An hour later, he was pacing the Cameron great hall when the door flew open with a bang. He rushed over to the door, blurting out the only thing he could think of at the moment. "Did you find her?"

He knew the answer by the look in Aunt Caralyn's face, wet with tears. Uncle Robbie said, "Nay. We had a possible trail with one other horse, but with all the horses in the area for the war, it was impossible to trail her. She has not come here? We'd hoped she might have ridden in this direction."

Jamie said, "Nay." His belly churned so hard he thought he might be ill. Images of the worst possible scenarios flashed through his mind—wild boars, reivers, Simon de La Porte. Nay, he could not let that happen. He had to find his wife.

"I'll go search outside for her," Kenzie said. "I'll not give up until I find her."

He started to say, "Kenzie, I doubt she's…" but Loki clasped his shoulder.

"Let him go. 'Twill give the lad something to do."

Kenzie dashed out of the hall. As soon as he left, Uncle Robbie asked, "My brother? How is he?"

"Aunt Jennie's checking him now," Jamie said, running a hand through his hair. "It does not look good. He's pale and weak. He only awakened when Aunt Jennie yelled at him. Tell me which trail you followed. I'm going back out after Gracie."

"I'll go with you," Finlay got up from the trestle table and said, "She has to show up somewhere."

They headed to the chamber when the door flew open a second time. Aunt Brenna flew past him with a short, "Greetings, all. I must go to my sister's healing chamber." Uncle Quade, Uncle Logan, and Aunt Gwyneth followed. The Ramsays had arrived. The churning in his belly slowed at their presence. Aunt Brenna was still renowned as one of the best healers in all the land, and she had taught Aunt Jennie. The aunts working together gave him new hope, gave them all hope.

Uncle Robbie said, "Nice work, Logan. That was fast."

Uncle Logan wiped the grime from his face with his plaid. Logan's gaze searched everyone in the hall, catching the slow but unenthusiastic nods. "He's still that bad?"

Slow nods followed.

Uncle Robbie said, "Glad to see you came along with my sister, Quade. How are your joints?"

"Riding horseback is easy. I know how she loves her brother, and after we heard how bad he is, I had to come. Fill me in while they work on him."

Jamie said, "Finlay, I'm going to check with my mother, then we'll head out."

His pacing slowed as he approached the room they'd been referring to as the sick chamber. Aedan Cameron stepped out of the chamber as he approached it. "Jamie, go on inside. I must go greet Quade and Logan. Have faith in your aunts. I do."

Jamie stepped inside the chamber, the smell making him wish to run the other way. He had no idea how healers could do what they did. His mother rushed up to him and grasped his hand.

He whispered, "Any change?"

"Hush, listen to Aunt Brenna for a moment."

Aunt Brenna and Aunt Jennie peered at the wound on the right side of Alex's belly.

"Based on the book that Aedan gave me, I think this is his liver," Jennie said, "and that looks to be where most of the damage is. 'Twas a clean stab. It did not go through the entire organ to his back."

Aunt Brenna nodded. "I wonder if he would have enough left to serve him if we were to cut out the small portion that is shredded. 'Tis a verra large organ, and he would still have most of it. Quade never suffered any lasting effects from the organ I once removed from him. Granted, it was small in comparison, but based on what I've learned, the liver does not have an inner cavity the way the heart or the stomach does. Mayhap he can survive with most of it left intact. The rest of it appears to be healthy."

"I think 'tis our only chance," Aunt Jennie said softly. "Otherwise, he will continue to bleed from all those tears. I think we cut here—" she made a motion across the organ, "—and sew him up to stem the bleeding. His outside wound is clean, so we'll stitch him up. Hopefully, he'll awaken before the fever sets in. We must try to get enough fluids in him."

"I think we must do this as quickly as possible. I do not like how slow his vessels are beating."

"Aye, 'tis Mama's most basic healing rule. Keep fluids in the body and keep it clean."

Jamie had heard many of the elders talk of his grandmama and her sire. They'd been amazing healers. All had admired her sire, but when his mother had grown of age, they'd worked together and done some wonderful things for the clan. It had been his grandmama that had pushed them to be clean about their wounds. Though he had no idea why, he had to agree that the cleaner a wound was, the less chance of fever.

"This is good timing. I just cleaned all of my surgical tools, so we do not have to take the time to do that. This time the water had come to a boil before I dropped the tools in. Surprised me how much easier they cleaned in the hot water. I hardly had to touch them. I'll wash my hands and get my tools."

Aunt Brenna looked up at them as Aunt Jennie went for her instruments. "I'm hopeful, Maddie. The bowel was not pierced, so that is the good news. I think we can repair his liver. Jamie, 'tis a good thing you brought him here. Caralyn does not do much surgery. Why not take your mother down to the hall? This may take a while, and if Alex wakes up, which I doubt, we will put him to sleep again."

His mother shook her head, but Jamie said, "Mama, 'twill not do him any good if you drop to the floor in here. Why not go into the hall and get something to eat? You'll need your strength to help him heal."

His mother nodded, her beautiful smile back. "Of course, you're right, Jamie. Brenna, if aught…"

"I know. I'll send for you. You look like you could use some rest, too. This could take several hours. There are many stitches for us to place."

As soon as they arrived in the hall, the door opened again.

It was Kenzie. "I found Gracie."

Jamie was so excited he flew across the hall, but Kenzie pulled out his small sword. "I am to take you to her, but only you and her mother. No others."

"Why, Kenzie? Where is she?"

"She's at Lochluin Abbey. Father MacKenny brought her here."

Kenzie rode with Jamie and Caralyn rode with Robbie, crossing the short distance separating the Cameron's keep from the abbey. Once they arrived, Jamie hopped off his horse and ran inside, Caralyn behind him while Robbie waited outside. He halted as soon as he saw Gracie, all dressed in white robes, standing in front of the altar in the chapel.

"Gracie?"

Gracie turned around slowly as Jamie moved up the aisle. Her hair was the same color as her robes, and she looked like the most beautiful angel in all the heavens. She clasped her hands in front of her and said, "Forgive me, Jamie, but I can never return to Clan Grant."

She looked down at her hands as though she needed strength to continue.

"I have requested to annul our marriage."

CHAPTER TWENTY-THREE

"WHAT? GRACIE, YOU'RE JUST CONFUSED from all the chaos. You should not have come out into the melee."

"I am not confused, but I have realized that I do not deserve to be a Grant. I've asked the abbess if she will accept me as a nun." She wanted so badly to make them understand, but she was not sure how.

Jamie stepped closer, but she wished he'd keep his distance so she would not have to look into his beautiful blue eyes, eyes that softened when he asked, "How could you say such a thing? How does one deserve to be a Grant? We love each other, 'tis all that matters."

"I have committed a travesty. Because of my careless actions, one of the greatest heroes of the Scots is on death's door. No one will forgive me, and the worst part is that they are not wrong."

Her mother moved forward, and Gracie wished she could wash the pain out of her mother's face, help her to understand that this was right and just. She would speak with her alone later.

Caralyn stood strong in front of her, as if she had something important to say. Gracie knew from experience to listen when she had that look about her. "Daughter, everyone loves you, and no one will fault you for what the baron did. 'Twas the baron's lies and selfish actions that caused the battle, not yours."

Jamie added, "My sire has not passed on either. I believe my aunts will save him."

She could see that Jamie would not accept this easily. With each comment he made, he came closer to breaking down her barriers, but she vowed to remain strong.

"I'm weak, Jamie, don't you see? Nay, I'm not worthy of your name. My sister put an arrow in the worst villain in our history, and my cousin killed the man. Sorcha will be as strong an archer as her mother someday. All of your cousins are strong, intelligent people. What am I?"

"You fought off that scoundrel. How much stronger could you be?"

"I did not stay and fight. I ran and ran. Had someone put a dagger in his heart then, this never would have happened."

"One woman against one man is not good odds. You did right to run away. He could have overpowered you or taken his sword to you."

"I should have learned how to wield a dagger as my sister did. But I'm not that type of person. I do not deserve…"

Jamie stopped her. "You have other strengths that your sister does not. You took care of three wee lassies when no one else could. That's a strength and patience I do not have, nor does anyone else in our keep."

Her mother asked, "Who do you admire and love the most of all the Grants and Ramsays, other than Jamie and your family?"

Gracie thought for a moment about the question, but she did not need to give it much thought. "Aunt Maddie."

"Why?"

"Because she has the biggest heart of all of us."

"Have you ever seen your aunt fire an arrow or wield a dagger?"

"Nay."

"Then why do you think you need to? Your heart is just as big as Aunt Maddie's. 'Tis why the wee ones flock to you. Stop comparing yourself to your sister. You have different strengths."

Mayhap her mother spoke the truth. She did love the wee ones. But there were other worries that weighed on her, private ones she hadn't shared with anyone other than her sister. It was time. "I think I carry bad blood from my father. There's a dark cloud over me, and 'twill follow me everywhere I go. I fear I have brought that curse to the Grant family. If it were not for my bad blood, this would not have happened. Look at all that has transpired simply because I said I wished to marry. I caused a rippling cascade of tragedies that may not be over. I'm going to stop it from ever hurting your clan again."

"You are my wife, and I will not give you up," Jamie said, staring at her with a fierce gaze. "You made a vow to me. We all know of your background on Grant land, and no one cares. We love you for who you are. Your suggestion of bad blood is preposterous. Where did you get such an idea?"

She just shook her head and said, "Nay, the only way to guarantee everyone's safety is for me to live away from everyone." Tears ran down her face. These dark thoughts had tormented her and nipped at her since she was a wee lassie.

"Gracie, that's enough." Her mother's voice was so forceful, it shocked her. "You will come down here and sit," she said, pointing to the back bench, "and listen to me. Jamie, get your uncle to come inside. He needs to hear this as well." While Jamie ran outside, her mother's hands settled on her hips, and she paced in a small circle, something she'd seen her do often when she was upset. What had upset her so?

"Hear what, Mama? What is it you wish to tell us?"

"Something I should have told you long ago, but I had hoped to protect you." She stared at the ceiling as if praying to the Lord before she continued. Her voice broke on the words. "I did my best to keep you from being hurt. I never wanted to hurt Robbie either."

Gracie stepped toward her mother, just now noticing the tears in her eyes.

Jamie brought Robbie inside, and her mother motioned for them all to sit on the back benches. She sat next to her mother on one bench, and the men sat across from them. Once they were settled, she said, "This is between Gracie and me." She paused, then added, "Robbie, I'm sorry I never told you before. I love you so much that I was afraid to risk losing you."

"Go ahead, Caralyn. She needs to know, whatever it is. Nothing could change my love for you."

"Gracie, I will tell you everything, but please do not interrupt me or I may not be able to finish."

Her mama's words frightened her, but she decided she would do as her mother asked. The need to know more about her sire—who he was and why he'd rejected her—had been building over the years, and now it was so strong, it threatened to knock her down so thoroughly she'd never rise again.

"First, know that I am not proud of my past," Caralyn said in a shaking voice. "Whatever I did, I did to protect you and Ashlyn. I did everything for my girls."

She paused to gather her thoughts, or so Gracie thought. Her mother had never told her much about the past, and though Ashlyn's memories of that time in their life were powerful, Gracie's were not. She remembered nothing before Clan Grant, yet somehow she had always known

Clan Grant was the best place for her.

"When Ashlyn's sire died in the fishing accident, my heart was broken. Every day I worried about how I would be able to feed her in the winter. Your sister went hungry many days, but then a man came along who promised to feed her, but only if I earned the food.

"He prostituted me and I agreed, and you know most of this. It was a horrible life, but your sister's belly was full. Before you came along, there was one man who came through our wee village every time he sailed through on his way up the firth. His hair was white like yours. He was a kind man, unlike many of the other men Malcolm sold me to." She reached over and ran her fingers through Gracie's strands, then lifted Gracie's chin so she could look directly in her gaze. "And his eyes were the same shade of blue. After a few visits, I made a big mistake. I fell in love with him because he was kinder than any of the others.

"He would bring me trinkets, and each time we saw each other, he would swear that someday he would have enough coin to take me with him, but in my heart I knew it could never be. You see, Malcolm controlled me, and he did not like this man. His name was Nicklas. When I found out I was carrying, I prayed every day that the child would be his and no one else's. Malcolm did not allow anyone near me while my belly grew. It was lovely, and he'd given me a couple of sacks of grain to carry us through. You have no idea how happy I was when you were born. You had Nicklas's blue eyes, which became more and more blue as you grew. Your hair did not come in strong until your second summer, but I was ecstatic to see that each strand on your head was almost white. Because Nicklas had a kind heart. I'm sorry I never told you, but I thought if I told Robbie I had loved another I could risk losing him. I would have done aught to keep from returning to that life, including keeping the truth from you.

"A moon after you were born, Nicklas came to see me. He fell in love with you, held you and kissed you. He would have been a wonderful sire, but 'twas not to be. Malcolm was jealous. I never believed he had any feelings for me, but he must have felt something, because he made sure Nick never returned.

"The other men said that Malcolm followed him out in his boat one night, waited for the perfect moment to stab him and toss him overboard. They said he pierced his heart and there was so much blood that he could not possibly have survived." Caralyn wiped her tears away, unable to stop them from pouring down her face.

"Malcolm told me I'd never see him again, though I didn't realize at the time that he'd killed him. I was furious, but he always had the final say. Whenever he visited, he brought food to hold in front of you and Ashlyn. I could not handle seeing you both hungry, so I did whatever he asked me to do. Nick never returned, and I felt certain that I'd lost my only chance for freedom and a good life."

Gracie did all she could not to sob. How horrible her mother's life had been. Tears blurred her vision, but she felt her husband move beside her and clasp her hand in his. Her sire had wanted her. She returned her focus to her mother, not wanting to miss any part of the story of her true sire.

"Fortunately, a few moons later I met Robbie Grant." She moved over to kiss Robbie's cheek before returning to Gracie. "Robbie has been the best father you could have ever asked for. I know Nick would approve of Robbie acting as your sire."

Gracie squeezed Jamie's hand and lifted her gaze to the ceiling of the building. She was not cursed. She'd been wrong. Her sire had wanted her. In a different world, her mother and Nicklas may have been happy together. Instead, Robbie had come into her life. How fortunate they'd been.

"I know, Mama. I did not intend to hurt Da by asking questions. Sometimes I just felt cursed. My thanks for telling me the truth."

"Nicklas would never have cursed you, and I believe with all my heart that he sent Robbie to us." She pulled out a linen square to mop her cheeks, then took something out of her sack. "This is for you. I've held on to it for years because I was afraid to admit to Robbie that I loved your sire. And I never wished to get your hopes up. 'Twas wrong of me, but I thought it would be best if you just accepted Robbie as your sire—if you forgot that there was another. Had I known that it bothered you so, I would have given this to you a long time ago."

Her mother took her hand and placed a gold pendant into her palm. "Nicklas found a few beautiful stones on the beach and had them set into this pendant. He said the blue one was for me, and the white shiny stone represented you. He asked me to give it to you when you were of age." Gracie brushed her thumb across the white stone, which beamed all of the colors of the rainbow depending on which way she looked at it. "Forgive me for not giving it to you sooner. Nicklas gave this to me the last time I ever saw him. Two moons later, two other fishermen told me about Malcolm's attack on him. I tried to throw Malcolm out, but 'twas impossible." She stared at the ground. "I hated him."

Gracie stared at the white stone, feeling an almost magical pull from the gem. Her sire hadn't hated her. He hadn't been a bad man at all. It was as if someone had released a tight grip on her heart, and she could mayhap be able to let go of all her questions. She whispered, "My thanks, Mama. And thank you for protecting me for all those years. You've always been a wonderful mama to Ashlyn and me." She hugged her mother as tightly as she could before moving on to Robbie Grant, who stood up and grasped her arms.

Looking into her eyes, he said, "I've always loved you and considered you my own, Gracie."

"I know, Papa, and I give you many, many thanks for it. I love you."

Robbie wrapped his arms around her, then kissed her forehead and stepped away to wrap his arm around her mother, who said, "We're returning to the Cameron keep. Know that you belong with Jamie, and we hope you come home to us soon, but if you need time to think at the abbey, we support you."

"Thank you both."

Kenzie, who'd been hiding in the corner, finally stepped forward to tug on her hand. "Gracie, I lost my true papa, too. But I love my new papa. You can love both."

Gracie said, "You are wise for your young age, and you are correct." She gave him a quick hug and he giggled.

He spun around toward the door, shrieking, "Wait for me, Uncle Robbie."

Once they left, Jamie wrapped his arm around her waist. "May I see your pendant?"

"Aye, 'tis quite beautiful."

He fingered the pendant, looking at it from different angles before he returned it to her. "You'll keep it forever. 'Tis quite a treasure. But why have you never said anything about your sire? Does Ashlyn know you've wondered about him?"

"Nay. I never said aught because of Robbie. I've always loved him, yet something inside of me wished to know the truth. It...unsettled me, more so than I knew."

He kissed her, the warmth of his lips spreading through her entire body. She had intended to push him away, at least until she had time to process what she'd learned, but she could not. She parted her lips and teased him with her tongue, and he growled, tugging her close.

His kiss became possessive and demanding, and she responded to him, giving herself completely to him, her husband, this man she adored. He thrust his tongue deep, forcing her to open wide for him, and she kissed him back with equal fervor, shocking herself with her newfound boldness. Strange sounds emanated in the back of her own throat.

He ended the kiss, panting for air, and finally whispered, "You're no nun, wife."

She giggled, pulling back to stare at him. "Nay, I think I must agree with you."

"Do you not know what you do to me? How can you think of leaving me? I would never be the same without you. None of us would."

"How is your da?" She cupped his cheek, and ran her thumb across his lower lip until he nibbled on it.

"When I left, Aunt Brenna and Aunt Jennie were preparing to do surgery. Aunt Brenna was hopeful. She did surgery on her own husband many years ago and had to remove a piece of his insides. It saved his life. He'd been gored by a boar. 'Tis how they met."

She thought for a moment, rubbing the backs of her fingers across the rough stubble on his jaw. "Forgive me. I've heard talk of many battles, but I'd never seen one before. It...hurt to see all of that violence."

"Does this mean you'll stay with me?"

She sighed. "Aye. I do not know what I'd do without you. 'Tis true I'm no nun around you." She rested her head on his shoulder, enjoying this quiet intimacy between them.

"If you do not wish to live on Grant land, we could live with Loki or Aedan or the Ramsays. I'll do whatever you wish. As long as we're together, it matters not to me."

"Nay. My heart belongs with the Grants. We have a wee niece or nephew coming soon. I promised Ashlyn I'd always stay at home, and I made her promise me, too."

He gave her a quick kiss. "Good. But if you change your mind, we can discuss it." He paused, then reached up to caress her cheek. "May I remind you 'tis our wedding night, lass?"

She lifted her head and played with the stubble on his chin.

"You like my rough beard?"

"Aye. I like everything about you. I always have, but some parts of you I would like to get to know better." She gave him a saucy grin and he laughed.

"Now you're teasing me..."

"I'll stop. Please take me to see your da," she said, feeling her smile slip away. "My heart will not rest until I see he's better. I...I cannot bear to keep thinking of Uncle Alex covered in blood on that battlefield."

"Aye, I need to see him, too."

CHAPTER TWENTY-FOUR

JAMIE SETTLED HER ON HIS horse and mounted behind her. Before they left, she had quickly changed out of her nun's robes and into her own clothes. She'd also briefly spoken with the abbess and Father MacKenny to explain her change of heart. He pulled her closer, enjoying every minute of having her in front of him—his wife, Gracie. He had to admit that he loved the sound of it.

Then reality settled in on him again, and he said a quick prayer for his sire, hoping that his aunts had been successful with their surgery.

When they entered the Cameron hall, everyone gathered around Gracie, welcoming her back, asking her about her trip, making her feel how welcome she was among her clan.

Robbie, who'd arrived just before them, settled it with an honest response. "Gracie just got a little lost."

"Da," Jamie said, "How is he?"

Just as he finished his question, Aunt Brenna and Aunt Jennie entered the great hall. While Aunt Brenna brought Maddie up to the sick chamber, Aunt Jennie addressed the rest of them. "We've finished the surgery. Alex looks better, but he's still verra weak. He did not wake up at all until after we finished. He's gone back to sleep, and Brenna has brought Maddie to sit with him. All we can do at this point is wait and pray."

"May we go see him?" Jamie asked.

"I think so." Aunt Jennie gave him a kiss on his cheek. "Make sure you do not speak of the battle around him. I think he hears everything, your father. And do not leave without seeing Brin in the lists. Gracie, you must chat with my lassies, too. They adore you." She gave Gracie a quick hug. "We were delighted to hear that you two have married. You're a perfect match."

Jamie kissed his aunt and then took Gracie's hand and led her toward the end of the hall.

They crossed paths with Aunt Brenna, who said, "Jamie, he's in the chamber next to the healer's chamber. My brother is too big for the pallets. Aedan sent some of his men in to move him to the place with the largest bed."

Gracie glanced at him, and he could see the tears in her eyes. He leaned down and whispered, "Papa is the strongest man I know. He'll fight his way back."

As soon as they stepped inside the chamber, Jamie's mother jumped off the stool to greet them. "Gracie, we're so glad you're here. Sit. There are two stools over there. Pull them up next to the bed. Your da would want you both close."

"He looks better, Mama," Jamie said, looking down at the bed. His sire looked at peace. Before his breathing had been ragged and labored. It helped that he was no longer covered in blood and dirt. His skin was still pale, and he had a long way to go to return to the powerful laird the Scots all knew. He still breathed, that was the important part.

"Aye. He's all bandaged and cleaned up. His sisters are so skilled. My thanks, Jamie, for pushing to bring him here. I did not want to be the one to argue, but I was not ready to give up on him. Your da is such a strong man…strong yet the gentlest man I have ever met. Why, when you were a bairn, he would carry you and Jake around strapped to his chest. He was always such a proud papa."

Jamie did not know what to say to that. He'd always known his father loved both him and his twin equally. Aye, sometimes he and his da fought, but he couldn't have asked for better parents. Listening to Gracie's questions about her sire made him grateful for his upbringing.

"Gracie," his mama said, "if I may, I'd like to say something."

"Of course, my lady."

"When I last saw you on Grant land, you had an expression on your face that I recognized. It was the same expression I had on my face when I first came to Grant land. I had this feeling that everything that had been done to me by my stepbrother and the evil man he wished me to marry was my fault. I believed that the injuries caused in the battle that followed were because of me, and it would not have happened had I not come to Clan Grant.

"You need not say aught. I know you well enough to know that's what you were thinking. Do you know it was this fine man in front of you who convinced me otherwise?" She squeezed Alex's hand, though he did not respond. "So I shall tell you what my husband would tell you if he could." Her eyes filled with tears, but she managed to blink them back. "You did not cause the baron's heart to turn black, it was always black. Those with black hearts are driven by things you cannot comprehend. They enjoy hurting others for the sake of it, and they like nothing better than using women as pawns. Please do not think it had aught to do with you being there. In fact, I doubt the baron came to our land for your hand, and I mean no insult by saying that. Alex told me it may have been an excuse to get past our defenses and get inside our castle. Even if it was not, I believe he was right when he said the baron was looking for an excuse to lay siege to our castle."

"I'd never looked at it that way." Gracie glanced at Jamie—a silent question—and he squeezed her hand. "I think Mama makes a good point." He reached over and brushed a stray lock of her hair back. "Take any guilt you are harboring and forget it, please."

"Do you think he'll improve?"

"Aunt Brenna said it will be a slow recovery for him, and we must get him to drink something when he awakens. She's says since he's older, he will heal slower than he used to, but she's hopeful."

"But what do you think, Mama?" Jamie asked. "Do *you* think he'll improve?"

To their surprise, his sire opened his eyes for a second and said, "Aye. You'll not be shod of me yet." Jamie saw him squeeze Maddie's hand before he closed his eyes again.

Jamie's mother gave him her biggest smile and said, "Aye, he'll get better."

They sat with him for a while, and after some time, Uncle Logan and Aunt Gwyneth came in for a quick visit.

"Maddie," Uncle Logan said, "he'll get better for you. Gwynie and I are heading home to be with the young ones. We'll visit when he's back at home over the summer. Quade and Brenna are staying."

"I so appreciate you for coming, Logan, Gwyneth. Send our love to everyone in your family. I'm sorry you feel in a hurry to leave. I hope all is well."

"Sorcha has been acting up. We know not what is going on in her wee mind, but she likes the lads a little too much to suit me," Aunt Gwyneth said. "She'll soon be eight and ten, and she's becoming quite vocal about her desire to do as she wishes." Gwyneth kissed Gracie's cheek. "So pleased you and Jamie finally found each other. Molly and Tormod are perfect together. Now we just need to find mates for Sorcha, Maggie, and Bethia."

"Bethia is so shy, and Maggie hasn't seemed too interested, has she?" Maddie asked.

"Not yet, but Sorcha's too interested. We must go calm her down." Gwyneth laughed and whispered, "She's the one who will turn Logan's hair gray."

Uncle Logan wrapped his arms around Aunt Gwyneth and said, "If I turn gray, you'll turn with me, wife."

"Aye," Aunt Gwyneth said, "we'll turn together. She's going to test us, Logan, in every way."

Maddie shrugged her shoulders. "She's a delightful niece. She's just having growing issues, those funny middle years."

Jamie smirked and said, "Uncle Logan, you had to suspect one of your daughters would be that way, did you not?"

"What do you mean? And remember, just because you're married does not mean I won't drag you to the lists."

Jamie replied, "You married Aunt Gwyneth, and she is far from a typical lass. 'Tis not surprising to me that Sorcha is not typical either."

Uncle Logan's gaze narrowed as he stared at his wife and then back at Jamie.

Maddie said, "He makes a fair point, Logan, though I might add that Sorcha reminds me more of *you*. You were wee bit wild for a time, if you recall."

Jamie had to chuckle when he saw the evil grin his mother tossed at Uncle Logan, something he rarely saw.

Gwyneth laughed. "I agree, Maddie. I think I can see Logan's mother Arlene saying 'tis his turn to deal with it."

"I cannot argue with you two," Logan said with a rueful grin, "but 'tis a different way of looking at the situation. Let's take our leave, Gwynie."

Once they left, Jamie asked, "Mama, are you staying here all night?"

"I'm not sure. Jennie said she'd find me a pallet nearby. You and Gracie go ahead, find your chamber. You are newly married, after all. We must not forget that." She stood and kissed each of them. "I think Jennie said she had the perfect place for you."

They took their leave and returned to the great hall. Some in their

party were already asleep on pallets, but Uncle Robbie and Aunt Caralyn awaited them. As soon as they stepped into the hall, Aunt Caralyn
bounced out of her chair.

"Come. Jennie has the perfect place for two newly married people,
and your father and I added a few things for you to make it feel a bit
special."

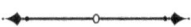

Gracie felt renewed by a surge of hope. She had dreaded sleeping
with her new husband in a crowded chamber or out in the great hall on
pallets. Their party was large and she had no idea how many chambers
there were in the Cameron keep.

Her mama and da led them outside, bringing them behind the keep.
Gracie stopped after walking a few steps to look into the sky. "Papa,
remember when we looked at the stars not long ago?"

"Aye. 'Tis a perfectly clear night for you to stargaze."

They stood still for a moment, all their heads tipped back to look up
at the sparkling forms in the inky black sky.

"Oh!" Gracie said.

"What is it?" her mother asked.

"I found a new favorite. When Papa and I were outside, I showed him
my favorite star way over in the corner, but this cluster is so much more
beautiful."

"Where?" her sire asked.

She pointed off to a westerly direction. "That grouping is the strongest, most beautiful bunch I've ever seen."

"They are lovely," her mother whispered.

"Those are my new favorites. I love them much better than that lone
star in the distance."

Her sire wrapped his arm around her shoulder, gave her a kiss on her
cheek and said, "Come along before you get too cold."

They made their way over to a small cottage hidden in the trees, way
off to the side. Her mother said, "Aunt Jennie and Uncle Aedan use
this place for themselves when they wish to get away from the bustle of
the castle. There is a place in the back where they sleep under the stars,
watching the sky while they fall asleep. 'Tis Aedan's favorite spot."

Gracie stepped inside and gasped. Beautiful did not seem strong
enough to describe this small cottage. A large bed sat in the middle,

piled high with furs and pillows. Many candles were arranged around the border of the room, across the shelf above the hearth, and in wall sconces. Dried flowers hung from the ceiling, giving the room a slight aroma of heather and lavender. Two cushioned chairs sat in front of the hearth with a small table between them. A basket of fruit and cheese sat on the table along with two goblets for wine.

"Aunt Jennie sent this wine and food for you. You must be hungry."

"Mama, 'tis lovely. My thanks for arranging this, and for everything you've done today."

Uncle Robbie tossed a few more logs in the fire, then said, "Come along, Caralyn. Let's allow the freshly wed couple to have some time alone."

He clasped Jamie's shoulder and said, "Well done, son. The entire day, well done." He kissed Gracie's cheek and whispered, "I love you. Have a wonderful night." He took his wife's hand in his. Caralyn kissed them both on the cheek and then hurried out of the cabin, pulling Robbie with her. Knowing her mother as she did, Gracie guessed she had chosen to leave before her tears started.

As soon as the door closed behind her parents, Jamie spun her around and asked, "What do you think?"

"I love it. 'Tis perfect. I admit I was a bit worried we'd need to sleep in the great hall as we often did as bairns."

Jamie pulled her close, wrapping his arms around her waist, and kissed her. "This is perfect. I'm not ashamed to say that I'm famished all of a sudden. That basket of fruit looks delicious. Shall we eat?"

Gracie nodded and took one of the chairs. "Aye. I do not think I've eaten a bite since yesterday."

Jamie cut and arranged the food on a linen square for them, then filled both goblets with wine. "While we're eating, there's something I'd like to share with you." He reached into his sporran and pulled out a folded piece of parchment and handed it to her.

Gracie had no idea what it could be. "Jamie, what is it?"

"My sire told me I was acting like an arse over all your suitors. Once he helped me see how foolish I'd been, he gave me this. I'd like you to read it. Mac, my old stablemaster, dictated it to my mother."

Gracie unfolded the paper. "Mac? He wrote you a note? Where was it all this time?"

"I guess he gave it to my parents. But 'tis quite special, and I'd like to share it with you."

She began to read it, and when she came to the part about the flower, her gaze lifted to his. "Is that what you meant when you said I was your flower?"

"Aye. You are my flower."

"Oh, Jamie. 'Tis such a beautiful letter. Will you miss your adventures? Do you still wish to go with Uncle Logan exploring?"

He shook his head. "Nay. This last fortnight has been more adventure than I'd ever wished for, so my answer is a verra solid nay. I'd prefer to spend my time with my flower at home. My purple flower because you smell of heather and lavender."

"I'd love to be your flower forever," she whispered, running her fingers down his jawline. Her husband was a handsome man.

"Aye, you're my purple flower. That's better than what Finlay called me."

"What?"

"All the while we traveled to the baron, he called me prickly, like the thorns of a flower. We were passing through a meadow of thistles, all the purple flowers just popping out. Mayhap he's right. I'm the prickly side to your purple flower."

"I love thistles."

Jamie broke off a chunk of cheese and gave it to her. "My mother told me stories about Mac and the horses. Something about how you would pet the big horses and I had my wooden sword to protect you from anyone else. I guess I even told Mac to stay away from you." He took a bite of the apple chunks on the platter. "And once I finally decided to go after you?" He snorted. "You would not believe how many people told me that we belong together."

She set the note down and gazed at her husband. He was so fierce, yet so tender. His skin was a light bronze from the sun, and his beard was a light brown stubble, a wee bit darker than his hair. His hands were strong and he kept his nails short and clean, something she liked about him, though they were not as clean as they usually were since he'd been in a battle that day. She ran her finger down his jawline and across his chin, likening it to the thorns on the thistle in the meadows, so vibrant in late spring and then again in late summer.

When she thought of all he'd done for her, her thistle, her eyes filled with tears. He'd followed her to the baron's, refused to leave, and then come after her. How had he known?

"Jamie?"

"What is it?" he asked staring into her eyes.

"Why did you come back for me? How did you know the baron had…when I was on the hill…" she trailed off, not wanting to say the exact words.

"I don't know. I was riding with Finlay, and somehow I just knew you were in trouble. I can't explain it."

"Make love to me, Jamie? But could we use the bed this time?"

CHAPTER TWENTY-FIVE

GRACIE LEANED OVER TO KISS him, but Jamie scooped her up into his arms and settled her on the bed.

"Aye, 'twas a bit cold and hard on the stone, was it not?" He smirked and kissed her neck before he stood up and dropped his plaid to the floor. "Tonight, I promise to keep you warm."

Then he reached for her, lifting her back off the bed so that she stood in front of him. "Last time, I did not get the chance to see your beauty. We'll not hide it tonight." He helped her with the ribbons at the back of her gown and then tossed it over a chair. "You'll not be needing this tonight."

She stood in front of him, the firelight warming her legs, but she watched his face, pleased to see an appreciative expression as his gaze traveled down to her toes and back up again.

"Gracie, you are so beautiful." His finger traced a line down her arm and then her hip before he changed to his other hand and repeated the caress.

She shivered.

"You're cold again. Forgive me, I'll settle you back in bed and keep you warm."

He moved to pick her up again, but she stayed his hands. "Nay, whatever you do, I will do the same." She lifted her brows and tipped her head to see if he would argue, but all he did was grin, so she proceeded with her task, trailing her finger down one of his sides and then the other.

She watched his manhood grow as she touched him, suddenly feeling a new sense of power. "Will you always do that if I touch you?"

He snorted. "Aye, especially if you're standing in front of me with naught on. That alone is enough to make me hard." He reached for her breasts. "They are perfect, as you are, the perfect size." His hands moved down her belly and out to her hips. "You have the perfect curves."

His hands on her hips tugged her closer until his lips almost touched hers, and he spent time caressing the globes of her bottom, something she found strangely tantalizing. "You are perfect. Every part of you is perfect, and I aim to know every last part of you."

His lips covered hers and she melded her body to his, enjoying his heat, his hardness from his chest to his belly to below. She broke away to whisper, "I love you, Jamie, and I know we'll be happy forever."

He lifted her and set her down gently on the bed. "I plan to show you how much I love you, and Gracie? We'll never be apart again. My heart knows it and so does yours."

She coiled her arm around his neck and kissed him, parting her lips to tease him with her tongue until he growled, taking control from her and slanting his mouth over hers in a rhythm that left her breathless. He ended the kiss and trailed a path down her neck and across the fine bone on her chest, then down between the valley of her breasts, stopping at each one for just a tease, a flick of the tongue to each nipple before he moved below.

She had no idea what he would do next, so when he kissed her *there*, she squealed, "Jamie!"

He lifted his head enough to say, "Hush, I wish to know all of you."

His tongue continued to tease her in the most sensitive area she had, stroking her until she gripped the furs around her, spreading her legs wider like a wanton, and his response was to growl and delve deeper.

"Jamie, please. Come to me, or I'll…" No longer capable of speaking, she writhed as his tongue continued to torture her nub until she screamed and climaxed in a frenzy. When she was totally spent, she loosened her grip on the bedcovers and stared at the ceiling. The only thing she could say was, "I had no idea."

Her husband chuckled as he kissed his way up her body, gathering her in his arms when his lips reached her forehead.

When she was able, she pulled back and said, "My turn." She started as he did, positioning him on his back and kissing the hard angles of his body, the slight indentations on his chest, the occasional dark spot from the sun. She teased his nipples as he had hers, surprised to see him react so strongly to the touch of her tongue, and the expression on his face told her he enjoyed it as much as she had.

She liked the small amount of coarse hairs on his chest, a light brown that followed down the middle of his abdomen to his male parts, where it blossomed. Anxious to see what he would taste like, she did not spend much time on his belly, but went directly to his erection, standing so proudly before her.

She touched her tongue to the tip and he bucked against her, giving a low moan as she ran her tongue around the edge and down the long length of him.

"Suck me," he whispered.

She did as he suggested and took him full in her mouth, her eyes closed. She only pleasured him for a short while before she felt him pull her away and toss her onto her back amongst the furs.

"You play with fire. I cannot tolerate such torture any longer." He kissed her, a kiss that was hot and demanding, a kiss that did not allow her to pull away, but one that told her how much he loved her. He devoured her and she surrendered completely to him. He ended the kiss, panting, with one word, "Enough. I want you now."

All she could say was, "Aye, now."

He positioned himself above her and teased her slick passage with the tip of his hardness. A smile spread across his face when she writhed against him, rubbing her mound against his hardness.

He entered her swiftly, and she took all of him, giving him more access with each thrust. He clasped her bottom to lift her so she could take more of him, and she wanted more, begged for more, wrapping her arms around him and clutching him as if she couldn't bear to let go. He plunged into her again and again, and when she felt her spasms begin, she yelled his name, gripping him and scoring him with her nails, plummeting over the edge of ecstasy that brought him to his own finish, a savage joining that she would never forget.

Jamie was hers.

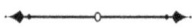

Jamie lay on his back, his elbow behind his head, Gracie's head on his shoulder as he stared up at the ceiling. Mayhap it was time to tell her all of it.

"Gracie? Are you still awake?"

"Aye." She tipped her head to look at him. "What is it?"

"My sire told me the reason I acted so foolish was because of what happened with Mac. What do you think?"

She ran her hand across his belly in a light caress. "I think you were afraid to get attached to anyone, including me. How exactly did he die, Jamie? Why did it bother you so?"

"It happened in a thunderstorm."

"Aye, but what exactly happened? No one wishes to talk about it."

"I headed up the hill in the back meadow to help him with two frightened horses when a bolt came out of the sky and struck him dead."

She gasped. "Jamie…how horrible for you. I'm so sorry."

"It hit him so hard that he flew into the air and landed quite a distance away, but Papa said he was dead before he landed in the dirt. It was so powerful that it knocked me down, too. I remember finding Mac on the ground and slapping him, trying to wake him up. My father had to pull me away from him. Then he and my mama kept me in their chamber for a while. I do not recall much except that I could not stop crying and hollering. My sire said I was so miserable that he had to take me down to Mac's stall in the stable many times until I understood he was not coming back."

Gracie sat up because something had occurred to her. "Jamie, I thought that storm was different, the one at Duncrub. 'Twas frightening, but there was something about the timing of it that was so perfect…"

"I do not understand."

She crossed her legs underneath her and turned to face him, though he was still flat on his back. "I was so confused, so frightened, that I could not find my way. I managed to flee the baron's keep, but I had no idea where I was going until a bolt of lightning crossed the sky and lit the way for me. I had no idea where the hill was, but I remembered it because the baron had shown it to me, telling me that it was the only way to get to his land, so I knew it was the only way out. When the sky lit up, I ran for the hill. Do you suppose…?"

"What? What are you trying to say?" Jamie rolled onto his side and propped himself up on his elbow.

"It was almost as if the storm started just for me, that it lit the way for me in the black of the night. And then it lit up again when we were both on top of the hill. I was so upset, so hysterical that I would never have seen you without that brilliant light. It was almost as if…"

"As if what?"

"As if the storm came along just for me, for us. It led me to you. Do you think Alice or Mac had something to do with it? That it was their way to watch over us?"

He tipped his head. "I know many people who would believe it. If so, maybe I need to look at things differently for the rest of our lives."

"How so?"

"Mayhap thunderstorms will be our friends from now on."

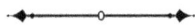

Gracie sat still in the chair in the wee lassies' chamber, doing her best not to wiggle. It had been nearly a moon since she and Jamie had married. Alex had survived, though he'd fought through two different episodes of fever, once at the Cameron castle, and once after they'd returned home.

Each day he looked better. Jamie and Gracie had their own chamber upstairs, not far from the wee ones' chamber. Maisie, Morna, and Maeve now slept by themselves, but she still worked with them each day, teaching them their letters and anything else Aunt Maddie wished for them to learn. Aunt Maddie spent a great deal of time helping Uncle Alex, and he was almost back to the hale, hearty man he'd been before the battle.

Almost.

"Lady Gracie, please do not move your head. 'Tis hard to curl it when you move," Maisie said.

Maeve looked very serious, her tongue protruding between her wee lips, as she placed flowers carefully in Gracie's hair. While she worked, the door popped open and three more lassies came in—Kyla's sister, Eliza; and Brodie and Celestina's daughters, Catriona, and Allison.

Catriona said, "We heard you were testing Aunt Lina's knew way of winding hair that she showed us at the last Ramsay festival, Maisie. Is it working?"

Maisie did her best to explain how she was wetting and winding Gracie's hair the way Eliza and Kyla had shown her.

Aunt Maddie came in to check on their progress. She clapped her hands together and smiled at the six lassies surrounding Gracie.

"Aunt Maddie, they are doing a fine job," she said without moving. She had thought about calling her mama, but Aunt Maddie had said either would do, and habit took over most times.

"Aye, they are. 'Tis so kind of you to allow them to practice on you. My, but you should see your cascading tendrils, Gracie. I wish you could see the back. Your hair is no longer straight. Aunt Avelina did create a new way of curling hair."

"And I love curling hair," Maisie said, "but Morna and Maeve are better at decorating it."

Maddie leaned down to whisper in her ear, "My thanks for being so patient with the lassies. They do love you so."

Gracie blushed at the wonderful compliment. She did not understand why sitting there allowing the wee ones to play with her hair made her wonderful, but she was not one to argue.

"Do you know that I had to promise your sister that I would allow you to be free for a sennight once she has the bairn? She is so afraid she will not know what to do with the wee one that she wants you there with her for as long as possible."

"Truly?" Gracie asked, feeling a huge grin spread across her face. "I would love that, Aunt Maddie. I cannot wait to see if 'tis a lad or a lassie."

Aunt Maddie said, "I have another favor for you when you're done. If you do not mind, I'm sewing a gown for Kyla, and I need someone to try it on so I can check the hem. Would you mind?"

"Of course. I would love to." Gracie was being quite honest. She would do anything for her husband's mother. Marrying Jamie was the best thing that had ever happened to her. She loved waking up in his arms every day. He often pestered her, telling her that he was sorry they'd married so quickly instead of having a proper wedding, but she did not mind. Their happiness meant more. What would have happened if they had not married the day they did?

She shuddered to think on it.

Aunt Maddie left and returned a few moments later, sneaking into the chamber with a dress. "Do you like it? Kyla chose the color."

The gown was a beautiful shade of purple, a deep lavender so enticing, she had to reach out and touch the fabric. "This gown is beautiful. What a fine job you have done on it."

"My maid, Alice, used to make many gowns. I try to sew as well as she did, but it is often difficult with the stiffening in my hands. I appreciate your kindness in agreeing to try it on as I wish to give it to Kyla soon, but she is tied up in the kitchens with Cook."

"Eliza, would you do me a favor, please? Would you run to my sewing basket near the hearth and bring me the white thread?"

"Aye, Mama."

"Take the wee lassies with you."

Gracie allowed Maddie to help her into the gown, and it was the only time since she'd married that she wished for her own special wedding. She fingered the ribbons on the bodice, but then stood tall while Maddie laced up the back of the gown, refusing to give in to those feelings. She truly could not be happier.

The girls weren't gone long when Gracie heard a yell from one of the girls.

"That was Maisie," Gracie said, whirling to look at Maddie. "I hope she did not fall down the stairs. I'll go after her."

"I'm done, go check on her, please."

As she approached the stairway, she heard Maisie's voice again, "Gracie, will you come and help me?"

Gracie sighed in relief. She did not sound hurt, just upset about something. She continued down the passageway and down the staircase, staring at her feet because the hem of the gown was long and trailing. She had almost reached the bottom of the staircase when she yelled, "Maisie, are you all right?"

Maisie stood at the bottom of the staircase, giggling with her hand over her mouth.

Gracie froze and glanced around the hall. Wrapped up in her worry about the lassie, she hadn't noticed the changes until now. She glanced over her shoulder to see Aunt Maddie coming down the staircase, a wide smile on her face.

The entire hall was full of Grants. Each trestle table was adorned in purple and green linens, with bouquets of thistles on each one. Thistles also adorned the hearth and had been braided into wreaths hanging around the room. At the base of the staircase stood her sire, dressed in his finest clothing. He held his arm out to her and she took it.

"Welcome to your wedding, Lady Gracie." Maisie clapped her hands and giggled, jumping up and down in excitement.

Gracie looked down at the skirt of her gown at the same time Aunt Maddie leaned over to kiss her cheek. "Aye, I made it for you. Welcome to your wedding. Jamie insisted."

Tears blurred her eyes and she swiped at them so she could see everyone. Her sire whispered, "Are you ready?"

Her hand moved to her hair. The flowers the lassies had woven into it so carefully had been white and purple. She nodded to her father, and she walked through the middle of the hall as her loved ones greeted her.

Kyla.

Her mother, who cried tears of joy.

Her sister Ashlyn, beaming like she'd swallowed the sun.

Magnus.

Jake and Aline.

Connor and Eliza.

Her brothers, Roddy and Padraig.

Uncle Brodie and Aunt Celestina with Braden, Catriona, and Allison.

Loki and Arabella with Kenzie and Lucas.

Uncle Alex was seated near the hearth, where Father MacKenny stood beaming.

And there, walking toward her from the side of the room, was her husband.

Jamie, who took her breath away in his red plaid and leine, came to her with his hand extended. "Will you marry me again, my purple flower?" He wore an armband of thorns on his right arm.

She laughed and threw her arms around him. "Aye."

She cupped his face and said, "You'll always be my prickly thorn, but I love you."

Jamie whispered, "But together we'll be something special."

EPILOGUE

JAMIE GLANCED AT HIS BROTHER Jake, the two of them standing at the entrance to the great hall, waiting to see why they'd been summoned to the keep from the lists. Jamie fidgeted every once in a while, unable to stop himself.

"Can you not hold still? You never could when you were wee either."

"Why?" Jamie whispered. "Does it bother you? Because if it does, I'll make sure to do it more often."

Jake gave him a wide grin. "I have two fists behind my back that might change your mind."

The hall was empty except for the elders seated at the dais. It was a special meeting that had been called, but neither Jake nor Jamie knew the reason for it.

At the table were three of the elders who had been part of the group, the *dearbh fine*, since Alex had been chosen laird. In their clan, the laird did the disciplining with his second, but Alex had always had two seconds—his brothers—so Uncle Robbie and Uncle Brodie were both elders. Nicol; Edwin, Nicol's sire; Taran, the eldest male in the clan and also Edwin's sire; and Solas.

Jamie glanced over at them: Taran, Solas, Edwin—the eldest three, and the newer members—Nicol, Robbie, and Brodie. After the laird, the *dearbh fine* held most of the power in the clan.

"I'm thinking this is about Da." Jake leaned toward Jamie, doing his best to keep his voice down.

"Why do you think 'tis about Da?" Jamie asked.

"Because he has not healed as fast as everyone thought he would."

"There's naught wrong with his mind," Jamie insisted. "He can lead from a horse, he just cannot do battle."

Jake sighed. "I agree with you, but I'm not sure Taran and Solas agree with us."

The door opened at the end of the great hall, the new area built especially for Alex and Maddie. Their mother held it as their father made his way through it with slow, deliberate steps. He used a whittled oak branch to keep him upright, something Kenzie and Loki had whittled until it was smooth as a stone plucked out of the bottom of a rushing riverbed.

Alex Grant nodded to the men at the dais and his two sons who'd been instructed to remain by the entrance to the great hall until they were called forward.

Jake whispered, "I still can't believe he survived. Damn good thing you were there to argue with me. I was sure our sire was a dead man. They say he may never get back to full strength."

"He does not need to," Jamie whispered. "He's the great Laird Alexander Grant. His days as the best swordsman in the Highlands might be over, but I think he'll swing one again."

Jake glanced at his twin. "I hope you're right."

"Mama and Papa love their new chamber. You did a nice job with that. They'll never go back upstairs," Jamie said.

Their sire would not be able to handle the keep's stairways for a while, so Jake had overseen the addition of a chamber near Uncle Brodie's tower, but at the end of the hall instead of in the corner. He'd added a hearth and a sitting area for their mother.

Once their parents had settled, Taran, the chief of the elders, asked, "For what purpose did you call this meeting, Laird?"

Jamie couldn't believe what he'd heard…his sire had called this meeting?

"I've called this meeting because I believe it's time for me to step down as laird of Clan Grant."

A huge uproar followed. So many comments were made that Jamie could not keep them straight.

"You cannot step down."

"Why is your wife here? She's a woman."

"Women are not allowed at our meetings."

"You'll be fine in no time."

"Who could possibly replace you?"

"Give yourself time to recuperate."

Alex finally brought his fist down on the table to gain everyone's silence.

They all stared at him wide-eyed, though Jamie was not sure whether it was due to his father's statement or his fist.

"You cannot mean that, brother," Uncle Robbie said.

"If I may, I'd like to continue."

Taran banged his hand down on the table in agreement. "I'd like to hear what he has to say. If he wants to step down, then we should vote on his eldest son, Jake, taking over."

Jamie glanced at his brother, who'd paled at that statement. He elbowed him, but said nothing. Jake's moment was finally here.

It was Jake's right as the laird's eldest son, and Jamie did not want to see it go to anyone but his brother. This was their clan, and they needed a sound leader.

"Allow him the opportunity to speak his mind, he's our laird," Solas said with an emphatic nod.

They quieted and gave his sire the chance to speak.

"First of all, I brought my wife along because she will have an important contribution to this meeting." Alex cleared his throat. "Understand, *dearbh fine*, that 'tis an honor for me to serve my clan, but I also firmly believe that I should be in this role only as long as I am fit for it. I would like to suggest that the lairdship be passed down to my sons."

"Sons?" Taran asked.

"Sons?" Edwin echoed.

"Aye, my sons. I suggest that the lairdship be shared equally between our firstborn sons, Jake and Jamie."

Jamie's knees nearly buckled, though he somehow managed to stay upright. This possibility had never occurred to him.

"But Jake is your firstborn son, Laird," Edwin said. "And our custom is to pass the lairdship over to the laird's firstborn son unless he is unfit. Jake is perfectly fit for the job, though the matter would need to be voted on."

"Is he our firstborn? Who on the dais can answer that question for me?" Alex leaned back in his chair and crossed his arms.

Taran glanced at the others at the table. "Robbie? Brodie? What say you?"

Uncle Robbie shrugged his shoulders. "I was not there. I cannot say for certain."

Uncle Brodie said the same. "I was with Robbie in the hall."

Taran turned to look at Jamie and Jake standing near the doorway. Jake said, "We were there, but I do not think either of us recall." Their comment gained a ripple of laughter from everyone in the council but Taran, who had a more of a scowl than usual.

Jamie and Jake exchanged a glance, grinning at each other.

"Who was there?" Taran asked. "Alex, you were there, were you not? Your poor wife was attacked in the middle of the long event. Did you not stay in the chamber after the birth? 'Tis the tale the minstrels tell."

"Aye, I was there. Besides the two of us, Maddie's dear maid, Alice, who has since passed on, was also present. So was my sister Brenna, who now lives with the Ramsays."

"Enough of this foolishness, Laird," said Solas, who was red in the face. "When the first bairn was born, what did you name him? Jake, was it not? Then it's Jake."

Alex looked at Maddie. "We did not name them until much later. I do not recall myself which one came out first."

Taran stood up, banging his hand on the table. "Here, here, Laird." His frustration was evident in the way the words spewed from his mouth, spittle flying everywhere. Taran had sat as the head of the *dearbh fine* for some time now. He was as old as dirt, according to the lads of the clan, and his long beard was a testament to his age. "We need not hear the details about women's work. Just tell us who was first."

Jamie could not believe the spectacle in front of him. All these years, he'd been told he was the second born. His sire had planned this perfectly. Of course, everyone knew the lads looked nothing alike—Jamie was fair, and Jake was dark-haired—but no one could openly accuse the laird of lying.

His father said, "I'll ask their mother. Maddie, what say you?"

"I was verra busy trying to deliver the second one to pay attention to the first. I cannot answer that. And we could not decide on names. We never even thought about it 'til after the bairns had been brought down-stairs into the hall and then back up to me. Then we decided to name the dark-haired lad after Alex's sire, John, because he had the same coloring, and the light-haired lad after my sire, James, for the same reason. It had naught to do with who came out first. John became Jake, James became Jamie, and there you have it."

Taran bellowed. "Again, must I hear about issues that took place inside a woman's chamber? I care not to think on it. Just tell us who was first.

The clan's *dearbh fine* commands you to reveal the truth." He sat down and stroked his grizzled beard as he awaited the laird's response, his beady eyes aimed directly at him.

Alex said, "Please calm down, Taran. With all due respect, I tell you this because in my eyes, it does not matter. Maddie feels the same way. We did not pay close attention because she'd had a dagger at her throat minutes before the bairns were born. But here is what I'd like to present to you. Our sons are two verra different men, and this past year has illustrated as much. Jake is the type of warrior who focuses on the big issues, while Jamie is more likely to concern himself with details. Jake is an expert on knowing how to do what's needed immediately, while Jamie recognizes what is needed in the long-term. They are two verra different leaders, and I believe we are best served by having them both lead our clan. Just as my two brothers, who have both been invaluable to me, are verra different, so are Jake and Jamie. Together, they will be more powerful."

Jamie looked into Jake's eyes as he thought about what his sire had said. He could see the truth of it. Was his brother appraising him the same way?

"He makes a valid point," Uncle Brodie said. "They worked together well both at our fight with MacNiven and Hew Gordon at Castle Dubh and in the battle with Baron Crichton."

"But it was Jake who led the battle against the baron," Solas argued. "I saw him do it. He was at the forefront of the battle all the way."

"True," Nicol said, "but it was Jamie who saw our laird go down and who called for our warriors to protect him. He was farther back. Jake had no idea our laird was injured."

Uncle Robbie said, "And if it had been up to Jake and me, my brother would not be here. He would have died within a day's time. Jake and I wished to allow you to die in peace. 'Twas Jamie and Brodie who said to take you to Jennie's, and your sisters are the reason you are still here."

Taran waved to Jake and Jamie, summoning them over to the dais. Jamie's head was spinning. What would come next?

Taran stood when they came to a stop in front of the dais. "Lads, would you accept our decision if we ask both of you to step into your sire's position as laird of Clan Grant?"

Jamie glanced at his brother, unsure how he would take this. They'd both believed their entire life that when the time came, Jake would become laird. He'd wait to see what his brother said first. It would be his choice.

Jake thought for a moment, then said, "Aye. I trust my brother's judgment. We often have different ways of approaching a problem, but we always seem to come to terms. I think the clan would benefit from having two lairds."

Jamie was shocked. He was about to be named chief of Clan Grant alongside his brother? Many times over the years, he'd thought of becoming the laird instead of his brother, but alongside him? The possibility had never occurred to him. He thought it was a sound plan.

"Jamie? Your brother accepts. We must hear from you."

Jamie nodded. "I am honored to be included. I would accept on one condition."

The elders looked aghast that he would consider making a demand of the elders.

"I'll hear that condition, Jamie," his sire said.

"On the condition that when you are strong enough to take the lairdship back, we will relinquish it until we are again needed."

His mother pulled a linen square out of the folds of her dress and dabbed her eyes.

"Accepted," Alex said.

Taran banged the table and said, "How many are in favor of this, say aye."

A chorus of ayes greeted him.

"Nays?"

Silence.

Taran said, "James Alexander Grant, John Alexander Grant, you are now the new lairds of Clan Grant, based on the *dearbh fine's* recommendation."

The entire table erupted into cheers and smiles.

Jamie looked at his brother and asked, "What have we done?"

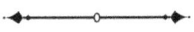

At the end of the table, Alex Grant looked at his wife of more years than he could count and said, "Does this please you, wife?" He kept his voice low so the others would not hear him.

"Aye, Alex, but I'm still surprised you decided to do this. You still have an able mind to lead."

"Maddie, I must tell you something." Alex had dreaded telling her this, but he knew it was time.

"What is it?"

"Did you know that all your hairs have turned white? I fear I must have put you through too much with this last injury."

"What? But I have had a few white hairs for some time now."

Alex tipped his head, his gaze traveling to the bound hair hanging down her back. "A few?"

Maddie grabbed the bottom of her plaited hair, tugging it over her shoulder and as far into the air as much as she could. She stared at her long tresses for a moment and then whispered, "Why, so it has. Why has no one told me?"

"Because you're still as beautiful as the day I met you. 'Tis time for me to spend all my time with you." He tugged her onto his lap and kissed her.

Taran barked, "Och, for the love of God. Look at the two of them." He tossed his hands into the air and scurried out the door.

THE END

NOVELS BY KEIRA MONTCLAIR

The Clan Grant Series
#1- RESCUED BY A HIGHLANDER-Alex and Maddie
#2- HEALING A HIGHLANDER'S HEART-Brenna and Quade
#3- LOVE LETTERS FROM LARGS-Brodie and Celestina
#4-JOURNEY TO THE HIGHLANDS-Robbie and Caralyn
#5-HIGHLAND SPARKS-Logan and Gwyneth
#6-MY DESPERATE HIGHLANDER-Micheil and Diana
#7-THE BRIGHTEST STAR IN THE HIGHLANDS-Jennie and Aedan
#8- HIGHLAND HARMONY-Avelina and Drew

The Highland Clan
LOKI-Book One
TORRIAN-Book Two
LILY-Book Three
JAKE-Book Four
ASHLYN-Book Five
MOLLY-Book Six
JAMIE AND GRACIE- Book Seven

The Summerhill Series- Contemporary Romance
#1-ONE SUMMERHILL DAY
#2-A FRESH START FOR TWO

Regency
THE DUKE AND THE DRESSMAKER

D EAR READER,

Thank you for reading *Jamie and Gracie*, the seventh novel in The Highland Clan. The Scottish thistle is the national flower of Scotland, and one legend does say that it had a role in the Battle of Largs in 1263. Read more about the battle in my novel *Love Letters from Largs*.

If you have not read my first series, The Clan Grant, you can learn about the elder generation of the Grant and Ramsay clans in those eight novels. Alex and Maddie's story is the very first novel, *Rescued by a Highlander*. You'll learn about old Hugh, Mac and Alice, and the mighty laird and how he gained his reputation as the best swordsman in the Highlands.

I have many more novels planned in The Highland Clan series, so stay tuned for more! We'll be headed back to the Ramsay's for the next Highland Clan saga—Sorcha's story. But I have another novel in the works before that, something different. You'll see!

If you want to know more about my novels, here are some places for you to visit.

Visit my website at www.keiramontclair.com and sign up for my newsletter. I'll keep you updated about my new releases without bothering you often.

Go to my Facebook page and 'like' me: You will get updates on any new novels, book signings, and giveaways. **www.facebook.com/ KeiraMontclair**

Stop by my Pinterest page:
www.pinterest.com/KeiraMontclair/ You'll see how I envision my characters and their settings.

Leave a review on retail websites or Goodreads. Reviews help self-published authors like me and help other readers as well.

Happy reading!

Keira Montclair
www.keiramontclair.com

ABOUT THE AUTHOR

KEIRA MONTCLAIR IS THE PEN name of an author who lives in Florida with her husband. She loves to write fast-paced, emotional romance, especially with children as secondary characters in her stories.

She has worked as a registered nurse in pediatrics and recovery room nursing. Teaching is another of her loves, and she has taught both high school mathematics and practical nursing.

Now she loves to spend her time writing, but there isn't enough time to write everything she wants! Her Highlander Clan Grant series, comprising of eight standalone novels, is a reader favorite. Her third series, The Highland Clan, set twenty years after the Clan Grant series, focuses on the Grant/Ramsay descendants. She also has a contemporary series set in The Finger Lakes of Western New York.